I0760728

Southern Lies

A MAX PORTER PARANORMAL MYSTERY

Stuart Jaffe

Southern Lies is a work of fiction. Names, characters, places, and incidents either are the product of the author's imagination or are used fictitiously, and any resemblance to any persons, living or dead, business establishments, events, or locales is entirely coincidental.

SOUTHERN LIES

Cover art by Mari Morgan

ISBN 13: 978-1-963517-20-0

First Hardcover Edition: March 2025

For Tim Zuk,

you'll know which scene in
this book is for you.

Also by Stuart Jaffe

Max Porter Paranormal Mysteries
Southern Bound
Southern Charm
Southern Belle
Southern Gothic
Southern Haunts
Southern Curses
Southern Rites
Southern Craft
Southern Spirit
Southern Flames
Southern Fury
Southern Souls
Southern Blood
Southern Graves
Southern Dead
Southern Hexes
Southern Hart
Southern Kin
Southern Lies

Nathan K Thrillers
Immortal Killers
Killing Machine
The Cardinal
Yukon Massacre
The First Battle
Immortal Darkness
A Spy for Eternity
Prisoner
Desert Takedown
Lone Star Standoff
The Puppeteer
Blowback
Prime

The Pathway Ring
Pioneers of the Pathway

The Ridnight Mysteries
The Water Blade
The Waters of Taladoro
Waterfire

The Parallel Society
The Infinity Caverns
Book on the Isle
Rift Angel
Lost Time
Pages of Glass
The Bold Warrior
City of Infinity

The Malja Chronicles
The Way of the Black Beast
The Way of the Sword and Gun
The Way of the Brother Gods
The Way of the Blade
The Way of the Power
The Way of the Soul

Gillian Boone novels
A Glimpse of Her Soul
Pathway to Spirit

Stand Alone Novels
After The Crash
Real Magic
Founders

Short Story Collection
10 Bits of My Brain
10 More Bits of My Brain
The Bluesman
The Marshall Drummond Case Files: Cabinet 1
The Marshall Drummond Case Files: Cabinet 2
The Marshall Drummond Case Files: Cabinet 3

Non-Fiction

How to Write Magical Words: A Writer's Companion

For more information, please visit ***www.stuartjaffe.com***

Southern Lies

Chapter 1

DESPITE THE END-OF-SUMMER HEAT, Max Porter stood in the alley of his office building picking up trash with a toy shark-head grabber — a long, plastic stick with a shark head on one end and a trigger handle on the other. When squeezed, the teeth chomped down. Max had won the silly thing at the Dixie Classic Fair the previous year, and it now feasted on burger wrappers, discarded papers, and several beer bottles.

Marshall Drummond, the ghost of a 1940s detective, poked his head out of the building's brick wall. Once a warehouse for Reynolds Tobacco — back when Drummond lived — the building had sat like a forgotten tomb for decades. But as Winston-Salem revitalized its northern section, this decaying brick shell found new owners in the Palasco Brothers. They divided the warehouse into office floors. The Porter Agency, along with its ghost, now called it home.

"I thought you'd left already," Drummond said. "It's getting late."

Max poked the shark head around a patch of grass and found an empty, crumpled cigarette pack to drop into the trash bag. "I'm taking a break. Then I'll be back up to finish my work."

"Sure, partner. Your work."

"What's that supposed to mean?"

Drummond floated closer. He flared his long coat back and stuck his hands in his pockets. With his head lowered and his Fedora obscuring his face, he said, "I know it's been hard on you and Sandra, but the situation is temporary. J will be back eventually."

"This isn't about J."

As Max tied off the trash bag and tossed it into the dumpster, he thought about how proud he had felt watching J cross the high school stage to accept a diploma. The young man beamed with joy and confidence, shook the principal's hand, and then looked into the audience, straight at Max and Sandra, and he raised his arms overhead in triumph. Max and Sandra weren't the only ones erupting in applause. Without warning, PB had arrived weeks earlier — said he would never miss his brother's graduation — and stuck around for a month. Max grinned. That had been a great start to the summer.

Even with Max's mother occupying J's old bedroom, the small house felt cozy, not cramped. PB and J were home, together, once again the Sandwich Boys. PB slept on the living room floor while J took the couch. They cared for Mrs. Porter while Max and Sandra led The Porter Agency through several simple cases. Life had become gentle.

But when June ended, PB offered to take J on a celebratory road trip. Two brothers bounding through America before the youngest headed off to UNC Charlotte and the eldest headed off to further his self-discovery on the highways. J loved the idea. Max and Sandra knew it would be a great experience for the boys and a great memory. Besides, they couldn't interfere with it even if they tried. But it was hard to let them go.

July and August turned into dreary, humid affairs. Mrs. Porter grew cranky. Work at The Porter Agency dried up. And Sandra spent far too much time with her brow knit tight.

Max took refuge in the office. He figured Drummond knew it, but the ghost was too much a man of his time to come right out and say anything. Besides, the ghost couldn't really complain. The latest addition, Drummond's bookcase, had been made of dark-stained woods, and Sandra had carved a protective spell into the side. That bookcase was his home and hideaway. When he needed a break from ghosts in the area or from those in the Other, he always had his bookcase to escape the world. And that bookcase came courtesy of The Porter Agency.

When Max re-entered the brick building, he felt his tense thoughts dissipate. At least, for now.

The Agency had slowly transformed into a pleasant space to

work. A second home. A well-lit, open layout that had room for their desks, for the bookcase, and a sitting area with a couch, coffee table, and chairs. Beneath the coffee table, a circular area rug depicting a swirling starfield covered the casting circle that Max had painted down. With the help of their assistant, Brenda, several prints had been framed and hung to warm the high-ceilinged room. They still had plenty they wished to do, but at least the office looked more than functional.

Popping up through the floor, Drummond said, "Look, I'm only offering to talk through this with you because I know you folks like to jabber and jabber about your feelings. If you'd rather stew in it, that sounds good to me."

"You want me to talk about J and my mother and everything, then you need to talk, too. You love J as much as the rest of us, and I know you want him here. It'll happen. Like you said, this is temporary. He goes to college, and when he's done, he plans to work here with us. So, how about you tell me why you're sad about it?"

"I'm not the one who likes these talks." Drummond disappeared in his bookcase.

Max smirked. He had noticed Drummond engaging more and more in *these talks*. In fact, the dead detective initiated plenty of them. *Maybe you can teach an old ghost new tricks.*

Crossing to his desk, Max tapped awake his laptop. His latest data compiling had finally finished. Without a major case to fill the time, Max had turned his efforts to locating his Aunt Jane Porter — a woman he hadn't even known existed until recently. But then, so much had changed in the last few months that learning about his father's mystery sister seemed rather minor. In fact, now that Max had come to terms with the inevitability of change, the world threw as much as he could stomach. And then it threw a little more.

Sitting back in his chair, letting it tip far enough to lift his feet off the floor, Max rubbed his face. Finding the right Jane Porter might be impossible. After all, the name was so common that he had come up with nearly a hundred thousand hits in the United States alone. Once he added in other possible spellings and listing variations — *Jayne, Jain, Janie, J, Jainy, etc.* — and opened his search to include other major English-speaking countries like England, Australia, and Canada, the number of hits reached a couple million. Plus, there was an author named Jane Porter, and it was also the name of the character that Tarzan fell in love with. Everybody knew Tarzan loved Jane. Few remembered that her full name was Jane Porter.

But Max had little more to go on than that name, and his mother proved unhelpful. She claimed to know barely anything about the mysterious sister, and the only photographs Max had of his aunt dated back to when the woman was a toddler. Of course, assuming she had not changed her name or created a false identity, he could eliminate any version of Jane Porter that had not been born in the United States. That cut out a substantial number, but doing so required the lengthy task of going by birth certificate names since she could have married.

He went down the road of using census data, too. This often was a great starting point, but in this case, it proved useless. One of the big problems with census data, especially older data, was that it could be incomplete or misleading. It depended on the individual census takers as well as who actually answered the questions. If Aunt Jane did not want to be counted, she could easily have kept her name out of every census since she was an adult.

With the list he managed to compile, he broke the entries down by region. Through several generations, the Porters had maintained a presence in the northeast of the country. Those Jane Porters born and raised in California could be cut without too much risk. Same for any from the rest of the West Coast and the Southwest. The closer to the Mid-Western states, however, and Max had to be careful. They were probably safe to remove from consideration, but he could envision scenarios in which Jane had been born in Nebraska but raised back east — an unplanned birth during a last-minute vacation, for example. Doubtful but possible.

Max took those names and created a separate list. These would be his backups if he came up empty with the ones he considered his best chances. This meticulous winnowing of the list had taken weeks, and though the total number of names had been reduced to the thousands, it still seemed insurmountable.

Before he could build greater stress about the task, his wife shoved open the office door. It whined but did not stick — an improvement. Sandra's expression, however, kept Max from making any comment.

"I know she doesn't have a long time left," she said, throwing her coat over the couch as she strode to her desk by the window, "but if your mother doesn't change her attitude, I swear I'm going to kill her." She slouched into her chair. Seeing Max's open laptop, she perked up. "A case? What are we working on?"

Drummond poked his head in, heard that comment, and made a fast retreat.

Sitting straighter, Max said, "Sorry, hon. No case right now."

"Then why are you here and not at home helping with your mother?"

"I'm trying to find my Aunt Jane."

"I see. You're hiding."

"I'm not —"

"Honey, you have got to step up. This is your mother, not mine. Her MS is getting worse, and she's never liked me to begin with. Those two things alone are making her act like a — well, an unmannered lady. And I'm not a full-time nurse."

"I know. I do. But we can't afford an actual nurse."

Sandra pointed to the pamphlet that had been sitting on the corner of Max's desk for over a month — *Parker House Independent Living Community: Freedom with Peace of Mind.* "There's that."

"We promised we wouldn't put her in a home."

"You know that place is far from a nursing home."

"We can't do that to her."

"Then you have to quit spending your days in this office when we don't have a case. Otherwise, she might as well be at Parker. She wants you around, not me. Everything I do is wrong. Even when it's right."

"That's not true. She said she liked the dinner you made last night."

Sandra raised her brow. "She said she liked the salad — which she knew came out of a bag."

"What about —"

"Don't. Whatever point in her favor you want to make, read the room and don't."

A tentative knock on the office door pulled their attention. With an awkward smile, an older woman wearing a tailored suit and enough diamonds to fund a small army entered. "Excuse me," she said, with Southern aristocrat dripping off each syllable. "Is this The Porter Agency?"

Drummond popped back in from his bookshelf. "Thank goodness. I was about to start haunting you both if you didn't stop bickering."

Sandra stood at her desk. "Yes, welcome. Please, come in."

Gesturing toward the couch and chairs, Max said, "This is my wife, Sandra, and I'm Max."

"Penelope Sidwell." She glided with the grace of a woman trained in ballet.

"Would you like some coffee?" Sandra asked.

"No, thank you." Mrs. Sidwell perched on the edge of one chair, letting Max and Sandra take the couch. Her nose wrinkled disapproval at the worn furniture.

"How can we help you?"

"It's my son," she said, gulping the words as she fought to maintain her composure. "Something is trying to kill him."

Chapter 2

AT MAX'S SUGGESTION, they moved to the conference room — a small area opposite the break room off the back hallway. It had plain walls, fluorescent lighting, and barely enough space to hold the long table and chairs picked up from an insurance broker's going-out-of-business sale. However, Max thought it would be more familiar to Mrs. Sidwell, more comfortable, since she probably served on numerous charity boards and such. Conference rooms would be a weekly occurrence for her.

Then again, he recognized he had made numerous assumptions about this woman merely by the way she spoke, dressed, and held herself. Then again again, most people made snap decisions based on these things. It was a survival instinct to help a human determine the possibility of danger when confronted with something new. Of course, such instincts evolved from cavemen wondering if those shadows in the bushes resembled predator or prey, but they still served people in the modern world. In the Porters line of work, the question of predator or client came up more often than Max liked to admit.

Settling into the faux-leather swivel chair at the head of the conference table, Mrs. Sidwell folded her slim hands in her lap. "I don't know where to begin."

Max and Sandra sat on either side of the graying woman while Drummond hovered further down, half-inside the table. "You found out about us," Sandra added, "and you chose to come here. So, you know we're the best hope of helping your situation, no matter how strange."

Mrs. Sidwell's lips trembled — her fears ratcheting up as she faced speaking them aloud. With a long, uneven breath, she lifted her head. "I am not sure I ever believed in the family curse, yet I do not see how I can deny it anymore. It seems that every Sidwell man has succumbed to it, and now it has turned its attentions onto my son. I thought it wouldn't come for him because I kept him away from the mill, but the curse refuses to stop until the last Sidwell is dead."

Max said, "Your son has been cursed?"

"I don't know the specific terminology, but what would you call it when every male in the Sidwell family line has suffered the same fate?"

Clicking his tongue, Drummond said, "There's nothing I can see surrounding her — no ghosts, no glow of a curse, nothing. She might be right about it only going after the men in the family."

"Please," Sandra said in a gentle tone, "let's start at the beginning. Maybe we can figure out together what exactly is going on."

"Of course." Mrs. Sidwell sat taller as she rolled back her shoulders. She looked as if she had been called to the witness stand in an assault trial and prepared to point out her attacker. "My son is Reginald Theodore Sidwell — he prefers Theo. His father, Robert Reginald Sidwell, waited until after we were married and our son was born to tell me about this situation that afflicts his family. I didn't believe him, thought it was merely superstition, and quite honestly, I still didn't believe him even after he died. I mean what was I supposed to think? He's talking about magic and curses and it struck me as rather ridiculous. Had Robert been a different kind of man, I would have suggested he see a therapist. Only an insane person would believe such nonsense. No offense intended."

"Not a problem," Sandra said. "You think different now?"

"Indeed, I do. Maybe I believed more than I want to admit. After all, I made sure Theo never worked at the mill."

"The mill?" Max asked.

"Sidwell Mills. We were one of the few textile mills that survived through the many decades. Of course, that's gone now."

"Your husband ran that mill?"

"He did. And he was the last because I would not allow Theo to work there. No Sidwell actually runs it anymore. I suppose, in reality, no Sidwell has been running it for a long time. Robert was the CEO, but there's been a Board of Directors for generations now. They hold controlling power; we get paid. That is why the mill closed and work moved to Vietnam. More profit that way. Nobody cared that Robert had spent most of his life at that mill. Died there, too."

Sandra said, "Have any board members been afflicted the way the Sidwell men have?"

"Not that I'm aware of. But if it was happening, I would not expect those vultures to admit to any of it. Not only because they would refuse to believe, but because doing so might jeopardize their position on the board. Besides, evidence shows that it has nothing to do with the mill. If it did, my Theo would not be suffering."

Cocking his head to the side, Drummond said, "Can we get to the point? Who is the witch we need to deal with? Where's the source of the curse so we can break it?"

Max glanced at his partner but didn't respond. To Mrs. Sidwell: "We're dancing around everything. How exactly did you learn about this curse? Do you know who's responsible?"

Mrs. Sidwell bit back a comment, but her perturbed wrinkling brow spoke enough. Still, despite the not-so-gentle prodding, she said, "Long ago, long before Robert and I were even born, the textile industry was cutthroat to say the least. Every kind of outside organizations you could imagine tried to influence what went on here in North Carolina. I even thought for a while that this family curse was really some type of mob connection. But I saw what this thing did to Robert, and I see what it's doing to Theo. There's something far bolder and far more sinister at work."

"Now, she's getting somewhere. And she isn't wrong," Drummond said. "When I was alive, if it wasn't tobacco, it was the textile industry. Those two were the juggernauts that kept North Carolina going. Wouldn't surprise me one bit to learn that organized crime had a hand in things. Organized witches, doubly so."

Sandra said, "Do you think one of your husband's rivals had him cursed?"

"Doll, that's good thinking."

Mrs. Sidwell said, "It would be a rival of an ancestor of my husband, but yes. I don't know exactly how it would have happened, though."

"Anybody could do it. Most would end up harming themselves. To do it right would require a witch."

Mrs. Sidwell paused. Max could see her swallowing down the idea that witches were real. She did not voice her surprise, though. Instead, she firmed up her jaw. "I suppose that's possible, then. Perhaps another mill owner cursed a bunch of the others. I don't know. I can only say what I have seen in my family."

"Tell us about that," Max said.

"It starts with simple symptoms that could be mistaken for anything. Fever, hunger, sore throat, and general achiness. And like a cold or a fever, you can treat the symptoms and in a few days it would go away. But what makes this different is that it keeps coming back. Within a week, most of the symptoms returned. Then came exhaustion. Robert would be so lethargic. He would move slow like old folks in the height of summer. Just wanted to sit out on the porch, drink some lemonade, and watch the day roll by. He often complained he felt sore to the bone. In the last years, he had to use a wheelchair. Same thing has been happening to Theo. In both cases, it lasted for years. The first time, with Robert, I didn't know what to make of it. This time, I've tried every folk remedy I could come across over the years. Nothing's helped."

"Now you've heard about us."

"I heard about you years ago, saw something on the television, but I thought you were charlatans. Once I had it confirmed that you were indeed the real thing, I didn't think I needed you." She shivered. "No, that's not true. I didn't want to think I needed you. I was determined to save my son on my own."

"What changed your mind?"

"Theo turned twenty-two last month. Within a week of his birthday, he started hearing the voices."

"Voices?" Sandra asked.

"Angry shouting. Sometimes chanting. Keeps him up at night." A tear escaped the corner of Mrs. Sidwell's eye. "You must help me. Time is running out. After the voices, soon he'll start seeing the dead, and then it'll be too late. I'm a wealthy woman. This is for the life of my son. There's no price I wouldn't pay. Name it."

Before Max could respond, Drummond clapped his hands together once, and Sandra said, "Don't worry. We'll take the case."

Chapter 3

THEY AGREED TO MEET at Mrs. Sidwell's home the following night. Sandra had pushed for earlier, but Mrs. Sidwell said that she had two charity board meetings and a fundraiser to attend. Max thought it strange considering the clock was ticking on Theo, but Mrs. Sidwell refused to bend.

"I simply must keep the Sidwell name intact. Theo is every bit as important, but he has yet to reach the final stages of this curse. He can certainly wait until tomorrow night."

Drummond suggested he could use the extra time to explore the Other — the netherworld where ghosts existed outside of the human plane — and maybe he'd run across one of the dead Sidwell men. Breaking a curse was a lot easier when they could find out about it from the victims. For Max, the respite would allow him to get some basic research done on the Sidwell family.

But when morning arrived, Sandra said he would have to take care of his mother. Sandra had to spend the day with Brenda. A major reason Brenda had started working for the Porters, and worked quite cheaply, was because Sandra tutored her in witchcraft. In addition to plenty of on-the-job training, they met once each week to further her studies.

"Does it have to be today?" Max asked. "I need to research our new client."

Sandra flicked his nose before kissing his cheek. "You can do that at home while you take care of her."

"I know, and I do appreciate what you've done."

"Don't add a *but* to that sentence, and you'll be winning for the day."

Max knew when to quit — sometimes. Thankfully, he knew enough that morning.

After turning the coffee machine on, he kissed his wife, wished her success, and went about setting up his laptop for a day of working at the kitchen table. His mother tended to sleep in late, so he figured he could get some solid research done before —

"Max?" his mother called.

He wanted to be frustrated, but the quiet, almost frightened tone in her voice, stopped him. Walking to her door, he said, "Morning, Mom. You okay?" When he pushed her door open, he could see that she had wet the bed.

She had her head facing the wall. "I'm having trouble getting my body to move. Can … can you help me?"

The morning whisked by as he cleaned up the mess, helped his mother get into dry clothes, and cooked her some breakfast. After two failed attempts at getting food into her mouth — her arms repeatedly spasmed and oatmeal splattered on the floor — Max took over, gently feeding her by the spoonful. When she finished, her face reddened. She looked away from him.

In silence, he cleared the dirty bowl and spoon, rinsed them off, and put them in the dishwasher. He tried to stifle the tremor that welled up from within. This callous, vile disease slowly chipped away at his mother. How long before only a shell remained?

"Max," she said, the word creaking out as a painful moan.

"Yeah?"

"I need the hospital."

"Something else wrong?"

"Everything is … woozy."

"If that's what you want, I'll take you. But we'll be stuck in the waiting room for hours, and you know what they're going to say. You're having a flare up. Stress and lack of sleep can cause that. Your doctor said that with the move to our house, you would have more flare ups for a bit. Until you're settled."

With a whip-sharp snap, she said, "I've been here for months. I know what I'm feeling. Take me to the damn hospital."

After fifteen minutes criticizing each step toward getting ready and then more complaints getting into the car, Mrs. Porter finally leaned back against her headrest and closed her eyes. She was exhausted. Though he didn't want to waste his day at the hospital, Max partly went along to avoid the joy of maneuvering her back into the house. Not that the ER would be any easier, but at least they could be in the car for a while. He'd be fine with sitting in the parking lot, too, if that's what she wanted.

As he navigated the city's morning rush hour, he thought about witchcraft. Again. The subject probably entered his mind every day, and whenever his mother had a flare up or displayed any symptoms of her disease, the idea of having Sandra use a spell to heal or lessen his mother's suffering always popped up. It would be so easy. A few symbols drawn on the floor, a few words spoken aloud, some concentration, some knowhow.

But, of course, nothing with witchcraft ever proved easy. To take such a step would carry a price, and neither Max nor Sandra would risk finding out what that price might be. Even if they hadn't recently extracted Mrs. Porter from the clutches of a witch deal, they knew anything involving witchcraft meant devilish details in fine print that no contract lawyer could ever hope to uncover. Made him wonder why anybody messed with spells at all.

"Why do we?" he muttered. He glanced over at his mother. She did not appear to have heard, but the question echoed loud enough in his head.

He knew how Sandra would answer. Besides the obvious point that the Porters fought against those who wanted to abuse magic and ruin others with it, she wanted to learn everything she could of witchcraft to make the world better, safer. She wanted to be one of the few good witches out there. It sounded right. Noble, even. But Max harbored plenty of fears for her. He trusted her, but magic went beyond a person's abilities, intentions, or motivations. Each time Sandra cast a spell, or worse, each time Max asked Sandra to cast a spell, they risked everything about her — her morals, her sanity, her life. She would argue that the risk was worthwhile when it meant standing against powerful forces that wanted to control or hurt the vulnerable.

But being heroic was hard. Max preferred spending his days curled up with his wife, ignoring the power struggles of the world, and enjoying living together.

He didn't want to spend the day sitting in the ER. By three in the afternoon, his mother finally got her turn. The doctors looked her over, listened to what she said, and concluded that she had experienced an MS flare up. Really? Shocker. Probably induced by stress or lack of sleep no less. Max thanked them for their time and escorted his mother back to the car.

Neither spoke on the ride home.

As the day wore on, Mrs. Porter's symptoms dropped away. She settled in her room, but clearly was back to normal — at least, enough so that she could take care of herself.

By the time the sun set, Sandra had returned, and they readied to visit Mrs. Sidwell about her case, Max was itching to deal with magic. Anything to get out of the house. And suddenly, fighting a witch's curse sounded like a great way to spend the evening.

Chapter 4

WEAVING THROUGH WINSTON-SALEM, Max and Sandra drove out to the Sidwell home. Their latest car, a used Toyota Corolla, strained when reaching fifty miles-per-hour, but luckily, the GPS stuck to the city streets. Drummond floated in the backseat. All was quiet until they turned off the main road and entered one of the richest neighborhoods in the area.

With a dark tone, Max said, "Crap. Nothing good ever happens here."

The Porter Agency had dealt with several cases on these blocks. Each one had been difficult. Perhaps the neighborhood attracted bad things because it was so old — many of the enormous homes had not been altered since their original construction in the early-1900s. While most parts of the world experienced something ugly at some point — something that left behind bad energy that could cause problems — some places endured worse than others. Max's experiences with these mansion-strewn streets pointed to a lot of *worse.*

Magnolias dipped and spread across massive lawns, and the ritzy cars parked in horseshoe driveways gleamed like the jewels Mrs. Sidwell had worn the day before. Every blade of grass, every blooming flower, every potted plant had been sculpted with great care. The streets were well-lit and not a pothole in sight.

Max found it sterile. No music, no laughter, no signs of life except the lone woman power-walking with desperation in her step. These mini-castles had been erected to wall away the world. Not just the lower-classes, but the world itself. Those things that ignited the sense — if they existed here, it was hidden away where nobody could witness it from the outside.

Making a sharp right, Max pulled up to a building that made

the word *mansion* seem quaint. The driveway was an intricate geometric pattern of brick and concrete with small lamps lining the way. Max felt a twinge of guilt driving over it.

"Jeez," Drummond said. "This is R. J. Reynolds-level rich."

Sandra craned her head against the door window. "Right out of *Gatsby*."

Parking behind a black, stretch limousine, Max turned off the car. "Can we focus on getting this over with?" He tried not to gawk at the building. Not out of pride or even a sense of decorum, but rather the enormous house loomed like a gargoyle. It gazed down on their car, on them, and with the aged trees crowding against its ancient walls, the mansion lacked anything that could be construed as welcoming. Max trembled as they approached the front door.

"Should we knock?" he asked.

"You planning to walk in unannounced?" Drummond said. "Scare the lady?"

"The lady of the house asked us to come."

"The lady of the house probably owns a gun."

"Look at the size of this place. It could be hours before she makes it to the front door."

"I think your mother's making you afraid of old women."

"Boys, stop it." Sandra stepped forward and raised her hand to knock, but the locks clicked. A moment later the door opened. A young, Hispanic lady dressed in a classic maid's uniform ushered them inside. After closing the door behind them, she curtsied, gestured for them to wait, and hurried out.

Max had been in several wealthy homes before – Reynolda House, for one, and of course, the Hulls' mansion, for another — but the Sidwells lived with an extravagance that reached the grandeur of royalty. The foyer alone boasted a cathedral ceiling, dark wood walls with hand-carved molding, marble flooring with Turkish runners, a massive crystal chandelier guaranteed to kill a man should it fall, and every inch of available wall space covered with original portraits and landscapes done in oil. If not for the electric lighting, Max would have expected candles in diamond-encrusted sconces.

Drummond pushed back his hat. "I don't know whether to be impressed or nauseated."

A tall, thin gentleman wearing a tuxedo and boasting a double chin approached in the stiffest way possible. "Mrs. Sidwell has requested your presence in the music room." He looked and spoke like a slim version of Alfred Hitchcock. "Please follow me."

Sandra shot a snooty look at Max as she raised her pinky. She tossed her head back and trailed after the butler. Snickering, Max followed.

The wide halls and endless rooms created a labyrinth of luxury that echoed their footsteps as they kept a steady pace. Max had to wonder how empty it must feel to live in a museum with no visitors. After all, the entire Porter home could fit inside that foyer, yet Sandra and his mother lived with him alongside J on occasion. PB would show up again at some point, and Drummond often spent his nights patrolling the neighborhood streets.

At one set of double doors which looked no different than several others, the butler bent slightly and slid open the entranceway. He gestured for the Porters to enter. "The music room," he announced as if to assure that he had taken them to the right location.

Once again, Max experienced the word *astounded.* Not only was the music room larger than the foyer, it had several small tiers set up to handle a mini-orchestra. A ramp lined the left side to aid in wheeling up large instruments like the full-sized concert harp in the back. Baffles had been hung at specific angles to improve the acoustics of the large space while also dampening sound from infiltrating the rest of the house. In front of a cathedral window, a grand piano waited. The bench had been pushed off to the side.

"I didn't think anybody played the harp unless it was a professional," Drummond said.

Sandra said, "We never found out what Theo did for a living. Maybe he's a classical musician."

"Or maybe," Max said, "Theo calls in every friend he has for an impromptu jam session."

Drummond crossed the room and stopped at the tympani on the back tier. "You think this guy has enough friends to fill out an entire orchestra?"

"Maybe," Max said. "Guys with this much wealth — they're either surrounded by tons of people wanting to get close or they got nobody in their lives."

"Yeah, but the ones with tons of hangers-on don't usually live with their mothers."

Max strolled to the massive window that looked out upon the long acreage behind the house. The dying grass paled in the rising moonlight. "Either of you picking up on anything?"

"Nothing yet."

Sandra said, "Feels like a normal house. Other than the massive size and extreme opulence."

Clicking footsteps approached, and Max hustled over to Sandra's side to await their client. The doors slid open, and the double-chinned butler entered. With a pompous scan over the Porters, he said, "Mrs. Sidwell and Mr. Theodore Sidwell." He then backed away.

From the hallway, Mrs. Sidwell said, "Thank you, Timothy. I will handle this from here."

"Yes, ma'am."

A second later, a wheelchair rolled in with Theo being pushed by his mother. She stood ramrod straight, her proud chin tilted upward as she guided Theo's chair toward the center. With a flick and wave, she indicated that the Porters were to pull up two orchestra seats.

Max chose to approach Theo and extend a hand. "Nice to meet you. I'm Max Porter and this is my wife, Sandra."

Until this moment, Theo's gaze had ignored them. From beneath a mop of straight blond hair, his focus had been on the piano. But hearing Max's greeting, the young man lifted his head. He had sharp, gray eyes that cut through the air, and despite being bound to a chair, his handshake showed strength. Max peeked down at the man's legs. They looked firm with solid muscle. He guessed Theo had only recently started using the wheelchair.

Speaking with a gentle timbre, Theo said, "I'm sorry my mother has wasted your time bringing you out here. There's nothing you can do for me."

Mrs. Sidwell jabbed his shoulder. "Enough of that. These kind people have gone out of their way to examine you. The least you could do is be polite and accommodating."

"They're not doctors."

"And that's a good thing because what you suffer from is not a medical condition."

Sitting in the chair she had dragged over, Sandra placed a hand on Theo's arm. "You don't believe in any of this, do you?"

"No, ma'am. I'm sorry, but I do not."

Drummond had moved in closer, his eyes narrowing on the young man. "He should believe. There is definitely something going on with him. I can see a haziness around him. That's an odd one."

Holding back the urge to look at the ghost, Max said, "My wife is excellent at seeing things others don't. You should listen to her. Give her a chance."

Theo pulled his arm away. "I appreciate your desire to help, but I do not condone people feeding into or off of my mother's misbeliefs."

"I had them vetted," Mrs. Sidwell said.

"How do you vet people like this?"

"I am no fool." The bite in her voice caused Theo to flinch. "These are legitimate investigators with a long list of satisfied clients. Their financials are sound enough, and there is nothing suspicious in their activities to suggest fraud."

Trying to ignore the invasive list of this vetting, Max said, "If you think about it, your problems haven't been solved yet by conventional methods. Why not give this a try?"

"I'm here, aren't I?"

"It sounds like you only came to appease your mother and make sure she isn't being swindled."

"Seems like a swindle so far. Do you plan to put on your little show or can I go back to my room?"

Sandra motioned for Max to sit before he got heated up. She then looked to Theo again. "It's okay. Lots of people think we're making it up."

Max crossed his legs and arms. "Most of our clients come to us as a last resort."

"But even those who refuse to believe in what they experience leave with the peace of mind that they tried everything in their power to fix their problem."

Theo gestured to his legs. "You're going to fix this?"

"Like you pointed out, we're not doctors. If the problem with your legs is medical, we can't help."

"See that, Mother? They can't help."

"But if the problem is something else, something related to what I'm seeing around you, that's a different matter."

Mrs. Sidwell covered her mouth. "What do you see?"

"Something unusual. A grayish haze. I can feel the cold from it, especially near the shoulders."

Theo's eyes snapped open wide.

Drummond pointed at the man. "That got him."

"Is that what's cursing my son? What does this mean?"

"Mother, be quiet." Theo locked eyes with Sandra as his bottom teeth dug into his top lip. "You're telling me that's what's causing this?"

"I told you what I see. Whether that's what is causing your problems is a different question. If we're to answer that one, you'd have to start accepting what we do."

"Listen to them, dear." Mrs. Sidwell's voice cracked briefly, but she pulled it back with a harsh sniffle.

Theo glared up at his mother. "I am listening. You can see that. And don't think I'm oblivious to your manipulations. I know you put this meeting in the music room hoping it would set me at ease."

"It's your favorite room. I just thought —"

"I know what you thought." He shook off his scowl and forced a calmer grin towards Sandra. "If I'm hearing you correctly, you're saying that you can see something that none of us can see, and that it might or might not be the cause of my condition. That's awful vague. You could have easily found enough on the internet about me to come up with this ploy."

Sandra said, "That's true. Except your mother came to us. Until yesterday, I'd never heard of any of you."

"You've clearly convinced my mother that you can get rid of this. That you can stop this curse."

Mrs. Sidwell said, "Now you believe me?"

Before Theo could argue with his mother, Sandra said, "I only promise that we'll give you our best. Whether that will be enough is not something I can predict."

"Are not predictions your thing?"

"I'm not a fortune teller nor clairvoyant. I don't predict anything. I'm only reporting to you what I can see. That's all."

"And what does your service look like? Besides Mother giving you money."

"The first step would be for me to cast a spell that would help us identify the kind of curse you have."

"A spell?"

"If it will help, I'll agree to do that spell now, free of charge. Would you allow us to do that much?"

Mrs. Sidwell said, "Of course, he will. I did not go downtown to hire and bring you out here for nothing."

"Mother, please."

Max couldn't help but hear a tinge of Norman Bates. Hopefully, that was as far as the similarity went.

Drummond's take was a bit different. "This guy is damn rude to his mother. I'd have been smacked upside the head for daring to speak like that. In fact, I'd like to crack him in the ear myself. At least, we know what he's going to say."

"I'm not sure," Theo said.

"Huh. Didn't think that was coming."

"Nonsense." Mrs. Sidwell rolled her son back several feet. "You will let them try, or you will you have to deal with me later."

Mother and son glowered at each other in a silent battle. Max took the moment to give thanks that he never had to deal with PB or J in such a terrible manner. He also wondered at how fluid their dynamic appeared. It was difficult to figure out who was in charge.

Plastering on a thick smile, Theo said, "I guess I'm going to play along. What do you want me to do for your magic spell?"

Chapter 5

THE SIDWELLS DECIDED THAT THE SPELL should be performed in the music room, and Sandra agreed. She liked the fact that it was Theo's favorite room — packing it with good emotional energy — and since magic worked by manipulating the energies already in an area, the better the energy, the safer for Theo. While these points meant something to Mrs. Sidwell, it seemed clear to Max that the old woman's concerns primarily centered on protecting her floors.

When she heard that Sandra would be drawing a casting circle with chalk, the discussion immediately turned to the music room. Theo suggested the ballroom, but Max saw the glint in the young man's eye — he was prodding his mother with that one. It was more than a gentle playfulness, though. There were years behind those eyes. Years of ugliness.

Max surveyed the music room once more. The room — the entire mansion, in fact — acted as Theo's prison. Perhaps even more than his wheelchair. The gilded cage, indeed.

Despite these undercurrents between mother and son, Theo did exactly as he had suggested — he played along. Rather than argue each point, he acquiesced to whatever choices were made. A few more jabbing remarks, but nothing too biting. And with the final decision on location made, he quieted down.

Sandra got to work.

Tightening his coat, Drummond drifted toward the doorway. "I'm going to explore this place. If there's anything odd, I'll let you know."

Thick raindrops drummed against the huge window. Though the room had plenty of lighting available, Mrs. Sidwell turned a dimmer to one of the lowest settings, leaving the space in a dull amber. "Sometimes bright light hurts his eyes."

Theo smacked the arm of his wheelchair. "That's not true, and you know it."

"There was that one day —"

"Once. That was it. My eyes are fine."

Max guessed Sandra would be a short while, so he thought it best to keep the Sidwells calm. He also might glean more information from them, and anything he could learn would be of benefit. "I was wondering," he said, drawing the attention of both, "Theo was kept from working at the mill to protect him from this curse."

"Which didn't work," Mrs. Sidwell said.

"But you thought it would. Why? You mentioned your husband's rivals. Anything you can tell me about them?"

Theo snorted. "Everybody was Father's rival."

With an embarrassed grin that got quickly buried, Mrs. Sidwell said, "When you are successful in business, enemies are part of the way things work. Some are jealous. Some are greedy. Some are both. And some cannot find any sense of accomplishment unless they are pushing others down. In its heyday, the textile industry was full of these types. Sidwell Mills had been quite successful, so you can imagine how it attracted the ire of such men."

"And you think one of these competitors is responsible for your family's misfortune. I understand that. But why wouldn't that enemy make himself known? Or did he? Did one of the smaller mills surpass Sidwell Mills unexplainably?"

She shook her head. "I have thought about that, but nobody ever claimed to be behind this. Then again, some people do not gloat when they think they have won."

"Most do, though. Perhaps this is a more personal attack. Someone who felt wronged by your family."

Theo said, "That would be a long list. You can't run a business without pissing off people."

"Somebody always has a grievance about something." Mrs. Sidwell shook her head as if weary of such things. "Working conditions, working hours, pay rates. Always an angle to try and take more from you."

"And Father wasn't shy about fighting back. Most of those vermin deserved what they got."

Theo would have fit right in running the family mill. The young man's disdain sounded as cold to the bone as they had described his father. Perhaps running a large operation required such icy attitudes, but Max doubted it. The Porter Agency would probably remain a small business, but should it ever grow into a large company, he saw no reason to regard his competition in such ruthless terms.

"What about specific rivals? Or specific employees? Even ex-employees. A disgruntled worker that felt unfairly fired."

"We'd be here all night listing those people."

"But this would be people who also had an interest or knowledge of witchcraft."

Mrs. Sidwell said, "If we had known such a person, don't you think I would have mentioned them from the start? There is nobody."

Drumming his fingers on the side of his chair, Theo said, "What my mother means is that we never tried to know our employees too intimately. Whatever they did when they weren't working on the mill floor was their business. My father always said that he'd be happy hiring serial killers as long as they showed up on time and did their job well."

Sliding through the wall, Drummond said, "It'd take me hours to comb through this whole building, but from what I've seen, everything checks out. Only found one ghost — an old servant. He refuses to move on while the house stands. Spends most of his time wandering around. Even tries to clean in the middle of the night. Nice guy. A bit too talkative, though."

Moments later, Sandra announced that she was ready. She asked Mrs. Sidwell to wheel her son to the center of the circle, then to step aside. Mrs. Sidwell did so, opting to sit on the piano bench and watch with a cautious unease.

"This shouldn't take long," Sandra said, "but once I start the spell, we can't stop."

Mrs. Sidwell said, "Will stopping hurt him?"

"No, nothing like that. But it will ruin the spell. I'd have to erase the circle, redraw the entire thing, and start the whole process over. So, before we get going, does anybody need the bathroom or a drink of water or anything?" Nobody volunteered a need. "Okay, then. Let's begin."

Kneeling at the edge of the circle, Sandra spread her arms wide and lowered her head. She chanted a string of words from one of the long-dead witch languages. Soft, open, vowelly sounds. Most witch chants had a harsher, guttural quality, and Max paused at this more musical version. He swore he caught a slim rise on Sandra's lips as if she knew what he thought. Maybe she did. Not because of witchy practices — though that was always a possibility — but from the years together.

He shifted his attention from his wife to Theo to Mrs. Sidwell and back again, trying to keep watch for any sudden changes or reactions. He knew better, though. Unless prepared ahead, casting spells took time.

Mrs. Sidwell fidgeted at the piano bench, wringing her hands as she mouthed silent prayers. She stood, took a few steps along the edge of the circle, then those same few steps back to where she had started. Max had no doubt that she wanted to lunge in and shove her son out of the room. He conjured a ridiculous, cartoonish image of this woman racing that wheelchair down the hall. Hiding a grin, he walked softly to her side.

Whispering, he said, "Have patience. My wife is the best at this."

Mrs. Sidwell did not respond, but she stopped pacing. Her fingers clutched together, pressing hard into the skin. A bit of an improvement. A breath later, however, and she shifted her weight from leg to leg. Until she saw positive results, she could not quiet the anxiety.

Lightning flashed, turning the massive window into a stark blaze before flicking back into darkness. Mrs. Sidwell jumped, letting out a short cry, and looked straight at Sandra. Again, Max leaned close. "That was a storm. Not my wife."

Thunder rolled in the distance as if acknowledging Max's words.

While Sandra continued her chanting, Drummond drifted close to her. He watched Theo carefully — but no. Max noticed Drummond's eyeline reached beyond Theo and a little higher. Not simply curious, either. From Drummond's posture and the grim focus on his face, Max knew the old detective stood at the ready for anything. Well, *floated* at the ready.

A brighter flash of lightning. The afterimage hovered before Max like a window-shaped spirit. With nothing to do at the moment, Max counted the seconds until he heard thunder — eleven.

Theo looked bored, gazing around the music room, itchy to be done with this charade. A few times, he lobbed his attention toward his mother and offered a sarcastic wave. *Hi, Mother. Nothing happening over here.*

A soft sizzling rose from the floor. Sandra's spell. Max thought she still had a bit to go.

Another flash of lightning. He counted — thirteen. The storm moved away.

When the fourth flash hit, however, it ignited the air within the music room. Max's hair stood on end, and the smell of electricity overpowered. It took Max's brain several seconds to recognize that this was not the lightning storm. This brightness erupted only within the circle.

Mrs. Sidwell shaded her eyes. Stark shadows danced along the walls as another blast of light snapped through the circle. Each time, Theo jolted. Concern mixed with fear in his tight grip on the wheelchair, but he didn't utter a sound. Max only heard Mrs. Sidwell's surprise and the distant rumble of the receding storm.

Sandra bowed her head, taking a quiet breath. As Max approached her, she sat back on her knees, paused for another breath, then wiped her hand across the circle, breaking the chalk line and ending the spell. With Max's help, she stood.

"Well?" Mrs. Sidwell said, hastening toward her son.

"That's it?" Theo said.

Rubbing the back of her neck, Sandra offered a gently nod. "The good news is that I see nothing to suggest a curse. In fact, I can't detect any magic used against Theo at all."

Relief washed over Mrs. Sidwell, and as Theo patted her hand, Max processed the full weight of what his wife had said. He frowned at her, but she motioned to wait. He looked over at Drummond. The ghost observed Theo with concern.

Seconds later, Mrs. Sidwell turned her attention to Sandra, and her brow crinkled. "You said *the good news.* That implies there is bad news. What are you not telling us?"

"Mother, please. She is not hiding anything. I told you this stuff isn't real. Now, Ms. Sandra, I don't know how you made that happen, and I'm impressed with the show you put on, but you didn't find a curse. You're welcome to leave."

Sandra lowered to be at eye-level with Theo. "It's not so simple. There is no curse, but I saw something attached to you."

"Oh really?"

"A ghost. That haziness I saw before — it's a ghost — and that worries me because I've never seen a ghost behave that way."

Theo scowled. "This is getting beyond ridiculous. You have outstayed your welcome. It's time to go."

"No," Mrs. Sidwell said. "I am the one paying her to be here. I want to know about this ghost. Who is it?"

Max snatched a peek at Drummond. The detective continued to watch Theo closely.

"I don't know," Sandra said.

"Of course not," Theo said. "And how much more will we have to pay for that nugget of magical information?"

"We only charge once. Nothing extra. And we're good at figuring these things out. Max and our team will uncover everything we can about this ghost, and hopefully, from that, we'll understand how to get it away from Theo."

"Will this ghost hurt my son?"

Wheeling toward the double doors, Theo shook his head. "No more. Ms. Sandra, Mr. Max — you both seem like a nice couple, but I refuse to let my mother spend another cent on this nonsense. I only went along this far because I thought it would ease her mind. But you're agitating her further, and I can't allow that."

Sandra dusted off her hands. "We'll leave. Our apologies for upsetting you."

"Nobody's upset. We just want you gone."

"One question, though. This ghost looked a lot like — and don't laugh — it looked like Ebeneezer Scrooge. Like the classic version of the character. Old, bent over, large nose, large chin, wrinkles everywhere and long white hair ringing a bald spot."

Theo's eyes darted to his mother. She returned the gaze with equal shock as she walked toward her son. "That could be lots of people," she said. "I doubt we know who that is."

"Probably somebody connected with the mill," Sandra said.

Theo forced his head to shake. "Doesn't sound familiar."

"Thought I'd ask."

Max gathered their coats and swiped Sandra's chalk from the floor. "I apologize that we couldn't be of more help. Since you don't want us around anymore, I suppose we'll get going."

"Wait." Not Mrs. Sidwell, but Theo.

Max and Sandra paused.

"If you were to investigate this ghost you saw, what would you actually do with the information?"

Drummond floated over to Max. "Give him the truth. I think he's ready."

"In a normal case like this, I'd say we'd find out why this ghost is haunting you, address the issue, and help the ghost move on to the afterlife he should be in."

Mrs. Sidwell said, "But this is not a normal case, is it?"

Stepping closer, Sandra said, "It's not that strange, either. The Porter Agency has dealt with things like this. Never specifically a hazy ghost, but we have a lot of resources to help figure out why this ghost looks so off and what it wants. If you give us the chance, we'll deliver."

Mrs. Sidwell's shoulders dropped slightly. "I truly appreciate what you've done for us. Unfortunately, my son does not agree, and I won't force him into —"

Theo cleared his throat. "Perhaps, well … can't hurt to try, I suppose."

His mother lowered to her son, her eyes glistening. "Truly?"

"I'm not changing my opinion, but this is obviously important to you. So, why not?"

Mrs. Sidwell knew when she had won. Max guessed most of the time she won through brute force of will. Getting her way through her son's apparent affection must have touched her deeply. She even permitted her right eye to shed a tear.

Chapter 6

A NEW CLIENT with what might be a complicated case — especially a wealthy new client with what might be a complicated case — always brought mixed emotions. On the one hand, Max was elated with the income that would help pay bills and put food on the table. On the other hand, that income arrived due to the misfortunes of others.

Of course, if The Porter Agency did its job, they would mend the Sidwell's miseries. That was the most important calculation. The Porters had not caused the trouble. They had been hired to alleviate it. Still, Max could not rid the guilt he experienced from feeling happy at this moment.

When he and Sandra entered their home, however, he noticed his mother's bedroom light shining around the cracks of her door. His joy deflated. He had hoped she would be asleep.

Rolling her neck with several crackles, Sandra said, "I'm taking a shower."

Max would have loved to join her, but he hung up his coat before knocking on his mother's door. She muttered a noise which he took to mean *Come in.*

She sat in a little reading chair, gazing out her window onto their small backyard. The storm had passed and raindrops clung to the glass, speckling her view. Her hands rested on her thighs, and the amber of the back alley streetlamp highlighted the wrinkles on her face.

"Hey, Mom, how are you?"

"The same as yesterday." She did not look away from the window.

"Any more pain today?"

"There's always pain."

He leaned over to kiss the top of her head. "I'm sorry we weren't around this evening. We got a new client, and they wanted to meet at night. That happens sometimes. It's one of the downsides of this job. We're at their mercy."

Folding her arms, Mrs. Porter said, "You know, the point of me being here is so that I can be closer to my family. But the boys are gone, and you're never in the house. When you are, you can't wait to get away. Doesn't seem like much of a family anymore."

Max noticed she failed to mention Sandra, but he let the insult pass. He had to pick his battles. "We're trying our best. Don't forget, nobody is forcing you to stay in this room. You should get out of the house."

"I'll take four steps and have to rush to the ER again."

"You could meet some people. We've got neighbors your age. Maybe they're nice."

"What's the point? How much longer do you really think I have left?"

"Don't talk like that. Other than the MS, you're a healthy woman."

"For my age. Don't forget that part."

Max clamped his mouth. They had gone through this routine enough times for him to know there would be no satisfactory outcome. She refused help from others and refused to socialize outside the home. She wanted a life centered on herself with Max as a satellite in orbit, but that meant accepting he could not be at the house indefinitely. He had to earn money. He had a life of his own. One that encompassed more than just her.

With a slight move of her chin, she indicated her bedside table. "Hand me my earbuds."

Suppressing a laugh, Max did as asked. While Mrs. Porter rejected most suggestions from her son, she loved listening to audiobooks on the earbuds he had bought for her. Took three weeks and four tries, but he eventually made her a convert.

He gave her a hug and another kiss, whispered *good night*, and closed her door as he left. Sandra already had the shower running, so Max went to the kitchen, filled a glass of water, and sat at the table. His mind battled between strong desires — to get started on his research or to go to sleep. Sleep appeared to be winning out.

But before he could act upon the idea, he received a text — from Theo Sidwell. The young man wanted to meet right away. Max shook his head. Some clients proved from the start that they would be a pain. Hardly worth the money. But not to the point of turning them away.

Max knocked on the bathroom door. After conferring with Sandra in hushed whispers, they decided he would bring Drummond along. Sandra would remain at home. She could watch over Mrs. Porter and get a start on her witchcraft bookwork for the case. Also, and perhaps most important, she had just finished a shower and had no desire to leave the house again.

Twenty minutes later, Max stood at the end of the observation overhang at The Quarry at Grant Park. Part of Reynolds Park — Max didn't understand the distinction — the land around the old quarry had been turned into a beautiful maze of snaking pathways dotted with activity areas for kids, open fields for families, and a long, graded spiral that ended at the overhang. The ground was soaked from the storm. Nobody was around. The park was closed for the night. But apparently Sidwell money could get it re-opened for a short time, and Max guessed that was why Theo picked the spot.

Drummond flew along the quarry's edge, making sure the place was secure. No reason to suspect an ambush, but they had both been through enough cases to know that even the most innocent client could prove otherwise. From the overhang, Drummond looked like a pale dot gliding over the water. With only moonlight and a couple pathway lamps, Max's spatial perception was thrown off.

"Looks clear," Drummond said when he returned.

Holding the wet railing, Max tried to shake off a sense of vertigo. "Any guess what this is about?"

"No idea. Maybe he knows more about this ghost than he let on. It's been haunting him for years. Hard to believe he hasn't learned a thing or two."

"He seemed pretty shook up finding out it was real."

"He also seemed pretty concerned about what his mother thought. And having a meeting right after having a meeting, picking a remote location, waiting until the storm had ended, keeping it shrouded in secrecy — either he's going to admit something awful, or he'll try to kill you."

Max flipped his middle finger. "Sometimes you're all charm."

"Right back at ya." Drummond flicked his fingers from under his chin.

The two chuckled in the ensuing quiet until a black van drove up the path. Though pretty sure cars were forbidden over here, Max knew that the ultra-rich could buy their way through every kind of prohibitions. After all, money got the park opened after hours, too. When the van parked, a middle-aged gentleman got out, walked around the side, and helped Theo detach from the van's wheelchair rig. The man started to push the wheelchair, but Theo smacked him away. Standing back against the van, the man watched carefully but made no further attempt at aid. Theo muscled his way up to Max.

"Thank you for meeting me," Theo said, huffing.

"No problem. I've got to ask — and I mean no offense — but why do you have a manual chair?"

"I prefer it." He growled the answer, and Max thought it best not to push for whatever simmered beneath those words.

Drummond said, "I've seen his type before, especially after the war. He doesn't want to admit he might always be in a chair. If he got a motorized one, that would be defeat. Maybe that's why he's such a jerk to his mother."

The air off the quarry water chilled the skin. Max tried not to shiver. Thankfully, Theo did not like pleasantries.

"I want you to know that the show you and your wife produced was impressive enough that my mother won't cease talking about it, and though I haven't figured out yet how you did it, I will. That's why you're here. Preying on my mother's weaknesses doesn't make you special. Lots of scum have tried it over the years. But it won't work. You won't get rich off us."

Max had wondered in which direction Theo would fall after the day's experiences. Most people when confronted with the reality of the supernatural either embraced the truth or doubled-down on denial. Clearly, Theo had chosen the latter.

Drummond moved in closer but still kept a good distance. That hazy ghost would be nearby. Max wanted to watch Drummond to get a better feel of where the other ghost floated, but he needed to focus on Theo.

"We're not con artists," Max said.

"That's what all con artists say. Look, my father was not a pleasant man to be married to, and with him dead, she's got a lot of money. That makes her an easy mark — I get it — but I'm telling you to stop."

"She doesn't strike me that way at all. She clearly loves you and wants to help. I think she's seen some terrible things—"

Theo shook his head. "You people never listen to reason. You're so bent on getting our money that you refuse to accept decency. Let me put this in terms you'll understand. Either leave my family alone, or I'll see to it that you are hurt. Badly."

"Want me to freeze him?" Drummond said. "Maybe that'll get him to accept my kind are real."

Max shook his head slightly. Not only did he think that plan might backfire, convincing Theo further that some trickery had been used, but Max didn't want his partner getting any closer to the hazy ghost until they knew more of what they dealt with. Besides, this wasn't the first skeptic they had ever encountered.

Hoping to sound relaxed, even light, Max said, "Doubting us is normal. Heck, it's hard to believe in any of this even after you've seen it. I also know nothing I say tonight will convince you that we're legit. But if you'll accept that my wife and I believe what we're saying, even if you think we're crazy or scammers or whatever, then you'll see that we can't walk away from this. It's our job to help you and your mother."

"We don't want your help."

"Your mother does, and you need it." Max waved off Theo's next argument. "This is the best I can offer as proof that we're not a scam — The Porter Agency will not charge your mother anything, not a single dime, until we solve this case. If, in the end, you still think we're trying to pull something over you, you don't have to pay us at all. Even if your problems go away. Think of us like those lawyers who only get paid if they win the case."

"There's no way for me to verify you'll have accomplished anything."

"It depends on what's happening to you. But let's say you're right. Let's say what we do produces no results you can trust. If it puts your mother at ease, if it ends the way she frets over you and fears and lives a nervous existence, maybe that's worthwhile enough."

"That sounds like you're trying to weasel —"

"Doesn't matter. You didn't hire us. Your mother did. I'm telling you that we won't charge her unless she's satisfied. Simple as that, and it's the best I can give you. Because we're not walking away from this. You have a ghost haunting you, and even if you don't want to do anything about it, we can't let it go on. Not just for you, not just for your mother, but for the ghost. Whoever he is, he suffers, too. We need to help him."

Theo's top lip curled. "I'll sue you for fraud."

"We get threatened with that one a lot. It won't work for the same reasons you can't sue a medium or a fortune teller."

"Then you admit that you're nothing more than an entertainment."

Max stayed silent. Nothing he could say would get through to the man. Theo would have to find out the hard way. Again. Maybe more than a few times. And if past cases were any indication, Theo had quite a few ghostly encounters coming up on his dance card.

At length, the young man spun away and propelled towards his van. "You better watch yourself. One slip up, one bit of anything that my lawyers can use, and your scam is over."

Max held still and stoic until the van drove away. Then he let out a long breath, held the railing, and bent over to loosen his taut muscles.

"Lovely fellow," Drummond said. "Can't even accept the obvious things in front of him."

With a short series of jumping jacks, Max burned off some of his adrenaline before getting in his car. “I’ve got to get home and get some sleep. We’ll tackle this in the morning.”

Drummond tipped his hat before vanishing. Max wished he could do the same.

Chapter 7

WHEN DAWN ARRIVED, the Porters were ready for an early start. Sandra called their witch-in-training, Brenda Byrd, and the two met at the Agency office to research ghosts seen as a haze. Meanwhile, Max stayed behind to watch over his mother. He set his laptop on the kitchen table — fondly glancing over at the alcove that had been his workspace for several years — and got busy digging into the history of Sidwell Mills. In particular, he wanted to find photos of every man who had died at the mill. Every so often, Drummond drifted into the kitchen to inspect Max's results. So far, none of the men resembled the ghost Drummond had seen.

"These guys are too young. Didn't you listen to your wife? Our man looks like Scrooge."

Max swallowed the urge to respond. One room over, his mother slept — and no matter her age, she still could hear whenever Max did something she would want to question. Talking to a ghost in the kitchen would absolutely ping her radar.

Returning to the laptop, Max remembered he could use the computer to type responses, but he wanted to focus on the work, not on Drummond's quips. He brought up the Sidwell Mills homepage once more. He had been methodically working through every page and every link, focusing on the historical events surrounding the mill as well. Not surprisingly, the company website painted a picture of joy, harmony, and great fortune through hard work. The employees were part of the Sidwell family, working together for a brighter future.

Other sites, ones devoted to the true history of the company, brought into focus the conflicts with unions, the abusive hours, the low pay, a handful of management-level scandals, and the eventual closing of the mill so Sidwell could make more money with cheap labor overseas. Though horrible, few of these incidents resulted in an untimely death, and those that did hardly seemed vicious enough to cause a ghost to haunt the Sidwell family for generations. But as Max clicked a new link for a deeper dive into the management side of things, his mother shuffled into the kitchen.

"Good morning," Max said, pleased she had walked out on her own. Perhaps today would be a good day for her. "You hungry?"

Dressed in a pink nightgown that hung limp on her shrinking frame, Mrs. Porter settled opposite Max. She placed a plastic pill case on the table, flicked open the section for that day, and dumped her morning regimen. As she lined the pills up, she gestured to the coffee. "Did Sandra make it?"

"Yeah. You want a mug?"

"I don't like the way she makes it."

Forcing a cheery smile as thoughts of a good day vanished, Max said, "You can always have orange juice."

"Not in this house. I can't stand the pulp, and the juice you have here has pulp."

"You only have to tell us. Next time, I'll buy the kind without pulp. Okay?" He poured a mug of coffee for her and set it on the table.

As she swallowed her pills one by one, taking a sip of coffee for each pill, she said, "I want to talk with you about something important."

Max tried to ease back in his chair, but his stomach clenched. "Is there a problem?"

"Other than losing my apartment, my strength, being in pain most days, and having to choke down a pharmacy every morning, I'd say all is well." With the last pill finished, she snapped the plastic container shut. "Thank you for taking me to the ER the other day."

"Of course. Anything you need."

"I know you think you know everything, that you have the answers —"

"I never —"

"Don't interrupt your mother. I raised you better than that." She sipped more coffee before continuing. "You and Sandra treat me like this is a hospice, like I'm going to die any moment. Maybe that's true. But even though my body is falling apart, my brain still works. My eyes and my ears still work."

Reaching across the table, his heart sank. "We never meant to make you feel like that. And it's not true — I'm not waiting for you to pass. I love you. I want you to be comfortable and happy."

"I'm not a fool. I know what's going on around here."

She had not responded to his offered hands, so Max scooted back in his chair. His stomach gripped harder as he tried to discern if his mother was lucid at this moment. "What is it that you think is happening?"

"Don't talk to me like I've got Alzheimer's on top of MS. I'm still your mother, and my belfry is free of bats."

Max snickered. "Okay. I believe you. But I really don't know what you think —"

"Your Aunt Jane. You're still trying to find her, and I told you not to do that."

"She's family. Not only that, she's family that's been kept away from me. Heck, her existence has been kept secret. How can I not try to find her?"

"Don't be dramatic. If your Aunt Jane wanted to be found, she would have popped up ages ago. It's not your place to out her now."

"*Out her?* About what?"

"About where she is. Pay attention."

To avoid a swift, angry rebuttal, Max brought up another article about Sidwell Mills on his laptop. Part of him wanted to open his folder on Aunt Jane, but he tamped that down. No point in being spiteful.

"Don't start pouting with me," Mrs. Porter said, crossing legs and arms at the same time. "You've been doing that your whole life and it never works. You won't get any answers out of me."

That got Max's interest. "Do you know where she is?"

"I don't. And I don't want to know. That woman brought

nothing but trouble to my life."

"But you know something. You implied you have answers."

Turning her focus on him in an uncomfortable manner, Mrs. Porter said, "You need to stop. There's no big mystery here. Definitely not the kind of pretend nonsense your clients bring to you. It's rather mundane, really. Your Aunt Jane is just a woman who wanted to be cut off from the rest of the Porters, and the family obliged. You don't need to know why or how or whatever questions you have."

"But —"

"No. I won't help you. It serves no purpose in your life. Until you found that photo album, you didn't know about her. Now that you do, what's really changed? Nothing. Stop obsessing and leave the poor woman alone."

"Um, partner." Drummond had lowered behind Max. "Sorry to interrupt your circular argument, but we found our ghost."

Max peeked up at the detective.

Pointing at a photo on the laptop showing a ribbon cutting for a new section of the mill, Drummond singled out an older, bent gentleman that bore a striking resemblance to the classic image of Scrooge. Max enlarged the picture and scrolled down to the caption beneath that listed the names of those shown. Trying not to visibly startle and gain the concern of his mother, Max re-read the name. It hadn't changed.

Robert Sidwell.

Chapter 8

RUNNING A BUSINESS that solved supernatural problems equaled danger and deception. No matter how often he encountered it, though, Max never lost that gut-churning sensation when he discovered he and his wife or his family were on the losing end of that equation. Learning that the ghost was Robert Sidwell knotted Max's nerves. Thankfully, Sandra was with Brenda and not with the Sidwells at that moment.

"That makes sense," she said over the phone.

Max pressed harder on the gas pedal as he drove toward the office. Balancing his phone on his right thigh, he said, "You expected this?"

"I wouldn't say I *expected* it, but you've got admit that Mrs. Sidwell and her son acted highly suspicious. I mean for a young man in a wheelchair who doesn't believe a lick of magic to suddenly allow himself to be placed in the center of a casting circle — no questions, no real protest beyond complaining. That was strange. He could have wheeled out of there at any time, yet he stayed put."

"The way his mother domineered him, I figured he cowed to anything she wanted."

"That's probably true, too. At least, for some of the time. But he didn't act too cowed last night at the park, did he?"

"He was belligerent. Said whatever he could to shut us down."

"Exactly. People get scared when confronted with anything that fundamentally changes their reality. Their brains will fight against it."

"Ghosts and magic are a very fundamental change."

"And you saw how they acted when we told them what the

ghost looked like. They knew who he was right away. If Theo didn't believe in ghosts before, he's finding it much harder now."

Taking a sharp turn, Max's phone slid across his thigh. He caught it before it could fall in the crevice between his seat and the center console. Slamming on the brakes to avoid colliding with a parked car, he received an annoyed honk from behind.

As he eased back into his lane, he heard Sandra say, "Are you okay? What happened?"

"I'm fine." He ignored the adrenaline racing through his system. "Will you please call the Sidwells and arrange a meeting? We've got a lot of questions for them."

Cutting through downtown Winston-Salem was no faster or slower than driving around the city perimeter. People called it the twenty-minute town because that's the time it took to get anywhere. It was true, too. Well, true-ish. When Max wanted to get someplace faster, traffic always conspired to turn the city into a forty-minute town.

While waiting at a stop, inching off the brake in little bursts as if that might urge the light to change, Max felt the cold of a ghost appear in the passenger seat. Drummond adjusted his hat.

"I went back to the mansion. Tried to see if I could talk with Robert Sidwell ghost to ghost."

"And?"

"No luck. I don't know why, but he's still nothing but a hazy blob. There was only that flash of him with Sandra's spell. Otherwise, he doesn't seem to be entirely there."

"Whatever happened to him — and my money's on something to do with witches — we'll get some answers later today. Sandra's setting up another meet with the Sidwells."

Drummond gave an approving nod. "You've got be careful when you approach a client that you know isn't being honest with you."

"It's not like this is the first time that's ever happened."

"Still, it's a good idea to —"

Garbling the next words, Drummond's head cracked back followed by his body. Fluttering half out of the car, he threw a punch upward and disappeared.

"Crap," Max said to the empty car. Something had attacked his partner, and he had good guess that it was one particularly hazy ghost.

As he turned onto a busy street that led further north out of the city, Max saw Drummond appear a few feet ahead. The car sped straight through the ghost who struggled against his unseen attacker.

"Keep driving," Drummond yelled as he slipped by.

Checking the rearview mirror, Max watched the ghost disappear once more. He glanced down at the glove compartment. Sandra had made an emergency ward, and he kept it there.

Shouting, Drummond popped out of the hood, his cheek smushing from an invisible fist. He elbowed behind, catching his assailant, but as the car ripped through the fighting ghosts, part of Robert Sidwell passed through Max. The icy chill that dug into his bones caused his legs to stiffen. The car sped up. Max wrenched the wheel, avoiding an accident with a building.

It happened in an instant. Seconds later, the brawling ghosts had departed, and a cascade of warmth rolled through Max's bones. Before he could adjust his thoughts, Drummond flailed into view, crossing the car. Another icy blast hit Max as Sidwell raced after Drummond, giving no concern for the living. Max swerved, struggling to maintain control of the car.

He reached for the glove compartment, his shivering fingers fumbling the latch.

"Floor it," Drummond said, appearing in the passenger seat.

Max frowned at his partner. "H-Huh?"

"He's coming back, and I got an idea. Floor it."

As Max pushed the gas pedal down, Drummond took a hit to the gut. The car charged along the street. Drummond reached out and clasped his seat's headrest. He screamed the anguish that only came when he touched the corporeal world. His fingers sank into the faux-leather, locking him to the speed of the car while the rest of his ghostly visage flapped back, his legs through the windows.

"Don't stop." Drummond roared at the pain in his hand as

he raised one foot and slammed it back. Though Max saw no enemy, he did see Drummond's strike connect with something in the empty air.

"How did you do that?"

"Don't overthink it."

"But —"

"Watch the road."

Snapping his focus forward, a car pulled out from a passing gas station. Max's tires screeched as he dipped around the near-accident. If he continued like this, some cop would eventually pull him over, suspect him for a DUI, and what could he say? *Sorry, Officer, but it's hard to drive while your ghost partner is fighting a hazy ghost in and around the car.* That would go over real well.

Max turned down a narrow alley. With any luck, they could avoid notice. Drummond massaged his burning hand as he darted his attention from one part of the car to the other.

"You lost him?" Max asked.

"He's a ghost. It's not like I can — watch out!"

Before Max could take in any information, the deep cold of the dead reached into his brain. A vulture of a man appeared half-inside the dashboard, his withered arm stretching straight at Max. This was hardly the first time a ghost had tapped into Max's head and lit up the ghostly realm, but the frozen pain felt sharper than previously. The ghost's old face did indeed resemble Scrooge — not only wrinkled and balding, but bushy browed with an unpleasant sneer curling his lip — and he twisted his hand causing Max to shriek.

Drummond dashed behind the ghost, wrapped his arms around the man's neck, and yanked back. Though Max tried to maintain control of the wheel, the pale blue of the dead world prevented him from clear focus. A migraine-level pounding shoved his gray matter against his skull. The car caromed off the alley wall, shattering the plastic door handles, scratching the sides, and flashing a few sparks.

Max heard a deep growl, and the pain ceased. He saw Drummond arching back as if carrying a heavy sack. The ghost twisted in the air and disappeared. Max slammed the brakes, though he was only coasting.

Panting in a cold sweat, he shivered. With each shallow breath, his shaking strengthened. His fingers clenched, his arms vibrated, his toes curled, and his legs bounced. A stone rose from his gut, into his chest, growing as it travelled, gaining momentum, until he finally opened his mouth and screamed. Tears wetted the corners of his eyes.

At length, he checked his sidemirrors, though the passenger one now hung limp against the door. As his eyes flew over the glove compartment, he flicked the small door down. Underneath his vehicle registration and insurance card, he fished out a small piece of wood with a string looped through. Arcane symbols had been carved into the wood.

He slipped it on. Sandra had designed the ward to repel any ghost except for Drummond. It worked well, for the most part, though Drummond complained that it made him itchy and gave him a headache. Max refrained from pointing out that the ghost lacked skin to be irritated or blood to pound his head. Then again, Max had no clear understanding of how the ghost sensed anything. He'd have to take Drummond's word for it.

The air chilled. Max braced his arms and legs. He held his breath and winced at the next attack. The pale glow of Drummond flashed against the hood as the detective punched downward.

Max caught his partner's eye, lifted the ghost ward, and the side of Drummond's mouth raised. He thrust the invisible opponent upward, hauled back, and released a devastating strike. Though Max saw nothing more, he pictured the body flailing back through the windshield and into the car. As the temperature dropped and frost appeared on the inside of the windows, Max felt the ghost ward heat up.

Then nothing.

The temperature rose to Drummond levels, and the ward cooled. A second later, the detective reappeared and drifted back to the passenger seat. "Don't worry. He's gone. That ward surprised the heck out of him."

"That was Robert Sidwell, right?"

"Without a doubt."

They still had a few miles to reach the office, but Max needed a moment to let his jittering hands rest. Though Drummond had sounded confident that they were now safe, Max noticed his partner remained vigilant in watching over the area.

"That was crazy," Max said, more to hear a voice than anything else.

"It was a sure sign that we've found something worth knowing."

"Any idea what that something would be?"

"Not a clue. But anything kept quiet this long that's suddenly met with an attack — you don't need more proof than that."

"Of what?"

"That we definitely want to chat with Mrs. Sidwell again."

Max eased the car down to a connecting side street and headed for the office.

Chapter 9

WHILE THEY WAITED FOR MRS. SIDWELL TO ARRIVE, Sandra listened at her desk as Max and Drummond detailed their harrowing encounter with Robert Sidwell's ghost. Brenda sat nearby on the beaten couch, sifting through several old books from Sandra's personal collection. Every so often, the two women would exchange a glance. Each time, Max paused, trying to discern what he had said to garner such a look.

Drummond concluded the retelling with a simple, "That's it. No more to share."

"I'm sorry to hear you had a difficult time," she said.

"Difficult?" Max slumped at his own desk. "I could've been in a major wreck. I could be in the hospital right now."

"If you had been explaining this from a hospital bed, I'd be showing far more concern. But you're not, hon. You're fine. I can see that right in front of me."

With a half-serious, half-playful pout, Max said, "You could pretend to be a little worried."

"Sure." She cleared her throat with a dramatic flair, then placed the back of her wrist against her forehead. "Oh, dear, dear Max. I was aghast to hear of your terrible trials upon the open road. How ever did you survive? Why, I swear, had you but a single scratch, I would have lost hope at sanity, my dire concern for you being so unfathomable."

"Thank you, hon. That's exactly what I needed."

She threw a pencil at him.

After a good laugh — including a few chuckles from Drummond — Sandra donned a ghost ward and handed one to Brenda. With all three protected, Drummond scooted to the back corner near the ceiling. From there he could see everyone but stayed out of the bulk of the ward fields. He scratched at his neck.

Sandra shifted into a serious tone, and Max perked his attention toward her. "We've been trying to find out what we can on what this misty, hazy kind of ghost means." She gestured to Brenda, and the younger woman stood.

"You want me to say this?" Brenda asked. She had been growing out her afro lately, and it had a slight bounce as she moved.

"The more you practice, the better you'll get at it."

"Okay." Brenda walked to Sandra's desk and pulled up their notes on a laptop. "Don't get too excited. We didn't find much. Really, we found a lot, but it's a bit of a mess. See, there's plenty of things written about blurry, hazy, unclear ghosts. Many kinds of versions of it. The thing is that they each indicate different possibilities."

"A little more concise," Sandra said with an encouraging smile.

Max said, "It's some type of witch spell, then?"

"It can be," Brenda said. "But not always. This haziness is like how when you have a fever, that fever can be a symptom of tons of illnesses. You need more information or to run some tests to figure it out. With this, it could be a curse, a spell, or a malformed ghost."

Drummond looked to Sandra. "Never heard of that last one. What is it?"

Sandra pointed back to Brenda. "Our ghost wants to hear more on that last one."

Smiling in the vague direction she thought Drummond hovered, Brenda said, "It's a ghost caught between states of being. Most of the accounts we found were of ghosts starting to become poltergeists, but something disrupted the change."

"Based on what you gentlemen have told us, I'd say Robert Sidwell's ghost might fall into that last category. His rage attack against you sounds a lot like the blind anger of a poltergeist."

Max said, "You think he's fighting it? Trying to stay in control? Maybe it could be enough to disrupt that kind of a change."

"Maybe. We haven't encountered many poltergeists, so we're mostly going by what Brenda and I can find in books."

Drummond said, "Be thankful. Insane, murderous ghosts are not a pleasant group to hang around."

"Why did he leave?" Max grabbed a pen and tapped it against his desk. "I had the ward, but that only protected me. I mean, he came in, hurt us both, and then left without finishing the job. Isn't that strange?"

"What part of *insane, murderous ghost* is confusing you?"

Peeking at the clock on his computer, Max said, "Mrs. Sidwell and her son should be here any minute. We'll get a better grasp on this Robert Sidwell stuff once we hear the truth from her."

The office door opened, and Mrs. Sidwell backed in, pulling Theo's wheelchair with her. She settled him near the couch. "You said something about the truth. Yes, I suppose you need that much."

"Well, well," Drummond said. He shucked his chin in the direction of the doorway, and though Max saw nothing beyond the Sidwells, he gathered that a certain hazy ghost floated shy of their wards' reach.

After pouring coffee for Mrs. Sidwell and setting it on the low table by the couch, Max slid back to give her space. All remained quiet as they waited for her to begin. Mrs. Sidwell lowered to the edge of the couch and raised her eyes upward. Theo made a show of impatience. He opened his mouth to complain, but Mrs. Sidwell pointed a sharp finger. He stayed silent.

At length, she dropped her focus to Max and Sandra while always keeping her nose tilted up. She had mastered the art of looking down on a person, and Max felt himself shrinking underneath her gaze. He couldn't imagine how difficult Theo's upbringing must have been. Max made a mental to note to forgive his own mother for her stricter moments — a little bit, anyway.

"Robert had a difficult childhood," Mrs. Sidwell said.

Theo bounced once in his chair, the other side of him overcoming his fears — the side Max had seen at the quarry.

"Are you kidding me? This isn't therapy. They don't need to hear every detail of his life. Jump to the end, and we can be done with this."

A withering glare and Theo's protestations ceased as if a fuse had shorted in his mouth. He tried to start up twice — his jaw vibrating but no sound coming out. She held her eyes upon him until his shoulders slumped. He shifted in his wheelchair, finding sudden interest in chewing on his thumbnail.

Satisfied that her son would remain silent, Mrs. Sidwell gave a little nod — Max thought she meant this for herself — and returned her focus to the Porters. "Robert had a difficult childhood. His father was an abusive man, and his mother was cold. I don't know the specifics, he never liked to talk too in-depth on such matters and I respected his privacy, but I saw enough in how these hardships shaped his behavior. His parents ruined him. I tried, I swear I did, but I lacked what he needed. I wasn't enough to fix him. Robert was never happy. Never satisfied. He had achieved a great deal, more than most men, yet it never completed him." She took a breath, glanced at her son, and as she exhaled, she said, "He never was faithful, either."

Theo's head snapped up. "He loved you."

"I don't doubt that. But love and loyalty were not synonymous for your father. I'm sorry you have to hear this, but if we're going to get you any help at all, then this much must be told." To the Porters: "Robert slept with many women over the years."

"That's not true."

"I made sure you never had to know, but I'm afraid it is what happened."

Drummond slid along his bookcase, inching toward the doorway while keeping a safe distance from the ward field. "Robert doesn't look too happy about what's being said." To answer Max's frown, Drummond added, "He's still a hazy mess, but I can read the body language. The ghost is pacing like a pissed off tiger."

Doing her best to maintain her dignity, Mrs. Sidwell said, "I would never dare broach the topic of his infidelity, so I cannot say why Robert did these things — other than his insatiable need for more of everything. I suppose temptation surrounded him. Those young women who worked in the mill, many of them attractive, enough of them willing to be a mistress if that got them off the floor and into a cushy secretarial position — I can't blame him for the whole thing. I saw the way they flirted with him, throwing themselves at him. A man can only be expected to endure for so long."

Drummond curled his nose. "With the way this guy looks, I'm thinking more than one of these women had been forced into it. What could they do when their boss gave them a choice to sleep with him or lose their job?"

"Why did you keep this from me?" Confusion and anger swirled across Theo's brow. "I could have handled it, and I could've been there for you."

"You were there enough." Mrs. Sidwell rested her hand on the back of the wheelchair. "Besides, it wasn't your burden to carry."

"Perhaps one of these women was a witch," Sandra said.

Max added, "He did have enemies in the other mill owners. Not that hard to believe one of them might hire a witch to get close enough to cast a spell."

Mrs. Sidwell's face opened with hope for a flash before her mouth tightened into a hard line again. "I'm sure of it. Could that account for his behavior? Perhaps he had been cursed from the start, from before I knew him."

Theo slapped his wheelchair. "Stop making excuses. Cheating is cheating."

"A minute ago, you wanted to defend your father. Now you're ready to see him swing?"

"I don't —"

"You don't know anything about him. Not really. And you should learn not to be so absolute in your rulings against people. If a witch had cursed him, if he had no say in the matter of his behavior, that would explain —"

"What? What would it really explain?"

A loud thump hit the door. The Sidwells both jumped. They

looked in that direction, paused into an intense silence, and waited.

"One warning only, pal," Drummond said, pointing at the doorway. "Do that again, and my fist is going to do the knocking."

Sandra ignored the ghosts. "Mrs. Sidwell?"

With a quiver in her throat, Mrs. Sidwell said, "Please forgive us. Things have been difficult lately."

"Of course. You've been living under a lot of strain for a long time."

With a mocking snort, Theo said, "If what you say is true, if my father is really a ghost that's haunting me, then you don't need some mystical curse for it to make perfect sense. The man despised me."

"That is utterly false." Mrs. Sidwell spoke the words with such power that Theo wilted back. "You do not understand. And if you would keep quiet and open your ears, you might learn a few things about your father, about who he really was, about why he pushed you to be greater than you are."

"Too weak. Too close to Mother. Not smart enough to run a company. Should I go on with the rest of the crap he would say to me?"

"What you should do is silence yourself. You are making a spectacle."

"I am showing the Porters exactly what they are dealing with. How else are they going to end this *magic* curse and get rid of the *spooky* ghost?

"There is no need for mockery."

Sandra stood with her hands clasped in front. She offered a hopeful tone. "I think we've heard enough to help."

The Sidwells gazed up at her, and with the same shock that Max felt, Mrs. Sidwell said, "You have?"

"Absolutely. My colleague, Brenda, and I have been discussing your case, and we believe that Theo has some of this correct."

"I do?" Theo's shock matched the look on his mother's face.

"Some. Mrs. Sidwell, you understand plenty, as well. From

what you have said, and from our research, it is clear to us that Robert refuses to let go of his power. He had spent his life accumulating money and dominating over people. He clearly took pleasure in bending people to his will — sometimes that took the form of infidelity. Robert can't accept the idea that his death would end that."

"Plus," Brenda said, "y'all said that he wanted Mr. Theo to be the same as him. He can't let go of that, either."

"If he can make Theo into the same mold as himself, then his life and the horrible way he lived it would be validated. Justified."

Theo frowned. "My father is haunting me because I'm not an asshole?"

Mrs. Sidwell slapped his hand. "Theo!"

"It's a possibility," Sandra said. "It would explain why we don't see a curse on him, yet he behaves and appears as if he did."

"But what about the other Sidwells? You said this was a curse."

"You said that. We've treated it like one, but I'm not so sure anymore. Robert has been stuck as if trapped inside a paranormal maze, and he thinks the path out is through Theo. Through changing him into the kind of man Robert wants. For many ghosts, vicarious living is still living."

Imitating his dead partner, Max clapped his hands together once. "We can work with that. Right, hon?"

"We absolutely can." To Theo: "If you're willing to go through another spell, I know I can free you from this ghost."

Theo glanced at the eager eyes of his mother, and his mouth turned downward. Max prepared for a verbal assault followed by the man wheeling out of the office. Probably would throw out a few four-letter words — both satisfying to rattle off, and Theo would enjoy the shock of his mother. But as he conversed with his mother through their silent eyes, Max caught glimpses of love, frustration, and defeat.

At length, Theo shrugged. "Why not? I'm already here."

Chapter 10

THE PORTERS GOT TO WORK IMMEDIATELY with Sandra orchestrating everyone's movements. After having Max and Brenda lift away the coffee table, she swept back the large circular rug. Beneath it, her casting circle awaited. For now, it was an off-white painted circle, but Max intended to make it a permanent one when he got the chance.

With Sandra's nod, Brenda walked to the supply closet near the bathroom. She returned with a box of assorted candles and chalk. Requiring no further directions, she knelt at the southern edge of the circle and drew the first of many symbols. She used green chalk. As far as Max knew, the color of chalk did not change the spell. Not like colors of candles.

"Max, please stand closer to the doorway." Sandra gestured toward the entrance. "Your ward will keep Robert from disturbing us until we're ready."

Drummond scratched his arm. "I'll be by your side, partner. Just in case."

"Excuse me," Mrs. Sidwell said, "but are you saying that my husband's ghost is here?"

"Of course, Mother. The damn man has been torturing me for years. Isn't that right? I'm the victim of a magic ghost."

Sandra said, "Both of you need to stay calm. We all do. Robert's ghost is in a precarious position right now. Intense emotions could throw him into a poltergeist state — a violent, non-thinking fury. If that happens, not only will we be in danger, but Robert risks getting stuck in that state."

Theo said, "Stuck how?"

"You've heard about truly haunted houses — bleeding walls and attacks upon the residents and such. Those are most often caused by poltergeists. They can't be set free. They can't move on. Not in that state."

A mixture of doubt and fear rolled across Theo's face, so Max thought it wise to explain, "If Robert can't move on, then neither can you. He'll be haunting you for the rest of your life. Far more violently, too."

Theo rolled his wheelchair closer to his mother. That clearly satisfied Sandra enough — she joined Brenda to work on the spell. They placed red, white, and black candles at various points along the circle and continued drawing symbols around the edges.

Standing with his back toward the office door, Max felt Robert's presence. The air behind him pressed like a strong breeze. The ward heated up even as his skin prickled.

He recalled many of the times Drummond had cracked a ward through brute force. The old detective would charge forward and slam into the protective field. Again and again, taking the painful hits, until the ward could no longer hold him back.

"You need to calm down," Drummond said.

Max thought to toss back a witty remark but then saw that Drummond had spoken through the door — at Robert.

"Look, pal, we've had our differences, but I'm willing to look beyond your attack on us in the car. I know you're not thinking too clear, but trust me — we're trying to help you get out of this mess."

A thump at the door, and Max felt it against his back.

"If you'll quit hitting that ward field," Drummond said, "I promise you're going to be reunited with your boy soon."

With the next hit, Robert must have slammed his full weight because Max stumbled forward several steps. He looked over his shoulder at Drummond. The concern on the old ghost's face did little to ease Max's growing worry.

After glancing at the door, Sandra doubled her efforts. "No, no," she said, jabbing a piece of chalk in Brenda's direction. "That symbol has to be in the line with the West black candle, otherwise, the path to moving on won't open."

"Sorry," Brenda said. She flipped back a few pages in her notebook and reviewed what she had written.

Theo said, "Do you even know what you're doing?"

"Hey," Sandra said, sounding more like a stern mother than a helpful witch. "You do not talk to my team that way."

For a second, Theo didn't know how to react. Even glanced at his mother for guidance. But there was a strange solidarity between women when it came to disciplining children. Max never quite understood where they drew the lines, but mothers seemed to know when it was okay to scold another mother's child and when it was inappropriate. Clearly, Sandra had not come close to crossing a line this time.

Theo must have recognized this, too. As if his own mother had reprimanded him, he lowered his head toward Brenda. "Sorry, ma'am."

"Thank you," Brenda said before turning back to Sandra. "I wrote it down correctly here in my notes but screwed up which black candle to use."

Sandra said, "We're running out of time for mistakes. This is very much a case of *measure twice cut once.*"

Max saw the pain on Sandra's face — she hated to admonish Brenda — but if they ruined this spell due to one careless misstep, there would be no second chance. Robert would inevitably become a poltergeist, and the Porters' problems would compound. Not to mention the threat to Mrs. Sidwell and Theo.

The door pounded again. Max thought he heard wood splintering. Heat rose around the ward on his chest as did the pressure at his back. "Drummond?"

"Not much I can do unless you want me to restrain him. I do that and —"

"Full-on poltergeist."

"Most likely."

To Sandra: "Hon, best to hurry up."

As she raised her head to throw a sarcastic quip, the heat on Max's chest ratcheted up. A bright light shot out from the center of the pendant. With a loud crackle, the ward split apart. Max felt a sharp dagger hit his sternum and pieces of the broken ward clattered on the floor.

The front office door bashed open. Max whirled around as an invisible wall of anger smacked into him. The wallop flattened him to the floor.

Though dazed, he watched Drummond race in and grapple with the unseen entity that was Robert Sidwell. Rolling one direction, then the other, Drummond let out a short grunt and doubled over.

"Stop." Sandra stood at the head of the circle, glowering at the empty space that Robert occupied. She removed her ward and snapped her fingers for Brenda to do the same. "You are welcome here. We are going to help you. I'm sorry that you had to be locked outside, but we needed to prepare." To Theo: "Get in the center of the circle."

Theo remained still until his mother pushed at his shoulders. He rolled across the lines of the circle, stopping in the center. Brenda struck a match and started lighting the candles.

Rubbing the back of his head, Max sat up. He looked toward Drummond. "What's happening now?"

Drummond reset his hat. "Your wife has an incredibly strong presence. That's what's happening. Robert doesn't know what to do being confronted by a human that can see him and isn't afraid."

"Come in, Mr. Sidwell." Sandra took a step back and gestured toward Theo. "Join your son. It's what you've wanted."

"Robert's approaching the circle," Drummond said. "He's moving closer, then backing up, then closer — he's a wild animal that doesn't know what to make of the situation."

Max said, "But he wants to be with his son."

In a soothing tone, Sandra said, "It'll be okay. Nobody's going to hurt you."

Waiting in strained silence, Max watched the empty space that both Sandra and Drummond focused on. Then:

"He's in." Drummond nodded in Mrs. Sidwell's direction. "You better watch over her."

Max agreed. He walked to Mrs. Sidwell. "Please back up with me. For your safety. And for Theo's."

With a stunned nod, she allowed Max to help her to her feet and escort her to stand behind his desk.

Drummond hunched forward and put his hands out — trying to appear nonthreatening yet ready to lunge into a tackle should Robert decide to bolt. At least, that's how Max perceived it. Of course, a ghost could disappear, so he didn't know what Drummond actually planned.

Flicking the brim of his hat and offering a click of his tongue, Drummond said, "You can trust these ladies. There aren't many good witches in the world, but these are two of them."

Sandra gestured toward Theo. "Join your son, Mr. Sidwell. We won't hurt you. It's taken awhile, but you've made your point. Your wife and son understand what you want of them now."

Max didn't know if that was true — doubted it immensely — but so long as Robert believed in it, so long as he held to that hope, then he would remain a ghost instead of a poltergeist. Nudging Mrs. Sidwell, he said, "Tell him she's right."

With her voice trembling alongside her hands, Mrs. Sidwell said, "I'll see that he does better. Theo can be what you want. Robert, you can trust me. I'll make sure nobody destroys the great work you've done."

"That's it. Come now." Sandra backed away, allowing Robert room to enter further. Her voice had shifted into her casting tones — deeper, a bit sultry, filled with concentration, brimming with emotion. To Brenda: "We can begin."

Sitting on her knees with her head bowed low and her hands spread wide on the floor, Brenda chanted a short phrase in one of the dead witch languages. Repeating it like a meditative mantra, she pulsed her torso like the beginning of a modern dance.

The air in the office tingled. Max had experienced this enough times not to be concerned, but the sensation would be new to Mrs. Sidwell. He leaned close to her. "Don't worry. My wife has complete control of this."

As if on cue Sandra walked behind Brenda and spread her arms in a T. Staring forward at Theo and Robert Sidwell, she started to chant as well. Except this was not the same phrase as Brenda repeated. Instead, Sandra created a melodic flow of ancient words that weaved in and around Brenda's phrasing. It was like listening to someone blend a rap song with a classic pop song — it should not have sounded pleasant, but it weirdly worked.

Within seconds of these two spells uniting, Robert Sidwell became visible within the circle. Mrs. Sidwell gasped. One hand went to her heart while the other reached for Max. "It really is him."

Robert's head snapped towards the sound of his wife. He scowled.

Drummond floated between them, careful to stay out of the circle. "Ease up, old man. You're almost there. Look at me — ghost to ghost. This is your chance. You can escape and move on to something better."

Max could not hear what Robert replied, but he did see the ghost's mouth moving.

Drummond tilted his head. "It's not a case of heaven or hell beyond this world. It's not like that. This — this is your hell. You get out of here, and you'll be much better off. I promise."

Brenda rose on her knees, her arms spread wide like Sandra as her eyes rolled upward. Her chanting grew in intensity as well as volume. Sandra's tones found the harmony to blend and match.

"Father," Theo said, staring directly at the ghost. "I know I'm not what you wanted. I'm sorry I couldn't be better. But I'm not like that anymore. I'll do everything I can to live up to your expectations. You can move on now. I won't fight against you."

Drummond said, "I don't think he's buying it. He looks ticked off."

Max could see that much for himself. But as Robert turned toward his son, his face scrunching with tightened strain, his fingers clawed, Mrs. Sidwell took a firm step forward.

"Robert, that's enough."

The ghost paused, hunched like a movie monster caught in a heinous act, and turned to face his wife. He spat out a litany that neither Drummond nor Sandra bothered to translate.

Mrs. Sidwell did not cower, though her hands wrung tight. "You spent your life taking me for granted, taking our marriage for granted, and I allowed it. I did not stop your indiscretions because I understood the price I paid for my security." She tilted her head toward Theo. "I turned a blind eye to the way you treated our son for the same reason. But you are dead now. You've had more than most, including time beyond the grave. It's over. Move on. You cannot have Theo. He belongs to me. Always has."

Robert's face dropped in shock. He hovered, and his forehead furrowed. But his moment of surprised confusion washed away as a wave of anger squeezed his features. He jabbed a crooked finger at his wife, once again spouting off words most could not hear.

Max worried that this new round of rage might push Robert into poltergeist territory again, but a peek at Sandra calmed his nerves. She wore a soft smirk on her lips. When Robert lunged at his wife, he never reached the circle's edge. He was too late.

A shaft of light appeared from above. Shielding his eyes, he gazed upward. In awe, his hands flopped to his sides. He mouthed some words, but even Drummond shrugged at Max's questioning eyes. Whatever Robert said to this light could not be heard by any but Robert. When he finished talking, he listened and smiled at the response. Offering a final nod toward Sandra and Brenda, he let out one long breath.

Robert Sidwell faded away. He had moved on.

Max sent warm vibes to Sandra. He didn't know if such things were real, but knowing that ghosts and witches and magic were real opened the way for a lot of common phrases to acquire new meanings. Even if the idea of *vibes* was only in his head, the loving way Sandra gazed at him was real.

"Thank you," Mrs. Sidwell said.

Even Theo looked relieved. Though he still asked, "Does that mean the bastard gets to go to Heaven?"

"That light wasn't Heaven," Sandra said. "Merely the next step after death. Heaven or Hell or some other place — no mortal knows what awaits us. But if there is any justice in existence, I'm sure Robert will face his."

Mrs. Sidwell rubbed a finger under each eye and repeated, "Thank you."

Another case closed. Another client saved from the supernatural.

Except as Sandra's brightness threatened to launch Max into a foolish romantic gesture — probably sweeping her into his arms and planting a strong kiss — the circle emitted flashes of pale light. Sandra's joyful expression dropped into a concerned frown. Along with everyone else, she looked back at the circle and Theo.

"Is that supposed to happen?" Mrs. Sidwell asked.

"Hey." Theo pushed at his wheels, but the chair wouldn't move. "What's going on?"

While Sandra and Drummond stared in shock, Max and the others only caught glimpses of what they saw. Each time the light within the circle burst out, he witnessed numerous hazy shapes trailing off Theo. They clung to each other, spreading out in different directions, flowing in invisible currents.

Drummond said, "That's a lot of trouble."

"Get me out of here!" Theo thumped his chair from side to side.

Standing slow and careful, Brenda reached a hand toward Sandra. Together they inched away from the circle, moving toward the opposite corner from Max. He wished they had come his way, but as long as they put distance from the circle, he wouldn't argue.

"The casting circle," Max said, "can it hold those things?"

Theo banged at the chair's lock mechanism. "Help me."

Mrs. Sidwell inched back. Her eyes widened as she shook her head. "Please, do something."

"Case not closed," Max muttered as he took a step forward. He scanned the circle, searching for any advantage — but he had no idea what he dealt with nor what he could do about it. Sandra was the expert here, and her frown suggested a similar amount of confusion.

But as he turned toward Drummond to ask for the ghost's thoughts, Max caught sight of one object that might help. "Grab the wards."

Too late, though. The ghosts attacked.

Chapter 11

MRS. SIDWELL SCREECHED AND SPUTTERED as if she had walked through a spider-filled web. With her hands flailing about, the undignified sight would have been amusing if not for the violence that followed. Violence first inflicted upon Sandra.

Pale flashes created a strobe effect throughout the office as one ghost after another broke out of the circle. The first to gain its freedom vanished from Max's view but clearly smashed into his wife. It lifted her from the ground, tossing her across the room. She logrolled until Drummond's bookcase stopped her.

A second ghost thrust Brenda back against the wall. Her head knocked into the hard brick. Max could hear the air forced from her lungs.

Grabbing Mrs. Sidwell and attempting to calm her panic, Max pulled her behind his desk. "You'll be safe in there." He waited until she crawled underneath. No way would that desk protect her, but in her alarmed state, she accepted whatever he said.

Stealing a look over the desk, Max spotted Drummond throwing punches, spinning with his elbow leading the way, rocketing towards the ceiling, and tackling towards the floor. To an untrained eye, it may have appeared as if he got the better of his enemies. But there were too many. For every punch he threw, his body jerked in one direction or another indicating strikes landed by his opponents. They surrounded him.

"Stay here," Max said to Mrs. Sidwell, hoping that hiding under the desk would keep her from doing anything stupid. He then did something stupid on his own.

Bolting into the open, Max raced for the circle. In the four steps it took to reach the ghost ward on the floor, he felt icy cold patches of air whisk about him. He snatched the ward with one smooth bend. With equal grace, he slipped it on and felt it burning into his skin.

Though he could not see the ghosts unless they passed through the circle — and he saw many passing through the circle — he experienced their chill and the results of their actions. The walls shook, cascading dust to the floor. Loose objects rose in the air only to be discarded seconds later. Lights burst on and off with no clear rhythm or pattern. The office was a madhouse.

While the wards would not protect for long, Max trusted Sandra's abilities. They would provide security enough. He rushed around the circle, snatched up the second ward, and headed straight for his wife.

Two strides and something bashed against his ward field. Max stumbled to the left, kicking a trashcan and banging his knee against Sandra's desk corner. Hurrying the last several steps to the bookcase, Max helped Sandra sit up. She kept blinking her eyes, her head lolling from side to side. With one hand holding her tight around the shoulder, he used the other hand to slip the ward over her head. Once he had the necklace in place, he gave her a strong kiss. "You okay?"

"Uh-huh," she said, barely opening her mouth.

"What the heck is going on? Where'd these ghosts come from?"

"I missed it." Sandra rubbed her head.

"Missed these many hazy ghosts?"

"I was only looking for one ghost. Didn't occur to me that the whole hazy blob was more than one."

"So, what do I do? How do we stop this?"

"Candles."

Near the ceiling, Drummond threw two sharp jabs and an uppercut. The satisfied look on his face suggested he landed at least one of those punches. From under Max's desk, Mrs. Sidwell cried out. He guessed she had felt the icy touch of a ghost. Though the strobe lighting from the casting circle had lessened, that only meant most of the ghosts were loose in the room.

"What about the candles? Do I need to light new ones?"

Sandra scooted her back against the wall and winced.

Speaking clear but strained, she said, "No. Don't do that. Things will get worse."

"Then what?"

"Snuff them out. Except the white ones. Keep the white candles lit."

Thrilled to have a clear mission, Max gave his wife one last kiss before crawling away. Like a battlefield soldier, he kept low to the floor, using his elbows to lead his charge. Later he would look back and wonder why he had chosen that method of movement — a ghost didn't care whether he stood or lay prone — but in the heat of battle, it seemed like the right thing to do.

Reaching the circle, he blew out the first red and black candles. Drummond growled from above. Glancing back, his partner threw several wild haymakers. Reaching behind with one hand while shoving his palm downward with the other, Drummond uttered a few well-chosen swears before disappearing. Max didn't know if he took any of the ghosts with him, and though he hoped so, he didn't want to find out the hard way.

Concentrating on his task, he crawled around the circle, blowing out candle after candle, making sure to skip the white ones. While he felt the cold of ghosts come near him, his ward heated up each time. They were attacking. Faster than he could move around the circle.

"Hold on," he whispered to the ward. It grew hotter.

From across the room, Sandra yelled, "Brenda, be ready."

Max paused long enough to catch Brenda stumbling to her feet. Seeing her stand made clear how silly he had been crawling on the floor. He pushed up to his feet, and with strong strides, he hastened around the circle until the last candle was out.

Though wobbling a bit, Sandra propped up against the bookcase and chanted. Her words came out fast and firm. Each ancient syllable gave her strength, turning her watery legs into solid pillars. Not through a spell. Rather, her knowledge poured out of her, filling her muscles with her confidence.

The actual spell, on the other hand, diminished the ghosts, slowing them as she slowed her chanting pace. Like a windup toy losing its energy, the chaos in the office eased toward stillness. Drummond reappeared swinging, but after only two punches, he stopped.

"Keep it going." He grinned as he grabbed one ghost after another and tossed them back into the circle.

Max saw them then. Little blobs of gray that bore out-of-focus faces. He noted only five in total. The fight with Drummond had seemed like a dozen.

Perhaps sensing Max's thoughts, Drummond said, "Some of them ran off into the Other."

Brenda said, "These here would be the ones truly attached to Theo. The others may have been caught up in whatever magic or emotion put them in this way to begin with."

"That's right." Sandra dabbed at the sweat on her forehead. "You're learning."

Climbing out from beneath Max's desk, Mrs. Sidwell straightened her clothes and reset her scowl. "I am learning that you are not in control of anything."

Max said, "You wanted us to free your husband, and we did. He's moved on."

She hastened to Theo's side. His head had fallen back, and blood dribbled from the corner of his mouth. Max checked the young man's belly — still breathing.

"Look what you did to my son." Mrs. Sidwell unlocked the wheelchair and headed for the door.

"We didn't do that. Those ghosts —"

"You put him in that circle."

"You didn't tell us he was haunted by more than your husband."

"How should I have known? That was your job."

"Did you, at least, recognize any of the ghosts?"

She thrust the door open — it didn't dare stick for her — and pushed her son into the hallway. Glowering at Max, she said, "I don't care who they were. They're dead now. The only thing that matters is that my son is safe. And he is clearly not. I am paying you to fix this. So, fix it."

Max waited for her to reach the elevators. Turning back to

the destruction in the office, he said, "She's not wrong."

Brenda collected the candles and chalk. "How could we have known there were more ghosts? Put them together, and it looks like one big, blurry blob."

"I meant about repairing the damage, about protecting Theo. We're being paid to stop what's happening to him. We thought it was just his father, but it's obviously more than that. The guy isn't out of the woods, yet."

Sandra hung a fallen picture. "That's why we're not going to stop."

"Of course not. We'll find the answers. It'll take a bunch of research, and thankfully, that's what I do best."

Snickering, Drummond said, "Oh brother. Delusions of grandeur strike again."

With a raised eyebrow, Sandra said, "Get to it, hon. We'll finish the clean up here. You need to earn the right for that boasting."

"Oh, I see how it is. My past victories mean nothing."

"Glad you understand. This is a *what have you done for me lately* type of job."

Max winked as Brenda and Drummond shook their heads. Sandra laughed. A few minutes later, Max had gathered his things and got out of the way. There were other places to work — secluded places, quiet places, favorite spots. And he had the perfect one in mind for this research.

Chapter 12

SPEEDY'S — A LEXINGTON BARBECUE INSTITUTION. Max had yet to try the restaurant, and he knew better than to waste an opportunity. As he drove out for a late-day lunch, he marveled at The Porter Agency's resilience. This wasn't the first time they had encountered violence from the supernatural, but they took their beating in stride. They understood the job still needed to be finished. It tied in with what Mrs. Sidwell could not comprehend — that even if they weren't being paid, the Porters would see this through. They needed the money, of course — they needed to pay the mortgage — but greed did not make the rules over their life's calling. In the past, they had let greed be their guide, and it left them hollow and filthy. No more.

On the edge of Lexington, Max exited Highway 64 and looped around to the side road that deposited him at Speedy's. He had heard good things about their new location. They previously were on Route 8 about a block over from where an odd and powerful witch once lived in a trailer with her main workspace beneath the ground. Most of the businesses along Route 8 had been forced to move for road expansion. At least, Max suspected it was for the road. There hadn't been a lot of progress over the last couple years.

In fact, the last time Max had come this way, he had encountered Cecily Hull in her makeshift office a few blocks over at the beginning of what would be her downfall. Perhaps Speedy's had been right to relocate. That stretch of Route 8 may have had a curse of its own.

The restaurant boasted a tiled floor, simple black chairs, black tables with wood trim, spread in a comfortable open space. Each wall had been covered with posters of different themes. One wall bore movies like *Frozen, the Avengers, Caddyshack,* and *Star Wars* while another wall had been decorated with various bits of 1950s and 60s memorabilia. But the most impressive wall could be seen from any angle — the one announcing the annual Lexington barbecue festival. Year after year lined the wall. Each one in which Speedy's had participated. Max felt like he had entered the best Lexington restaurant he could ever ask for. His mouth watered.

He ordered a plate of chopped barbecue, hushpuppies, and a salad. As he waited, he heard Sandra in his head — her last words before taking Brenda to drive out to the Sidwells.

"We can't let them give up," she said. "Without us, they'll either end up prey for other witches or dead by those ghosts."

She couldn't have been more right, and Max would do his part. The food came quickly, and while he ate, he used his phone to conduct some basic searches. That didn't last long, though — the massive mound of pulled pork demanded his attention. For a few minutes, the world and its myriad of problems ceased to exist. Max's taste buds overtook his other senses, and he enjoyed the simple pleasure of eating the most delicious food in all of North Carolina. Possibly in all the universe.

When he finished his meal, he set up his laptop. This late in the day, nobody would bother him for taking over a table. Hardly anybody was in the restaurant anyway. But when they neared the dinner hour, the place would get packed, and he would have to leave for the paying customers. No problem, though. He was determined to succeed within a short time.

The search began by going through his previous finds. The first time around, he'd been looking for an image to match the ghost that Drummond had seen — Robert Sidwell. This time, however, Max combed through the information for details about the company, its history, and its employees. Though the same as before, his focus had changed. He no longer saw the number — employees, daily output, profits — but instead, searched for any terrible thing that might stand out as a catalyst for what they had experienced. A mass fire that killed a dozen employees or a sole employee serial killer would be the right sort of horror.

Unfortunately, no light shined upon any single moment.

The previous generations of Sidwells had run the mill hard and generated great profits. They were ugly, mean-spirited men who bought into the classist beliefs which propped them up. Max stumbled across a few instances of weird stories and one ghost story about the mill, and despite spending over an hour digging into those avenues, he concluded they were merely urban legends. With only a half-hour to go before the dinner rush forced him to find a new research location, Max learned of the numerous labor strikes the textile industry had undergone over the decades.

For much of the 20th century, textile mills flourished in North Carolina like oil wells in Texas. Drummond had not been exaggerating. If a town wasn't devoted to tobacco, its lifeblood was textiles.

Every such town either had a mill or supported the mill workers. Some had been created by the mill companies themselves, and these mill towns operated much like an old mining town with employee income paid in company scrip and employee expenses going right back to the company.

Sidwell Mills came late into the game. Others had been finding one way or another to screw over their workers for decades. Max discovered the Harriet-Henderson textile workers strike as a good example of what occurred many, many times throughout the state and throughout the years.

The textile industry and North Carolina had been working hand-in-hand since the 1840s. In 1959, at the Harriet Mills and the Henderson Mills — both located in the mountains near Henderson, North Carolina — workers became fed up with the state of their affairs.

Across the entire state, people labored longer hours for less money than ever before. Managers forced them to produce faster and faster, setting target goals near-impossible to reach. Most of the machinery was dangerous, at best, and managers started controlling bathroom visits as well as overseeing workers during breaks.

At these mountain mills, the workers' reaction to these

changes came fast. Most joined the Textile Workers Union of America. This shocked a lot of folks because there were few textile unions in the state. There were few unions of any kind in the state. By November 1958, the union and management could not agree on terms for continued work.

"That's a mild way of putting it," Max said to his computer. He pictured the smoke-filled meeting room, and the angry, unveiled threats between parties. Far more than simply not agreeing, unions versus management could be a dangerous, blood-soaked situation.

In this case, the workers went on strike, forcing the mill to close for several months. By February of the following year, the mill owners hired scabs to break the strike and get money flowing again. If a few heads broke, too, then all the better.

Matters grew worse as the strike lingered on. The town needed the mill workers to make money to support the local businesses, and the strike took that money away. A rift cut through the streets. Shootings, bombings, and other violence occurred. In one local paper, a banker said that the merchants "are afraid to ask payment for bills lest dynamite aimed at non-strikers be aimed at them." The governor called in the police and National Guard, but the unrest continued.

By April, management came to the table and agreed to a new contract. They quickly abandoned it once work resumed. So, another strike went into action.

Despite their stubborn bravery, the workers could only last so long. The company had deeper pockets. Still, the strike went on for more weeks and months than anybody had expected — officially ending in June 1961. By then, though, the union had lost its power in Henderson. Many of the strikers never worked for the companies again.

The outcome of this strike, as well as many like it in North Carolina, resulted in the state having the second lowest percentage of unionized workers in the country. In Henderson — the townspeople continued to be divided for many years.

Max gathered his research, popped one last hushpuppy into his mouth, and relocated to his car. He considered driving back to the office, but his skin prickled in anticipation of ghost chills. Though he knew the attack was over, it would take more than a few hours research to clear his emotional reaction.

Logically, he should head out to the library. Any one of them. Instead, he opened his laptop and got to work in the parking lot. Not that he couldn't use the library, but his mind had already devoured each bit of research he had found. Like an athlete, he was in the zone. He didn't want to disrupt that.

Especially when researching the mill strikes had led him to the most famous of all in North Carolina — the Loray Mills strike of 1929.

Chapter 13

LORAY MILLS IN GASTONIA, the largest mill in Gaston County, worked its employees to the bone. Worse than at any other mill at the time. Lured in by a decent income — as high as $12 a week — that soon changed for most. They called it the stretch-out system — forcing workers to labor ever faster for the same money, while others lost their hourly income as their jobs were reclassified to piecework. Often, two young boys would be asked to do the work of five grown men. Or worse.

Max typed a few notes as he stared at the forlorn, exhausted gazes of children in work clothes of the era. They looked into the camera as if they wanted to shout at the viewer but lacked the energy to even tell off the cameraman.

Leading up to the strike, the workers notched a few small victories. In 1928, a manager that implemented the most ruthless rules had been driven from town. But even as the workers celebrated, some of them understood that there would be a new manager to replace the old. The stretch-out would continue. Yet despite other economic pressures — including those that would lead to the Great Depression — the workers could take no more.

Much of the strike followed the same patterns that would be repeated in the decades to come. Union organizers in the north that heard about Loray Mills rushed down to help organize and lead. Violence became a nightly ritual. Local press got local attention, and most people tried to wait it out.

But unlike many other strikes at the time, the Loray Mills situation got picked up by the national news outlets. Some of the names involved achieved short-term fame such as Ella Ford, Fred Beale, and Ada Howell. But it was the murder of Gastonia's police chief, Orville Aderholt, and the beloved singer for the strike, Ella May Wiggins, that truly brought focus to the events at the Loray Mills.

"Nothing like a murder to sell more papers." Max slowed to focus on the details. What stood out was less the crime itself — nothing to suggest witchcraft — but rather the aftermath. Ella May's songs had garnered plenty of attention from unions throughout the country. Her death pulled international attention to the unfairness of punishments brought against her killers — namely, North Carolina failed to punish them at all. The authorities barely put in any effort to uncover these murderers. Company money outweighed the law, and striking workers went against both.

The killing of the police chief, however, drew swift justice. Several mill workers as well as key union leaders were accused, arrested, and went to trial with great speed. They received vicious sentences.

"Not much of a shocker," Max muttered. Probably wasn't a shock back then either. But the juxtaposition of the two murders, both victims involved in the same tense situation, put a spotlight on the inequity of it all.

In the wake of the lengthy strike and its violent conclusion, one in which the workers mostly lost their jobs and the mill continued raking in profits, the townspeople ended up as divided as any other mill town before or since. In fact, Max found articles about the townspeople in Gastonia today arguing over what to do with the abandoned mill buildings. Some structures had already been converted into museums featuring the strike while others had been refurbished for commercial use or even loft apartments. However, most of the buildings sat fallow and untended.

"Hey, partner." Drummond appeared in the passenger seat. "Sandra asked me to tell you that she and Brenda succeeded. Also, you're to pick up Chinese food for dinner."

"Really?" Max lifted his head from his laptop. "I mean about Mrs. Sidwell, not dinner."

"That lady wasn't too happy, but she did witness her husband moving on as well as the other ghosts still assaulting her son.

What choice did she really have?"

"You think she didn't know about the other ghosts?"

Drummond pursed his lips. "Hard to say. Even if she did know, she had no idea they were so angry. The part that confuses me about this — why are they after Theo? Seems like they should have been plaguing Robert Sidwell. Now that he's moved on, I'd expect some of them to move on, too. Those that can't get over whatever wrongs he did to them, I suppose they might go back to where the source of those problems originated and hang around haunting those places for a few centuries."

"Yeah. That's bothering me, too. I've been doing this research into the textile mills. It isn't pretty, but it has nothing to do with Theo. Barely has anything to do with Robert. The guy was clearly an ass, but as far as employers go, he was rather soft compared to some of these others." Max shifted in his seat. "You were alive during a lot of this. You mind if I ask you about it?"

Drummond tipped his hat back. "Fire away."

Turning his laptop so that Drummond could see the article on Loray Mills, Max said, "You remember this one?"

"Hard to forget. It was in the newspapers every day. The politics behind it got nasty. The Commies had raced down from the North to take advantage of hard-working folks. They led the strike because they led tons of workers' strikes throughout the country. Rise of the proletariat sort of thing."

"You don't think workers should have rights?"

"I was never against the workers. I just hated seeing the Commies try to take advantage of the situation. They cared less about winning the strike than hoping they'd convert people to their cause. Most of the workers weren't taken in. Too smart for that. They only agreed to let those carpetbaggers run things because everybody knew that these New York folks had more experience organizing a strike.

"The politicians mostly sided with the mill owners. No surprise there. They wanted the graft to keep coming in. No real regard for the fine people working into their graves to make that money, so long as the owners and politicians got their profits."

Max said, "Doesn't sound like much has changed."

"Maybe not in the big picture, but those strikes — even the failed ones — helped make the little, daily picture better. You kids today don't know how good you have it. Not really. One side of you screams about whether or not you can work from home. You take for granted the forty-hour work week or that children aren't allowed to work in sweatshops or that the equipment you use isn't a deathtrap. The other side whines about regulations when getting rid of those rules would only turn those people into monsters who disregard human life in the name of profit. The whole thing is disgusting."

With a snicker, Max said, "Don't hold back how you feel."

"You got to understand, I was in my early-20s when the Loray Mills strike went down. I saw the faces of nine-year-old girls that should have been picking flowers in the fields. Instead, they looked like haggard middle-aged women with a thousand-yard stare that would rival any soldier back from the front. That kind of things stays with you. Even after you die."

Max thought of the photos he had seen that day. He nodded. Tapping at the arrow keys, he scrolled through the current article, skimming for any detail he had missed, any crumb that would illuminate a path forward. Because he had to admit this research may have been worthless. He had followed his instincts down this hole, yet he had no proof that any of this connected to the case. Nothing beyond the fact that the Sidwells had once owned a thriving textile mill. For all Max knew, Robert had cheated one too many times on Mrs. Sidwell, and she made a deal with a witch to curse the man. Maybe that deal had soured, and Theo's troubles were the result.

"I know what you're thinking, and you're wrong." Drummond stared at the screen. "This is worth pursuing."

"Why? The Loray stuff doesn't line up with anything about Robert Sidwell. I mean, yeah, it's terrible and there was a murder and a trial that looks more like a coverup than anything else, but none of that gets us close to a reason for attacking Theo."

"Oh, I see a reason."

"Yeah? What?"

Drummond pointed at a black-and-white photo of a little girl on the laptop screen. "Her. She was one of the hazy ghosts at the office."

Chapter 14

MAX HAD NO DESIRE to sit through another uncomfortable dinner with Sandra and his mother. That night, in particular, he wanted to hole up in the office or a library and spend hours discovering whatever he could about this ghost girl that Drummond had picked out. He had her name from the article — Estelle Lynch — and Max needed little else to do his magic. But if he left Sandra and his mother to eat as just the two of them, there might be a dead body at the end of the meal. It might even be his.

For the first ten minutes, nobody spoke. The clink of cutlery against plates mixed with chewing and swallowing and the occasional gulp of a drink. Mrs. Porter sulked. She scooped up a mouthful of fried rice but ate little. Sandra, on the other hand, stabbed at her Pork Lo Mein like it might scurry away if she moved too slow. Grinding her food, her frustrated bites matched her fixed glares across the table.

To bring Sandra up on the latest, and perhaps mollify her with some work, Max launched into a quick overview of what he had learned about the textile industry in North Carolina as well as the difficulties with striking workers and brutal owners. He stayed clear of anything remotely connected to ghosts. With any luck, Mrs. Porter would listen, become intrigued, and perhaps participate in the conversation, too.

But Mrs. Porter only offered little complaints about using paper napkins instead of cloth, and how tired she was of the loud music somebody on the block played in the afternoons. "Shouldn't they be working?" she said.

Ignoring the comment, Max finished up by saying, "After the murder trial of Police Chief Aderholt, there were appeals."

"Naturally," Sandra said.

"Made it right up the ladder to the North Carolina Supreme Court. By this point, it's 1930 and the entire country knows what's going on. Even Thomas Harwick, a former US Senator from Georgia, got involved. But here's the thing — most of the defendants were the New York communist leadership. The same people stirring up the strikes and trying to form unions. In fact, one of the appeal points was that the judge, Judge Barnhill, screwed up because he allowed a witness's credibility to be attacked solely on the fact that she was an atheist — which, back then, might as well have been synonymous with communist."

Sandra said, "I'm guessing that didn't go over too well."

"What would you expect?" Mrs. Porter said.

Max fished out his phone to bring up a specific set of notes. "The prosecution countered by bringing up a statute from 1777. They said — and this is a direct quote — *There can be no doubt that under existing law in North Carolina, an atheist is wholly disqualified from testifying as a witness.* Can you believe that? And that worked. A few months later, when the court gave its decision to dismiss the appeal, they made a specific point of saying that going after an atheist's truthfulness was perfectly fine."

Mrs. Porter wiped her mouth. "Probably should still be the law."

"What?"

"I'm not saying these people should have been convicted for something they didn't do, but an atheist has no moral compass. Everybody knows that. Lying under oath would mean nothing — they're not swearing an oath to anything they believe in — and frankly, atheists have strange ideas. So why should we believe in somebody who doesn't have the sense to believe in the Lord?"

Max stared at her, dumbfounded into silence. But only for a moment. Heat welled up in his chest. "Atheism isn't a belief system. It's one concept."

"It's wrong."

"Do you understand it? It's simply that there's no evidence for a god. Not that there isn't one, but that so far, there's no evidence. Nothing else. No other beliefs."

"That's word games. An excuse for not being religious."

"Sandra and I aren't religious."

"That explains quite a lot. I suppose you're going to tell me that you're atheists."

"No. But that's not really the point. Atheists have every right—"

"I wouldn't say that."

"What about Muslims or Hindus or Jews? Do they get a pass for you? Is it only atheists you dislike?"

"I raised you proper."

Max reared back. "What does that have to do with anything?"

"People are quick to denounce their upbringing, but you should listen to me. I'm your mother, so I know what's best for you. These people who believe in nothing have no way to know anything about anything. I've heard you talking about your business — yammering about witches and nonsense. I don't say anything, but don't you bring that to me like it's okay. You want to take advantage of fools who have lost their way, I can't stop you. But when your time comes, when you have to face judgement for your sins, you remember what I've said."

Placing his fork firmly on the table, Max tried to take a calming breath. It didn't work. "I'm going to assume your MS has flared up today and put you in a really bad mood."

"You know what they say about assuming."

"Why are you trying to pick a fight?"

"I'm not." Mrs. Porter placed a hand on her chest like a shocked southern girl. "I was trying to be part of the conversation. You're the one who has gotten bent out of shape."

"Because you're being insulting."

"To who? A bunch of heathens who can't accept the obviousness of the Lord?"

"You were never religious when I was a kid."

"I made sure you had a proper upbringing and appreciation for church."

"We barely went. It's only now that you're …"

Raising her eyes with a question while her mouth gritted a

firm line, she said, "You have something to say? Now that I'm what? Dying? This MS is terrible stuff. I'm in pain a lot of the day, and yes, I'm quite aware that those days are numbered. That doesn't mean I can't have an opinion, and it doesn't mean I can't become closer to the higher power that guides us all."

Max looked to Sandra, but she held still with her focus resting on her plate. This wasn't her fight. She was merely stuck in the same room.

Until Mrs. Porter made a mistake and said, "Sometimes I wish the Lord would come and take me now. At least then I might get a homecooked meal. Your wife needs to learn how to use a pot and pan. It's not that difficult."

Sandra blasted to her feet. One hand formed a fist on the table. "If you feel so mistreated here, we can make other living arrangements."

"You'd like that. Get rid of me, throw me into an old folks' home."

"Stop it," Max said. "Nobody's going anywhere. Mom, you need to accept that we are both working people. We've got a client right now, and when we're on a case, we don't always have time to make a meal for everybody. But even though you don't like what we do, these clients put a roof over your head. So, if sacrificing homecooked dinners is what's got to happen, then that's what happens. No complaints."

Thrusting her napkin on the table, Mrs. Porter screwed her face tight as she reddened. "I've got plenty of complaints, and at my age, I'm allowed to let them be heard. This isn't the old days when a woman had to be quiet about what she feels."

"I see. You have a list of problems with us?"

"I've been ignored, treated like a piece of unwanted furniture, made to feel like I'm an obstacle. You both live around me. You act like I'm dying every moment, like this is a hospice and you're merely counting down the days."

Sandra said, "That's not how we —"

"Whether you want to admit it or not is your problem. But I am still here. Still alive." With a series of grunts, she rose from her chair. "I shouldn't be surprised that you have no use for my opinion. You both ignore everything I say."

"That's not true," Max said.

"Really? Didn't I tell you not to pursue your Aunt Jane? Yet you're still trying to find her. Oh, stop looking surprised. You leave your laptop open all the time because you forget I'm even here. I've seen the work you've done looking for her, and now that you found her living in South Carolina, you probably think that she's so nearby you'll be able to walk up to her house, knock on the door, and have a happy reunion. If you'd listen to your mother for once, you'd know that there won't be anything happy about it."

"I can't believe you'd snoop onto my laptop."

"I can't believe I raised a son who treats his mother so poorly."

Sandra stomped on the floor. "That's enough. From both of you." She grabbed a few plates with sharp motions. "Dinner is over. Go to your rooms and cool off before you say anything worse to each other."

"But —"

"Now."

Sandra's fury burned at Max. He gave his mother one final glower before storming to the master bedroom. As he left, he heard Sandra say, "You, too."

Max couldn't hold back a smirk at the shocked huff from his mother.

Chapter 15

THROUGHOUT HIS LIFE, Max had felt plenty of anger towards his mother. It was only natural. From his angsty teens to his risk-taking twenties and beyond, his years with her had been filled with the typical ups and downs of any mother-son relationship.

This was different.

Pacing his bedroom, he continued the argument in his head, muttering his points, his comebacks, even his insults. He heard that biting tone, that self-deprecation that somehow diminished him while propping her up in praise, that sense of failure no matter what he said. But he quickly accepted that his fuming had little to do with her tone. He had heard it before. Many times. Nor did he rage against her positions on atheism or religious doctrine or any of it. He didn't think she cared much about those things, anyway. She never lived her life as if those things mattered. But what she had said near the end, admitting that her eruption of venom originated from feeling isolated, ignored, lost — that caused his gut to twist.

In her loneliness, she had lashed out. Max and Sandra were the easiest targets. That didn't make things any simpler to accept. In fact, part of his seething grew out of guilt for feeling any of these emotions in the first place. He shouldn't get mad at her. She was dying, after all. She knew it, he knew it, and together they swirled around each other like high pressure systems. When they collided, massive reactions flowed hard.

Getting called out for continuing his research on Aunt Jane had not helped matters. Another thing to feel guilty about. Because his mother had indeed requested that he cease. He should have listened. Yet how could he be expected to ignore the possibility of another family member? When his mother was gone, he would have nobody left in his bloodline. Finding Aunt Jane could create a connection he never knew existed.

Yet his mother had made it clear. Perhaps she feared that by finding Aunt Jane, her own death would hasten. Max could see how his mother made that leap. He had plenty of experience with the machinations of her mind. The way she probably saw it — if she remained the only blood relative, Max's interest in keeping her healthy would be stronger.

Of course, he didn't think that way. Nobody would. However, his mother's rationality waned with every passing day. Feeling the constant breath of Death on the back of her neck had to have a damaging impact. Plus, she had plenty of time to imagine that Max counted the days until she died, wishing to find a way to cart her off to some home — out of sight, out of mind.

It was the same thinking he knew she would have about Parker House. Sandra had brought the pamphlet home and set it on his nightstand. Seeing it now, he wanted to rip it apart and burn it. But he also wanted to pound his mother's door open and throw the pamphlet at her.

Crap.

He would have to take steps towards easing her stress. He opened his laptop and pulled up his file on Aunt Jane. Though he had no plans to delete it, he could archive it for now. Once the day arrived when he buried his mother, then he might open these files again. Until that time, he could respect her wishes, and let this go. For now.

But as he moved the cursor to close the file, he paused. His mother had said something — that Aunt Jane lived in South Carolina. Max pulled up the latest narrowing of listings and searched for South Carolina addresses. There was only one. Without pause, he pulled up the email he had been sending to every potential Jane Porter and made a copy for the South Carolina version.

He hesitated. He should heed his first instinct. Treat his mother with that much respect.

Still, the urge to shed light on this dark hole in his past refused to be ignored. He moved the cursor toward the send button.

Before he pressed it, though, the bedroom door opened.

Sandra entered, closed the door behind her, and turned to face Max. Her eyes narrowed, her jaw set, and her left hand went to her hip.

Max waited. When she said nothing, he swallowed hard. "What?"

She raised an eyebrow.

"I know. I know."

Her other eyebrow joined the first.

"I'm sorry. But —"

She cocked her head to the side.

"All I'm saying is —"

Her right hand went to her other hip.

Max held still as if caught in a crosshair. He sighed. "I will apologize to her."

Sandra walked over and kissed his cheek. "You're a good son. Better than she deserves." She kissed him on the mouth.

Max dropped to the corner of the bed. "I don't know why I let her get to me like that."

"She's your mother. Not only does she know how to push your buttons, but she installed some of those buttons. You can't really get away from that."

"That doesn't make what she said right or okay."

"No, but at her age, we've got to make some allowances. Unless you want to screw up your relationship with her a short time before she passes away and moves on."

Max rubbed his forehead. "She better move on."

"You've got to stop that, too. We have no reason to think that she would end up —" Sandra's brow dropped as she looked at Max's laptop sitting on the dresser. "Is this the case?"

"Don't worry about that."

She leaned close to the screen. "You're still going after your aunt?"

Squirming on the edge of the bed, Max said, "I don't know. I haven't decided."

"It looks like you've decided."

"I don't see a better option."

"You could listen to your mother and drop the whole thing."

It was Max's turned to stare back in silence.

"Yeah, I know you're not going to do that."

Max joined his wife at the laptop. The name Jane Porter and the South Carolina address burned through the screen as if the other graphics did not exist. The brighter those words grew in his mind, the more he saw them sizzling in the air. "It's strange. Right now, it's nothing but a bunch of pixels. Some digital signals. But if I send that email, she might become real."

"Are you looking for permission?"

He gave the question serious thought. "Maybe. I mean what could be so wrong about this woman? Unless you think my mother's warning me because Aunt Jane's a serial killer."

"Or a witch."

"Or a serial killing witch."

Sandra pulled Max off the bed and into her arms. Smoothing his shirt and plucking at bits of lint, she said, "I doubt it's anything serious. Your mother is being protective of you, that's all. It's the way she's always been when it comes to you. This time, she's trying to save you from being disillusioned. Your Aunt Jane acts like a loner. Whatever bad blood she had with your father, she never tried to resolve it. According to your mother, the woman's been content to not get involved with the family ever. She's never reached out to you, never showed interest. This is a woman who doesn't want to be found. Not by family, anyway. Your mother understands that if you pursue this, the result will be hard to take." She pulled Max into a deep hug. "I worry about it, too."

When he stepped back, he looked at the laptop screen once more. Sandra's words carried the weight of truth, and he hated to disappoint her. However, she had to understand. Researching people and places, finding the reasons behind the stories, making sense by making connections — these were the things that gave Max's work meaning. The fact that the person, the story, all of it this time, flowed from his own bloodline only gave the work a greater heft. He wanted to lift it. He had to know the answers — even if he would not like what he learned. That same determination helped make The Porter Agency thrive, and it would help him deal with his aunt no matter the outcome.

"I'm sorry." He tapped on the word SEND. "I've still got to try."

Sandra rubbed his shoulder. "I know."

Whirling her into his arms, he held her tight. "Please understand. I don't want you to think I've betrayed you."

"Of course not. I love you."

A cyclone of raw nerves spun through his body — rage and fear, love and trust, confusion and clarity. Sandra's warm breath on his neck heated his blood throughout. He could barely breathe. They kissed.

Having his mother under the same roof had made moments of intimacy difficult and scarce. He often felt like a teenager stealing away secret moments to explore the adult world — only in this case, the other "teenager" was his wife. Yet he didn't care now. If his mother heard them, then so be it. This was their house. This was their marriage. Their life. He kissed her harder.

Sandra's fingers dug into his back, forcing a soft groan to roll up his throat. He reached down her thigh and pulled her leg up against his side. Heart racing, breathing tight, he looked into her eyes, and she nodded. Her hands grabbed the sides of his head as she pressed her lips to his. Her curves leaned against him.

And his phone rang.

They both stopped, looked at each other, and laughed — part embarrassment, part chagrin, part a promise for a rain check. Extracting from his arms, Sandra reached onto the dresser and snatched up Max's phone. She frowned.

"Theo Sidwell?" she said.

Unable to tamp down the growl in his voice, Max answered.

Chapter 16

CLOSE TO AN HOUR LATER, Max and Drummond entered Baggerz Saloon. Neither man nor ghost were in a good mood. Both had endured a difficult day, and both had been interrupted from a better evening by this call. Max, through the actual phone call, and Drummond, through Max contacting him for back up. During the entire twenty-minute drive across town, Drummond ranted about how this meeting had ruined his date with a roller-skating waitress from 1952. Max let the ghost get it out. He figured better now than while they met with Theo Sidwell.

Baggerz Saloon had a strange location. In the southwestern stretch of suburbs outside Winston-Salem, the bar sat in the middle of a small strip opposite a cemetery attached to Mt. Carmel Global Methodist Church. A body shop and a rumpled house completed the area. Fields and trees filled in the background. The single-light crossroads of Ebert Road and West Clemmonsville Road led off to housing in each direction. However, when Max entered the bar, he understood why it existed in this remote area — it was a biker bar. Nobody would bother these folks. At least, not the dead across the street.

Inside, the place was quaint. A few pool tables, a few places to sit, eat, and drink, a simple set-up for the bar itself, and a long, open area that could be used for a variety of events. That night, the event was a live band.

Max didn't catch their name, but they looked like five old guys reliving their dreams of being blues-rock stars as they banged out one classic tune after another. Most of the band members looked rather short — a fact made more apparent by the towering bassist who stood on the floor while the rest of the band played the stage a foot higher. The drummer appeared to be having a great time, guzzling beer and banging away while the guitarists kept their heads down to focus on their instruments. The lead singer, also behind a guitar, hit most of the notes. Not much in the way of stage presence, but they produced a decent sound that probably kept them gigging as much as they wanted. Shame there weren't more people to listen — the bar was mostly empty.

That brought Max's attention to his reason for being there. Drummond noticed it, too. He said, "Remote bar. Mid-week. Fairly empty. This guy sure likes his private conversations."

"Our office is plenty private."

"Yeah, but he has to be the one in control. He picks the place."

"Then where is he?"

"He sets the time, too. One time for us. Another one for him. I had to deal with plenty of rich boys like this in my life. Hate it that in my death I still have to."

Two songs later — a good rendition of *Crossroads* followed by a deep-cut Hendrix tune, *Come on (Part 1),* had Max deciding he liked these old guys. Theo finally arrived. The same man that had brought Theo to the quarry pushed the wheelchair to a table in the corner farthest from the bar and the band. He bent close to listen to Theo, offered a short bow, and took a seat at the bar. Not before casting a side-eye at Max, though.

Cracking his knuckles, Drummond said, "Might as well get this over with. If we're lucky, we can get back to our ladies before the night is out."

Max moved toward the table. "What's the ghost situation?"

"They're all around him. Hard to count how many, since they have that blurry, hazy thing going on. They blend together."

Max hesitated. "Are they dangerous now?"

"I don't think so. Before, that was because of Sandra's spell and the sudden loss of Robert Sidwell moving on. They panicked. Or maybe they almost went poltergeist. Right now, they're more like a blob on his back."

Sitting at the table, Max noticed the way Theo hunched forward. Those ghosts may not have been a threat to Max or Drummond, but they had a clear effect upon Theo. The young man's haggard face suggested his afternoon had not been pleasant. While Max assumed there had been plenty of arguing with Mrs. Sidwell, he now suspected these ghosts had more to do with it. At least, Theo would be more willing to work with the Porters than before.

"I want you to stay the hell away from my mother and me," Theo said.

Well, not the first time Max had been wrong.

Staying calm — Max had been fuming enough for one day — he said, "I've already explained that your mother is paying our bill, not you. I also offered to do our work for free unless we provide results. I'm pretty sure we provided more results than you expected."

"You call that dog-and-pony show *results?* Are you joking?"

Drummond shook his head. "I thought he might fall back into denial, but I didn't think it would be so quick."

With an incredulous grin, Max said, "You really think we made that happen with — what? — string and some fancy cameras?"

"I have no idea how you did it. Maybe Penn and Teller could figure it out. But I know you staged that."

"Let me make sure I got this right — you don't believe anything you experienced happened, yet you called me to come here, ruining my night, so that you could tell me to leave your mother alone. You could have said that on the phone."

Signaling to his assistant, Theo waited as the man strolled to the table. He moved with efficiency, taking his time to approach so as not to look like an overeager servant yet also arriving with speed and care. A nod from Theo, and the man reached into the pouch behind the back of the wheelchair. He removed a thick envelope, placed it on the table, and returned to the bar.

"Ten thousand dollars," Theo said.

Drummond chuckled. "Well, well, this guy keeps surprising me. A bribe is one thing — you expect that from the rich — but that's usually the first move. He started last time with threats. Now he moves to money. Either he's never done this before or he's really scared about something and doesn't know how to get rid of you."

Max had been thinking the same thing. "That's a lot of money."

"You can count it," Theo said. "But this is a one-time payment. I won't be blackmailed."

"Blackmailed?"

Drummond said, "He has no clue what he's doing."

"I want you out of my life, out of my mother's life. Take the money and leave us alone."

"He's scared too."

Max said, "Did somebody threaten you?"

"You did!" Theo's outburst garnered a few odd looks. In a lower voice, he said, "You didn't have to say it. I felt it at your office, and I know it whenever I hear the things you want me to hear."

"It wasn't us. We are not trying to blackmail you. We want to help. That's it."

"Take the money." Theo sounded more desperate with every word.

Pushing the envelope away, Max said, "I'm sorry, I can't accept that. If your mother wants us to stop, then we'll stop. You need to talk with her."

The band finished a song, and in the buzz of their instruments, Theo's spoke louder. "Please. I'm hearing the voices, okay?"

The drummer counted off four and the band ripped into Tom Petty and the Heartbreakers' *Running Down a Dream.* Max leaned closer to speak. "You hear the ghosts?"

"You wanted that. I know what you people are like. You did it to my father and my grandfather. If not for money, why would you hurt us like this? Why for so long? I never did anything to anybody. Whatever your family beef is with mine, let's end it now. Ten grand isn't enough? I can double this. Maybe triple it. More than that and my mother will notice, but if that's what it takes, I'll work something out."

Max held still. He wanted to assure Theo that The Porter Agency was not trying to shake him down, that they would free him from his suffering, but anything he said would be twisted into further threats. Theo grasped at the idea that this was a mental torture scheme to blackmail his family. The man was being attacked by ghosts, hearing them, feeling them, maybe even glimpsing them, but until he accepted that reality, nothing Max said or did would change things.

Scooping up the envelope as if it cut into his hand, Theo said, "I won't let you hurt my mother. I won't."

"For the hundredth time — we are not trying to hurt you or your mother."

Drummond said, "He's not actually listening. He came here to vent at you because he can't deal with what's going on."

Though Max knew his partner was right, it didn't make listening to Theo any easier. And did Drummond use the word *vent?* Max glanced over his shoulder and the ghost shrugged.

"I'm trying to stay with the times. Trust me, you don't want me to fall back into the days of groovy or rad."

Rubbing his face and sighing, Max said, "Mr. Sidwell, please, you've tried several times to get us off this case, but clearly your mother does not feel the same way. I understand your desire to protect her. So, what can I do to convince you that The Porter Agency only has your best interests, and hers, in mind?"

"I've told you. Leave."

"If we do that, you know your mother's going to come to our office and insist we return. And we both know denying your mother what she wants is not a good idea. Which brings us right back to the same question — what can I do to convince you?"

"Convince me that this con-job is real? Nothing."

Another hand motion brought his man back to the table. As Theo was wheeled toward the door, Max had one final thought. He stood, making a lot of chair noise so that Theo would look back.

"Tell me about Estelle Lynch." Max watched the name hit Theo hard.

"Never heard of her."

"That's a shame. She's one of the things haunting you. It would've been easier for us if we knew why."

Theo turned away, urging his assistant to get him to the car fast.

As the band finished their version of Muddy Waters' *Hoochie Coochie Man,* Drummond swung into view. "When you mentioned her name —"

"I saw it. Theo knew her."

"Maybe. Maybe not."

"Did I miss something?"

"Only that one of those hazy ghosts flew over his head and nosedived into his back."

"Estelle Lynch?"

"I assume so. I'm thinking you better find out who she is fast. After what happened at the office, those ghosts are acting ticked off. It would've been bad enough to have Robert Sidwell go poltergeist, but to have those ghosts turn violent —"

"Theo won't stand a chance."

Chapter 17

DRUMMOND LEFT FOR THE OTHER before Max reached his car to drive home. "Those legs flashing from that tiny skirt. If that carhop isn't waiting, I'll pop the ghost that tried to take her from me."

With a wink before he vanished, he left Max thinking the detective hoped for the chance to fight. Maybe throwing his fists around for the affections of a dead waitress appealed after getting beaten by enraged, confused ghosts that teetered on the edge of poltergeist insanity. Or maybe Drummond was pissed off at wasting a good evening because of Theo Sidwell. Max could understand either possibility. He felt a little of both.

When he entered the kitchen through the side door of his house, he found most of the lights off and a note on the kitchen table. *Too tired to stay up. Wake me if you need something for the case. Raincheck on the rest of tonight. xxx ooo.* Max slouched into a chair and let his head fall back. A part of him had hoped she would still be awake; however, if he were honest with himself, he was too tired to fully enjoy anything that might have happened.

He decided that if he was too tired for Sandra, he was too tired for research. Sleep called him, and everything else could wait until morning. He endured a twinge of guilt for Theo and Mrs. Sidwell, but those hazy ghosts had been haunting the Sidwells for a long time. One more night wouldn't change much.

At least, Max hoped so. He could barely keep his eyes from closing.

Over breakfast, Max detailed his odd meeting with Theo while Sandra downed a bagel and some scrambled eggs. Mrs. Porter stayed in bed, blaming a migraine and muscle fatigue. While Max wanted to look in on her, he decided she might prefer space from him after the previous night's argument. Perhaps a cooling down period between them would help. It often did.

"I suppose," Sandra said, "you want to spend the day researching Estelle Lynch."

"I think I should. It's our strongest lead right now."

"You'll need to break it to your mother. She'll be on her own today."

"Where are you going?"

"Brenda and I have our own research project to do. If we're going to get those ghosts to move on, I'll need a much stronger spell than what I used for Robert. We can't go after them one-at-a-time. Too dangerous."

Looking toward the hallway, Max said, "I don't suppose I could bribe you into talking to her for me."

"It'd cost you a lot more than ten grand."

Snickering, Max left the kitchen and approached his mother's bedroom door. She barely responded when he knocked, but he heard enough noise to suggest he could enter. She stared out her window, refusing to look at him. He explained she would be by herself for the morning, maybe longer, and that she should consider walking the block, perhaps meet a few people. She shrugged.

Suppressing the urge to shake his mother, force her to deal with him, to deal with the world around her, Max backed out of the room and closed the door. He wished he could have his mother return. This woman she had become so little resembled the one that had raised him.

The routine of getting ready for the day — cleaning up breakfast, brushing teeth, packing up for research — helped push his mind from obsessing over those things he had no control of. By the time he kissed Sandra goodbye, he had reached a level of mental normalcy that allowed him to function. Part of him wanted to use the office, force his brain into an even greater sense of routine, but Sandra and Brenda would be doing their work at the casting circle. Best to let them concentrate in peace.

Instead, he headed downtown to find a quiet corner of the Forsyth County Central Library. He loved this library for a few reasons. One of them was the amusing address — right on 4 1/2 Street West. Max tickled at the idea that anybody would number a street with a fraction. Another thing he loved about the place — from the outside, it looked like a boxy, utilitarian, government building; inside, it held the glory of a well-run library. The smell of books permeated the air. The rows of stacks and the quiet calm created the perfect milieu. Finally, Max chose this library because it was the County library. It held numerous unique books containing data about the county and its residents stretching back to the 1700s. Things a researcher couldn't love more.

Since Sidwell Mills was in Forsyth County, any obscure information about the employees, owners, or the mill itself should be found in this library provided it had been made public. Even some of the private matters might be here as historical records. Either way, Max guessed this would be his best chance at uncovering some truths. But before he dove deeper into the Sidwells, he wanted to follow up on Estelle Lynch.

Settling at a workstation with a computer, Max began with a simple search under the girl's name. He had expected a listing of her time at the Loray Mills and perhaps an obituary — especially since she died young. But the first page of results brought up a different Estelle Lynch. Not a problem. Searching a name often returned numerous people sharing that name. But what caught Max's eye, what caused his pulse to quicken, was that the first Estelle Lynch listed had been employed in the late-2000s at Sidwell Mills.

"What are the odds?" he said to the screen.

The answer, he decided, was slim. Very slim. Two Estelle Lynches, both working in the textile mills, both working less than a hundred miles apart, both working in North Carolina, both young when they died — near impossible.

The references listed in the library had not been digitized yet. Max copied down the book locations, but before he searched through the stacks, he decided to give the internet a chance.

After all, even if official documents had not been digitized, most information could be found online somewhere.

After running several searches for Estelle Lynch coupled with keywords such as *mill worker, Sidwell Mills, 2009,* and *North Carolina*, Max had to admit defeat. He had turned up empty. He found a couple Estelle Lynches that did not meet all the criteria, but they were dead ends. For better or worse, a name like Estelle Lynch was not commonplace anymore. On the better side, there shouldn't be too many false positives. On the worse side, not finding her suggested the Estelle Lynch he sought information about might have left the state. However, she should have a Facebook page or an Instagram. Some kind of online footprint. Yet he could not find a crumb to follow.

"You may not be online, but this library says they know something about you." Max pushed back from the computer. "Time to do this the old-fashioned way."

Like most libraries, the lower levels were reserved for large collections of catalog data, years and years of magazines, and any other resource that required large amounts of shelf space which would only be accessed infrequently. As the fluorescent lighting blinked awake — they never kept the lights on down here — Max followed the signs leading to the employment registers of North Carolina. When he finally found the listing, it confirmed that she did exist and that she did work for Sidwell Mills. It also provided her last mailing address. Leave it to the old book keeping techniques to dox a person.

Max copied down the information, but before leaving, he had one final idea. He returned to the library computers upstairs and with a few calculated searches, he found what he wanted. Back downstairs — not too far from where he found Estelle Lynch's mailing address — the library had a collection of Sidwell Mills annual employee directories. These were meant to be a way for employees to feel more like a family, more connected. Max thought the real purpose was to act like the company cared without having to put in effort. Didn't matter, though, because of the internet. Somebody at Sidwell Mills agreed with him because they ceased making the directories in 2012; however, searching through the last several years, Max found a 2009 entry for Estelle Lynch. The same info he already had, yet it also included one new, valuable piece — an employee photo.

Estelle had dark hair that curled at her shoulders and a bright smile. Very photogenic. Whereas many of the other women on the page looked weathered, beaten by time and labor, Estelle had a perky glint in her eyes. She was young, eager, and seeking opportunity. Max guessed that if the directory had continued for ten more years, he might fight a depressing photo of the same woman. One lacking any spark.

Grabbing his phone, he took a photo of her photo, and headed for his car.

Chapter 18

THE ADDRESS BROUGHT MAX back to the southwestern part of the county. Not far from Baggerz Saloon where he had met Theo the previous evening. A row of mobile homes lined an unpaved, dead-end road. Max parked near the last home.

While none of the places had been well-kept, the one that belonged to Estelle Lynch looked decrepit. Two windows had been boarded up and a third had been shattered. The screen door hung off one hinge at an odd angle. Vines crept up the back end of the place, engulfing the top corner, and mold striped the siding. No car. No motorbike. No vehicle of any kind. Nothing suggesting anybody lived here. Still, Max went up to the front door and knocked.

"You stupid?" A middle-aged woman called out from across the street. She wore grey pajamas, a pink robe, and sat on a folding chair. "Ain't nobody living there."

Max crossed the road and offered a friendly smile. "I'm looking for Estelle Lynch. This is the address I have for her."

"She ain't there now."

"You know where she went?"

The lady popped a cigarette in her mouth and lit it with such speed that Max guessed she smoked a pack-a-day, if not more. "Now, why would I tell you anything? I don't know you."

"Sorry. I'm Max Porter."

"You a cop?"

"No."

"Lawyer?"

"No. Nothing like that. I'm not here to cause her trouble."

"You working for Sidwell, ain't you? You coming to cause her more grief, no doubt."

Falling back on the tried and true, Max put out his hand. "Ma'am, you got me mixed up with other people. I'm none of those things. I'm a writer for a little online magazine about Forsyth County history. Doing some research on the old Sidwell mill, and Ms. Estelle's name came up. Did you know her well?"

Stretching her legs out before crossing them, the lady said, "You want to know about Estelle and the mill? Pull up a chair. I know everything about it. I'm Pauline Michaels, by the way." She then spelled out her name to make sure he got it right for his magazine article.

"Did you work at the mill?"

"I did. But I got the lung troubles." She took a long drag on her cigarette. "Kills my stamina. I'm on disability now. Going on eight years."

"But when you did work at Sidwell Mills, you worked with Estelle Lynch?"

"That's why we're talking, right?"

"I know she was a secretary. Is that what you did?"

"If I was a secretary, I wouldn't have had to worry about my stamina. Although with Mr. Feeler, that may not have been true."

"Mr. Feeler?"

"The boss. Mr. Sidwell." She slanted closer and said in a quieter voice, "To say he was a groper is being nice. He was a perv."

Max pulled out his phone. "You mind if I record this?"

Pauline glanced around the area. "I'd rather you not."

"Fair enough." He put the phone back, making sure to keep his smile even and warm. "How about you tell me in your own words whatever you know about her time at the mill. Okay?"

Taking one final lengthy drag, she flicked her cigarette butt toward the road. Exhaling smoke and coughing at the tail end, she pointed at him as if he had made a smart decision. Once she got control of her breathing again, she cinched her robe and faced up at the afternoon sky as if she could see her memories in the clouds.

"I don't know how much I can tell you that's useful, but I got stories. Estelle was hard to get to know. Didn't have many friends. Don't recall her ever having company, if you catch me. She was a lonely loner, as my pappy use to say.

"Now, I was working on the floor for about a year before she joined us. Her station was one over and a few back, and nobody really had time in the day to chitchat, so it could be rough on a new girl to join in, make friends, that kind of thing. But during our breaks, she would sit near the other girls. Kept quiet. Didn't talk much. Fact is, if she hadn't lived right across from me here, I probably would've never gotten to know her at all."

Max glanced back at Estelle's mobile home. Alone and unconnected. It didn't fit with the other homes on the road. Not because of the way it appeared but because of how it felt. The others belonged to struggle and survival. But Estelle's home looked more like a poverty-stricken mausoleum. Except nobody was buried inside.

"She was a pretty gal," Pauline went on. "That's how we knew she wouldn't last on the floor long. Mr. Feeler would pick her out of the crowd in an instant. Sure enough, less than a month later, he came rolling through — he was in a wheelchair, you see — and surprise, surprise, she got promoted to a secretarial position. She acted like she had won the lottery. For those of us too old or not pretty enough to get his attention, we knew we had it better. We only had to deal with his occasional wandering fingers or the *accidental* touch of a breast — stupid stuff like that. But his secretaries were the ones who found out what a monster that man could be."

"How bad are we talking about?"

"I can't say for sure, but I'd heard stories. Whatever put him in a wheelchair, he still could work below the waist. So I'm told. Anyway, about a week or so after Estelle got promoted, she came home late at night. I was out here drinking a beer, and I saw a company car drop her off. She looked upset. Hair was a mess. So, I called her over and gave her a bottle. I knew what had happened. Saw it in her eyes. I'd seen that look in other women's eyes before. Had it my own once or twice. Just about every woman in the world probably seen that look."

Pauline grew quiet. When Max reached a point that he

thought she might need some prodding to continue, she surprised him. She scooted up in her chair, took a hard sniff, and gazed across the road at Estelle's old home.

"This is a strange, stupid game we play. We pretend nothing's happening, but every man and woman knows — we've always known. Why do we do that? If the decent men would speak up, call it out for what it is, or if the wives would make sure their husbands paid a price for the cheating, or if — oh, I don't know. But it ain't right."

"Did he actually …"

"Rape her? Are you stupid? What do you think we're talking about here?"

"I knew he coerced some women, but I hadn't heard about rape."

"No difference. Sidwell was a foul-looking man and far too old for those girls. He forced them into his bed. Not always with violence, mostly with threats of losing their jobs, but violent or not, it's still rape. I told her so, too. See, that girl who barely ever spoke nothing to me, well we talked about it for hours that night. She sat right where you are and drank and let me hear it all. Here's something for your article — she was upset and hurt and such, but I kept seeing this weird look slip through now and then."

"Weird how?"

"Like she was calm and satisfied about something. It was kind of a scary look, and that's how come I remember it. Don't think I'll forget it."

"Did she go to the police?"

"For what? They ain't no help. I said that if she needed a friend, she could count on me. She thanked me and went back to her home. I think it mattered to her a little, but I also knew right then that she'd never take me up on my offer. Not sure how much longer after that everything happened."

"What everything?"

"Mr. Sidwell died. Couple weeks, I guess. The official story was that he had a heart attack while working at his desk. None of us believed that one. If you ask me, he did have a heart attack, but it was from choking down too many boner pills before calling in one of his secretaries. Serves the bastard right."

"Did the police look into it?"

"Don't you listen? They don't care about us." She put up her hands. "Things were a bit chaotic, so I wasn't paying much attention to that kind of thing, anyway. See, the board didn't want Theo Sidwell to take over, or maybe his daddy didn't want it, I never quite knew what the full story was. We went through a bunch of different people running the place, each of them changing up how we would get paid, how our hours were scheduled, everything. It was a real mess. And the minute we got comfortable with the new way of things, they'd switch out for a new boss, and it would change again. Not long after, they moved the mill overseas and I was out of a job. Somewhere in that, Estelle left."

"She leave a forwarding address? Any indication that she was going somewhere?"

"Nothing. And nobody's ever come looking except you."

"Before she left, did you notice anything odd about her? Not her quietness, but did you ever see her out in the middle of the night, looking up at the moon, or —"

Pauline gave Max a queer gaze. "What are you on about?"

"Anything strange about her behavior?"

"Other than that one look? I guess there was an odd thing."

"Oh?"

"She never got mail. Her box was next to mine and in all the time I knew her, she never once got any mail at all. After she was gone, nothing came either. Not even junk mail. I think she may never have owned that place. Just squatted there."

Max thanked Pauline for her help, promised to quote her in the article, and made his way back to his car. He intended to drive to the library, see if he could find anything more about Estelle Lynch from 2009, and if not, focus on the original Estelle Lynch of Loray Mills from 1929. Later, he could confer with Sandra and Drummond about their findings. With any luck, either Sandra and Brenda would have come up with a spell that would solve their problems or Drummond would have found a ghost in the Other who could shed light on the situation.

But those plans vanished when his phone rang — his mother. Hoping to remove any sound of annoyance from his voice, he answered. Before he could utter a word, though, his mother's strained cry shot through him.

"Help."

Chapter 19

THERE MUST HAVE BEEN A LITTLE MAGIC in the air. Max blazed through the streets, ran every red light, zipped by the stop signs, and acted like an ambulance racing to an emergency without the warning sirens. Which, he guessed, summed up his situation. The entire trip, he never saw a single cop. Never came close to getting pulled over. Magic, indeed.

When he arrived home, he found his mother sitting in the bathroom with an icepack against her bruised forehead. She had wrapped her arm with a towel, and blood stained both the towel and the floor. Her face had sunken, and her skin had paled.

"Thank goodness you didn't abandon me," she said as he knelt to look at her injuries.

"Are you okay? What happened?"

"What does it look like? I fell."

"I can see that. More detail would be helpful."

"Don't get smart with me."

Max removed the towel. A shallow but long cut had opened the skin around her forearm from her elbow to about midway. It looked well-clotted. Her paleness must have been shock or fear more than blood loss.

He grabbed the first aid kit from under the sink and tried to tend her wounds properly. Less panicked now, he said, "How did you fall?"

"I don't know. I guess I stood too fast when I finished in here. I got up, flushed the toilet, and next thing I knew I was on the floor."

Max pulled her hand and icepack off her head. She had a goose-egg but no cuts. Looking at the blood on the floor, he noticed a wet spot on the corner where the cabinet under the sink jutted out a bit. The incident became clear. Mrs. Porter stood, got light-headed, and fell to the side. Her forehead banged the sink, tumbling her body, and her arm scraped in an arc on the cabinet corner as she spun to the floor.

"You could've gotten hurt far worse."

"I'm fine." But the shaken look on her face had not left yet. Not even close.

Max turned her head to face him straight on. "Did something else happen?"

She hesitated. "I'd felt strange."

"Not light-headed."

"Cold. I stood, and I felt ice run down my back."

Max tried to contain any outburst. He didn't want to further upset his mother, but her unease compounded within his bones. As firm and calm as he could manage, he said, "Stay here."

"Don't leave me." She tried to stand, but he placed a hand on her shoulder.

"I won't."

He wanted to go into the living room, but with her level of agitation rising, he figured it best to stay close. That meant falling back on the old, reliable phone trick. Pulling out his cell, he pretended to swipe around to make a call. After a moment of acting like he heard a ring, he said, "Drummond, pick up."

Soon, his partner materialized in the bathroom doorway. One glance at Mrs. Porter and Drummond started searching around the house. "I'm not seeing anybody. How long ago was she attacked?"

"Ah, yes, hello. My mother had a little accident," Max said into the phone. "Just an accident. Of sorts. I'm hoping you can send out a guy to look at our heating system."

Mrs. Porter said, "You don't need a service call. That's expensive."

Covering the phone, Max said, "You felt an icy blast right before you fell. I'm getting that fixed."

Returning to the bathroom, Drummond said, "*Icy blast?* You think a ghost attacked her?"

"Yes," Max said into the phone. "I'm not sure what's going

on, but that shouldn't have happened. Do you think you can do something about it?"

"First thing, I'll go let Sandra know. The protection spells around the house haven't been recast in months. Either they need a boost, or they aren't the right spells for these weird ghosts."

"That sounds good. But do you think we can get this worked on right away?"

"I'm not following. What else do you want done?"

Max winked at his mother, pointed at the phone, and gave a thumbs up. "You will? Great. How soon can you get out here? I'm pretty sure my wife and I have an appointment with a client tonight."

Drummond nodded. "Okay, got it. I'll have Sandra set up a meeting with Sidwell for tonight."

"That's right, and usually my mother is home, but she'll be with me at the meeting."

"I'll warn Sandra about that, too."

Max pantomimed ending the call. He turned to his mother. "All set. Somebody will be out to fix the house."

Mrs. Porter set the icepack down. "You're a good boy."

"Tonight, you come with me and Sandra."

"I'd rather not. I'd like to get in bed."

"You shouldn't be by yourself, and I've got nobody to be here while I'm out."

"I can take care of myself."

"Unless there's another burst of cold air."

"Don't you do that." She raised her index finger overhead like a knife. "I know what you're thinking, but you are wrong. I don't need to be in a home."

"I didn't say —"

"You implied."

"I didn't imply anything. But since you brought it up, I do think you ought to at least look at some of the facilities. They're not like what you're picturing."

She crossed her arms and glared at her feet. "I won't go. I don't want to be surrounded by a bunch of old people, abandoned by their families, waiting for the end to come. I suffer enough. Here, at least, I've got you to look after me."

"That's the problem. I can't always be here to do it."

"And you don't have to."

"The bump on your head and the gash on your arm suggest otherwise."

"One fall and you're ready to cart me away. I taught you to be stronger than that. Show some backbone, and trust your mother. I'm absolutely fine."

Max cleaned up the floor. "Maybe. But we're not taking chances tonight. No argument. You are coming with me to a client meeting. If you have a concussion or something worse, I don't want you stuck here alone."

"But —"

"Mom, trust your son."

Chapter 20

CLOUDS OBSCURED THE MOON as another night storm gathered to drench the city. Sandra arrived at the house to pick up Max and his mother. Drummond made sure not to brush by Mrs. Porter — she'd had enough interactions with a ghostly chill that day, and they needed her to remain relaxed. Not that she acted at ease, but Max thought he saw a glimmer of calm in the way she sat in the car as if going out for a nice meal at a favorite restaurant.

When they arrived at the Sidwell mansion, Mrs. Porter became far more engaged. Max stifled a laugh and forced back the urge to tease her. She responded to wealth like many people — thinking better of those who had it, thinking they were smarter. But Max had spent the last days learning how the Sidwells and their friends screwed over the company employees at every turn. They acquired their fortune by forcing workers to endure harsh, unsafe conditions with little mercy for anything that cut into their profits. This beautiful home had been built upon the backs of decades of abuse. Look further into the past, and they had the bodies of unionizers and children poured into the foundation of their family fortune.

As they stepped out of the car, the entranceway opened and Timothy, the tall butler that sounded like Hitchcock, emerged. He approached with a stiff step to his gait and an unpleasant sneer on his lip. "Mrs. Sidwell apologizes, but she no longer requires your services."

Sandra said, "We have an appointment to meet with her."

"I'm aware, and that appointment has been cancelled."

"You could've called us before we drove the whole way out here."

"This was a last-minute decision."

Max said, "We're here now. My poor mother could use a break from the car. How about we take a few minutes to rest inside? We can finish up with Mrs. Sidwell directly."

Drummond pulled down the brim of his hat. "I'll go check out what's happening. It doesn't sound good, though."

But as he flew by the butler, the front door opened again. Mrs. Sidwell stepped out. She looked unsteady and some of her hair had escaped her tight control.

"Let them in," she said.

Timothy turned towards her, his entire body moving like a pillar on wheels. "Ma'am, you told me that you didn't want more of their —"

"I know what I said, and now I have changed my mind."

"Perhaps Mr. Theo —"

"I appreciate your concerns, but this is not the time to express them. Please bring the Porters inside before it starts raining."

The butler tilted his head and returned his attention to Max and Sandra. With his nostrils flaring, he offered a perturbed grunt. "Follow me." He led the way inside.

Once they stood in the foyer, Mrs. Sidwell gestured at Mrs. Porter. "Who is this?"

"I'm Max's mother. And you are?"

"The one paying their bills."

Max took his mother by the shoulder and guided her to a reading chair in an adjacent sitting room. "If it's okay, my mother will be here while we conduct our business." To his mother, he added, "Please stay put."

She turned her head and tapped her earbuds. "I've got a good book to listen to. You go do your work. Don't worry about me. I won't bother anybody."

"Thank you."

As he turned back to Mrs. Sidwell, his mother cleared her throat. "I could use a glass of water."

Fighting to keep a pleasant grin, Max looked to Mrs. Sidwell. She, in turn, snapped her fingers at Timothy. He appeared as unhappy as Max, but he bowed and exited to fetch the water.

Sandra pointed down the hall. "Is Theo in the music room?"

"No. I'll take you to him, but I need to know that you really can help this time."

"*This time?* The spell at our office worked."

"My son was attacked."

"We were trying to get Robert to move on, and he did. You neglected to mention the other half-dozen ghosts haunting your son."

"I thought he was cursed, not haunted."

"Had we known about the other ghosts, we would have handled things differently."

Mrs. Sidwell looked at a door to her right. "I do not like excuses. Either you can do the work or you cannot. Evidence suggests the latter."

"I'm the best witch you're going to get."

"That doesn't say much for witches."

Before Sandra could make a fist, Max jumped in. "If you're so dissatisfied, then why did you bother with this meeting? Why not fire us already?"

"I'm not sure I have time to hunt down another agency like yours. It was difficult enough to find you." She glanced at the same door. "Perhaps this was a mistake."

Drummond shoved his hands in his pockets. "I hate the indecisive ones. Makes our job so much harder."

As the butler returned with a crystal glass of water carried upon a silver tray, Max said, "You can take that back. Your boss can't make up her mind. We're leaving."

Timothy turned away, but Mrs. Sidwell put out a hand to stop him. "No need to throw a fit."

"I'm not," Max said. "But we put ourselves at great risk dealing with these ghosts. I'm pretty sure one of them attacked my mother." Max peeked over at Mrs. Porter who sat in the reading chair with her eyes closed as she listened to an audiobook. "We want to help your son, but if you can't commit to the work we're doing, then you're not only wasting our time and safety, but you're wasting your own. You'd be better off hunting down someone else to help — though, I'd be very careful about that. A lot of con artists out there, and a lot of mean witches."

Mrs. Sidwell grew quiet, and Max worried he had pushed too far. Part of his anger had been genuine, but most had been posturing. All he said was true, but he had no intention of leaving if he could avoid it. He figured Mrs. Sidwell needed a strong nudge. It was like chemotherapy — Mrs. Sidwell understood her son's illness required spells to cure, but she balked at putting him through that harrowing experience more than once.

The butler stood between them all, the glass of water rippling as he awaited orders. At length, Mrs. Sidwell covered her mouth with one hand, and through tearing eyes, she nodded. Timothy returned to Mrs. Porter, bowed down and offered the glass. Max's mother opened her eyes, thanked the man, sipped the water, and set it on an ivory side table before closing her eyes again.

"I am sorry my family's troubles have hurt your mother."

Max flapped his hand as if fanning away a stench. "How about we start over for this evening? Your son still has a ghost problem, and we are here with whatever we can do."

She trembled a nod. "Please, come this way."

"Finally," Drummond said. "I'm for giving a client the time they need to talk about these things, but it's not like we haven't dealt with Theo already."

As she led them down a hall, away from the ballroom door, Sandra hurried to her side. Mrs. Sidwell appeared to appreciate Sandra's presence, though neither spoke. They turned a corner and stopped at a swinging door — presumably for waiters and other staff to reach the ballroom from the kitchen further away.

Mrs. Sidwell placed one hand on the door and mumbled to herself. A prayer, most likely. Then she pushed the door inward.

They entered a prep area. Several chrome tables dominated the center while two stations with microwaves, a small oven, and a refrigerator took up one wall. Another side looked to be for coffee and desserts, and the wall nearest the door would be used for dirty dishes and other items ready to be returned to the kitchen.

"I do apologize again," Mrs. Sidwell said.

Sandra said, "That's not necessary."

"Speak for yourself, doll. I think this back-and-forth requires plenty of apologies."

"You must understand that with what Theo has gone through, I want this to be over. I'm not foolish. I knew his recovery would be slow and difficult, but I thought I could handle it. Then he cried blood. Actual tears of blood. That is why I agreed to meet with you. Except it cleared up, and I thought … I don't know what I thought."

"You hoped," Sandra said. "A little bit of wishing this was over."

"I suppose so. But I went to check on him before you arrived, and now …"

Mrs. Sidwell opened the swinging door to the main ballroom. Max took the lead and entered.

Large enough to house three chandeliers, a wide stage, a lighting rack, sound system, not to mention the oversized portraits on the walls — the high-ceilinged room belonged in a hotel. Unless the Sidwell mansion had become the hot place to hold conventions, Max had difficulty understanding why someone would want such a cavern in their house. Sure, they might hold a few large parties in a year, but this place could have held enough people for two weddings and a political fundraiser and still had room for a private function in the corner. But this ostentatious flexing could not mute the horror in the center of the room.

On the dancefloor, under the main chandelier, Theo floated four feet above his wheelchair. He arched back with his chest toward the ceiling as if a barbarous fiend had yanked him up with a meat hook. Dangling there, his body twitched and spasmed. His eyes were open wide, but Max got the sense that the man didn't see anything. A blue mist surrounded him.

Stepping next to Max, Mrs. Sidwell squeaked out, "Please. I can't lose him."

Chapter 21

THE PORTERS CREPT CLOSER TO THEO, their eyes turned upward as their steps echoed in the echoing room. Drummond rose in the air, his head cocked as he inspected their floating subject. Only Mrs. Sidwell remained behind, uttering muted cries, drawn to watch what they did but horrified by what she saw.

Max wanted to say something to assuage her fears, but he couldn't think of anything. Her fears were warranted.

"Estelle Lynch?" Drummond called out.

That must have gotten some reaction because both Sandra and Drummond perked up. Max waited for an explanation. When Sandra returned her attention to Theo and Drummond circled from above, Max guessed Estelle didn't offer much in the way of communication.

"Why aren't you drawing on the floor?" Mrs. Sidwell stomped her foot. "Don't worry about ruining the wood. Save my son."

"It's not that simple," Sandra said as she came alongside Max.

"You did it before."

"And look at the results."

"Yes, but like you said, you didn't know about the other ghosts. You know about them now." Mrs. Sidwell's momentary firmness fumbled. "Surely, there aren't even more hiding up there."

Max turned the question toward Drummond with a glance.

The old ghost squinted into the haze. "Not as far as I can tell. But they don't appear any happier than when we saw them at the office. When I called the one by name, they all pulsed real bright. Not in a pleasant way, either."

Wrinkling her nose, Sandra said, "Do you smell that?"

Max sniffed — a sour, sulfur rot. To Mrs. Sidwell: "Does this house use gas?"

"No. It's electric."

Not a gas leak then. The odor strengthened.

"This is more than a suggestion," Drummond said. "You should leave this room."

Sandra gazed up. "Oh, crap."

Before Max or Mrs. Sidwell could ask, Theo's body turned clockwise as if the invisible chain that hung him in the air started to spin. A breeze arrived from nowhere. The chandelier tinkled a soft tune like windchimes on a gentle day. But Theo's turning sped up along with the breeze. The gentle tune became a rough sound as the chandelier swayed.

"Time to get out," Drummond said.

Max took hold of Mrs. Sidwell's hand. "We have to go."

"No," she said. "Help him."

"We will, but not now."

The ward around his neck brightened like a lightbulb receiving too much electricity. Before he could react to the heat buildup, its light camera-flashed and the ward cracked. An unseen hand shoved Sandra back several steps. Her ward heated up like an ember until it also flashed bright and cracked.

The wind grew to a full gust. Shards of glass flew off the chandelier, smashing into the walls in a variety of notes creating a dangerous song. Max tugged on Mrs. Sidwell's arm, trying to get her moving without exerting too much force. No good would come from a rougher approach — she would dig in more. Though, if he needed to, he would throw her over his shoulder and carry her out.

"You have to stop this," she said, yanking her hand out of his grasp.

Sandra grabbed Mrs. Sidwell's shoulders and shouted over the wind. "We can't help him if we're hurt. Neither can you."

With one final gaze at her son, she offered a weak nod. Max and Sandra hurried back to the prep room. But before they reached the door, a large table dropped from above. It covered the doorway as it crashed against the floor.

Max moved to push it aside, but Drummond yelled, "Duck!"

Flattening to the floor, Max heard the rapid-fire hits of chandelier bullets cutting into the wooden table. The wind howled. Peering over his shoulder, he saw Theo whirling around, arms spread out by centrifugal force, hair like a flag in a storm, eyes never closing.

"The front door," Sandra said. She grabbed Mrs. Sidwell and headed across the ballroom.

As Max pushed to his feet, he saw blood dribbling from the mouths on several of the wall portraits. The ground rumbled. Light fixtures and electric outlets sparked.

Above, Drummond acted as if nothing happened. He had his hands in his pockets and a sly grin on his face. An act, of course, but Max couldn't see how it would help.

"This is impressive," Drummond said. "I never went in for the haunted house look myself, but if that's what you want, you nailed it. Thing is — there's a better afterlife for you than this."

Okay, then. Trying to keep these raging ghosts from a point of no return. Max wanted to help, but first, he had to not die.

Hustling to catch up with his wife and their client, he dodged a tumbling chair. Sandra kept one arm around Mrs. Sidwell. The older woman hugged herself and had her head turned down against the wind.

The sulfuric stench overwhelmed the ballroom. Little bits of dirt, wood, and glass spit through the rushing air. Max knew they all had received small cuts and hoped none would be too serious.

Fifteen feet ahead, the double doors to the hallway stood. Beautifully carved, dark wood works of art with brass hardware that Mrs. Sidwell probably had purchased thinking they would suitably impress those who approached. Max was not impressed — not if the doors were locked.

But he never got the chance to find out.

A loud creak like the hull of a ship in a storm pulled his attention upward. The last chandelier swung hard. Over the screaming winds, Max shouted, "Sandra! Freeze!"

She halted, yanking Mrs. Sidwell back. Max heard the support bar snap — a metallic ping — and the chandelier descended with an odd grace. Its dying splendor forcing the chaos around it to slow and still. For one solid second, it continued to fulfill its purpose — mesmerizing with its kaleidoscopic display of glittering light while sparks from the torn wiring danced around it.

Then it hit the floor.

A high-pitched explosion of glass awoke the storming world around them. Max tackled the women, taking the brunt of abuse with his back. Bits of chandelier peppered his coat and the floor. Cuts on his head and legs stung.

"Wow," Drummond said, his voice distant and echoey. "You ghosts really know how to pull out the stops."

Sitting up, Max squinted at the door. The massive chandelier blocked it now. Trying to weave through to get to the exit might have been possible, but not while a team of unhinged ghosts threw a fit. Too many chances for a large crystal shard to slice somebody open.

"What other way out is there?" he asked Mrs. Sidwell.

She pointed off to the side next to the stage. A green room, perhaps. Taking his wife's hand, Max rushed for that small door. He heard enough clicking shoes behind him to know that Mrs. Sidwell joined them. But he still had to look back. He had to make sure. Whatever panicked rush propelled him forward could not overcome the guilt of leaving anybody behind.

In that single glance, Max caught Drummond's face drop from gentle and kind to dark and worried. He saw Mrs. Sidwell's mouth gape as if she witnessed the same invisible horror as Drummond. He noticed Sandra's hair standing on end as a new energy charged through the air.

Then light blasted.

The entire ballroom blazed with sunlight. Max tripped. He rolled into a ball, covering his eyes. The blinding shine cut through the dark of his hands and his closed eyelids. He saw the red of his blood, and even that turned pinkish under the spread of this supernatural sunshine.

When it finally dimmed, Max managed to stand. He blinked away the dancing afterimages burned into his vision. Nearby, he glimpsed his wife on her knees, hands covering her mouth. The raging winds had ceased. The howling had silenced. Ten feet ahead, Mrs. Sidwell crouched next to Theo's empty wheelchair. Above her — nothing. No mist. No son. Nothing.

"Where's my boy?" she said, the words scratching as she lowered her head and wept.

Max held still. Partly out of respect. Partly out of discomfort. He thought it would be awkward if he tried consoling their client. What could he do? Pat her on the back and say *there, there?*

However, Sandra did close to that exact thing. She didn't mutter such inanity, but she did walk over to Mrs. Sidwell and rested a hand on her back. She did murmur kind words as the older woman sobbed.

Damnit, Max thought, *when did I become so callous?* Perhaps spending most of his days dealing with the half-truths of witches had warped his view of people. He would have to be more careful.

— *Mother?*

Theo's voice spoke as clearly as if he sat in the ballroom. Max and Sandra exchanged a surprised look as Mrs. Sidwell jumped to her feet.

"Theo? Darling? Where are you? I'm here for you."

Drummond said, "Don't ask me. The boy isn't here. Neither are his tormenting ghosts."

— *I feel strange.*

The voice bounced from wall to wall. Sandra narrowed her eyes as she tried to get a read on where the sounds emanated from. Feeling his pulse quicken, Max tried to fight the urge to race around the room calling out to Theo — it wouldn't help and would probably confuse things. But the need to do something crawled through him, nudging his muscles, begging him to take action, any action.

Finally, Sandra snapped her focus up. "He's in this house. We can find him."

Chapter 22

POINTING AS SHE SPOKE, Sandra threw out orders with a commanding tone that brooked no questions. “Max, search this floor. Every inch. Drummond and I will take the upstairs. Mrs. Sidwell, keep talking with your son. Keep him grounded to this world. Don’t let those ghosts take him anywhere beyond the house.”

They headed out to the prep area and into the hallway. As they hurried toward the stairs, Max said, “Do you really think he’s still here?”

Sandra said, “You know how painful it is for a ghost to touch the corporeal world. Imagine how bad it would feel to try moving an entire person — one that is fighting every step of the way.”

“That’s right,” Drummond said, gliding alongside them. “And while they’re not the easiest ghosts to see, I can hear them loud and clear. Even with the craziness going on in there, I guarantee they would’ve been screaming if they had moved Theo out of the house.”

“As long as Theo can still be heard like he was just now, he’s still connected to his body. He can still be alive.”

They walked by Mrs. Porter. She didn’t glance up, preferring to sip her water and listen to her audiobook.

Stopping at the foot of the stairs in the foyer, Max said, “Assuming everything you’ve said is correct — and that’s a safe assumption — what the heck happened to Theo?”

Sandra gazed up at the second-floor balcony. “Find him first. Then we can work out the rest.”

As she climbed the stairs and Drummond lifted in the air, Max retraced his steps to start at the kitchen on the far end.

Sweat stung his numerous cuts. He rubbed the back of his neck, but that caused his wounds to sting worse.

When he entered the kitchen, he considered getting some ice to soothe his irritated skin, but the smell of cigarettes stopped him. He ran his hand along the nearest wall and found the light switch. A professional kitchen appeared before him. In the back, the butler sat at a small table, enjoying a hip flask and a smoke.

When he made no motions to hide his behavior nor any effort to offer assistance, Max said, "Shouldn't you be looking after Mrs. Sidwell?"

Timothy's derisive glare matched his careless attitude. "I'm off duty, and she's too cheap to hire a nightman."

"You live here?"

"Of course. Do you think rich people would pay more than they must? They always throw in a room and access to the kitchen so they can knock down the salary."

Max walked around the large kitchen but saw no sign of Theo. "Where's your room?"

"All the servants' rooms are down that hall." The butler indicated a door at the back. "I'm the only one living here right now. Sometimes there's a maid who doesn't work for a service. But not at the moment. Why are you asking?"

"Trying to find Theo. He's — playing with us, I guess."

"I'd start with the music room, if I were you."

"Right. I should have thought of that."

The butler swigged back his flask. "Perhaps I should have your job. Does it pay well?"

"Not usually."

"Shame. I'm getting a bit tired of this. But when you're born into a family business, it's not hard to get stuck on that path. Theo doesn't know how lucky he is not to have to take over running the mill."

"You knew Robert well?"

"Just at the end. My father was Robert's butler. Both men are dead now, and their sons still struggle with their ghosts."

Max paused at the comment, but the way Timothy knocked back his flask was a clear answer. Before Max left the man to wallow, he said, "Did you hear anything from the ballroom?"

"It's been quiet. Why?"

"Just curious. Have a good night."

No reason to ruin the man's maudlin buzz. He would find out in the morning that a monumental mess awaited his cleaning efforts.

Max knew he should check the empty servant rooms, but the butler had been right — Max should have started with the music room. He hustled through the halls and returned to the sitting room. This time, Mrs. Porter raised her eyes to watch Max race into the foyer. He thought she made a short grunt, but she never said anything. His cuts offered another round of stinging as he reached the music room.

Turning on the lights, he found no sign of Theo. In fact, everything looked exactly as when they had left it the other day. Odd. Considering that this was supposedly Theo's favorite room, why hadn't he come in here?

He had seen some terrifying things in the last two days, experienced those things. It would be reasonable to think that he would find solace in some music. Or perhaps by sitting at the piano or picking up a violin or playing on whatever instruments he knew, Theo would be able to express the inexpressible, find some way to deal with the idea that reality may not be what he had thought it was. Yet nothing had been touched.

No, no. Max knew better than to start putting thoughts into the heads of his clients, thoughts he had no way to know except through conjecture. To suggest that Theo had something to hide or some ulterior motive to not have used this room in a time of need required Max to know what Theo felt and thought. Not only that, but Max had to admit that there was an equal, if not greater, chance that Theo didn't have the time to return to his favorite room. His mother was also upset at the last spell casting. Perhaps she required his attention.

Max turned to leave when he noticed the framed photos on a shelf that was part of one wall. He approached one ivory frame with his stomach grumbling — not hunger, though, but concern. Heart hammering, breath thinning out, he locked eyes with the slender woman in the photo.

The photo was black and white. The woman wore jeans and a plaid shirt, had dark hair that curled at her shoulders, and she sat at the piano, smiling for the camera. And the woman in the photo? Estelle Lynch.

Max's phone chimed a text from Sandra. It read: *We can't find him up here. Meet in the ballroom.*

Before leaving the music room, Max snapped a picture of the photo and texted a copy to Sandra along with a simple: *on my way.* As he walked back to meet the others, his mind whirled at what this old picture meant, if anything at all. He would have to think on it. Too much going on right now. It could wait until the morning.

A scream rang out through the halls. Not Sandra. Not his mother. It had to be Mrs. Sidwell. Max sprinted across the house, garnering an annoyed glance from Mrs. Porter.

Closing in, he heard more wailing. "No, no, no!"

Max burst into the ballroom. There he found Sandra and Drummond with somber expressions as they watched Mrs. Sidwell. She sat on the floor, howling her heaving cries.

"Get out of my house! Don't ever come back!"

Draped over her legs, her son lay dead.

Chapter 23

NOBODY WANTED TO TALK the rest of the night. Nor the following morning. Max and Sandra meandered through their routine without experiencing any of it. They awoke, showered, brewed coffee, ate breakfast, cleaned up, and sat. Even Mrs. Porter acted stunned — though she only knew that a young man had died the previous night and that everybody was upset. She had no idea why or what happened, and either she had the good sense not to probe around for an answer or she was too shocked by her evening ending with death that she stayed quiet.

Over the years, the Porters had chalked up their fair share of failures, but Max could not recall the death of a client. Witches had died. Enemies had died. In fact, some clients had died as the natural order of the case — helping a client move on, helping a client break free of a curse sustaining their life, that sort of thing. But to have The Porter Agency's absolute failure be the direct cause of death — that was new and unwelcome.

As the morning dragged on, Drummond appeared, took one look at Max and Sandra, muttered something about the Other, and left. Not a bad idea. Max would go batty if he spent the whole day wallowing in this loss. But he didn't feel safe leaving his mother alone, and he didn't feel right asking Sandra to spend her day stuck doing the things he wanted to escape from.

As if reading his mind, Sandra sat next to him on the couch and put a hand on his knee. "We need a break. I'm going out for a few hours. Brenda and I will look into what happened with those ghosts. Figure out where we went wrong."

"We never had a chance to do anything last night."

"But we did force Robert Sidwell to move on. We did cast the initial spell looking for a curse. I've got to make sure neither of those spells caused this."

Max covered her hand. "Your spells did not backfire."

"All spells have a level of unintended consequences. That's why we witches are forever refining the design and casting of our craft. If there is any small change I can make so this never happens again, I need to do that."

He bumped his shoulder against hers. "Of course. But I still think you're in the clear."

"When I get back, it'll be your turn."

"For what?"

"For getting out of this house for a few hours. Go do something. Eat some barbeque. Whatever. I'll take care of your mother."

He hugged her. "I love you more than you'll ever know."

"Oh, I know."

The rest of the morning, Max remained in the living room and watched YouTube videos about the history of Scooby Doo, the science behind the formation of planets, and the stupidity of people eating far too many baked beans. At some point, his mother had rustled into the room and settled in a chair. She had her earbuds in and her eyes closed. Though Theo was nobody to her, Max figured she might need some human contact to help process the night, too. Death was death, after all. At her age and with her disease, any reminder would be disturbing.

But what could he say? From the first days when she arrived in North Carolina, she had been exposed to the paranormal world. Their last big case had been about extracting her from a witch deal. Despite it all, she refused to accept the truth. She never had. He had no clear picture of how she dismissed everything she had encountered, but she did. She could not handle reality. Better, he decided, to say nothing. Just be present for her.

Yet when he rested his head back and started to close his eyes, his mother cleared her throat until he looked at her. "I'm scared," she said.

He inched toward the edge of the couch and placed his laptop on the coffee table. "What happened last night is not going to hurt us here." He hoped that was true but recalled the cold blast that had caused his mother's recent injuries.

Pulling out her earbuds, she gazed at him with her most motherly smile. "You're a good boy. I know this can be hard — watching me at the end of my time — but you're handling it well. I love you for that."

"Would you like to talk about it?"

"If that's what you need."

Typical. She told him she was scared, then turned it around on him. Why couldn't she say what she wanted?

But at the sight of those little girl eyes glistening before him, he swallowed his complaints. His mother faced a frightening moment, one that nobody could soothe. Even if she had been a devout believer in any religion, she would still have to wonder about what came after. Only the most blindly faithful person could possibly face death and not think about such things. Even then, surely that person would have a sliver of worry that they had not lived righteous enough.

Max wanted to tell her that he knew a little about the afterlife, that she would be okay. After all, Drummond had moved on once, and if that waitress-chasing, cantankerous old ghost could go to a peaceful, pleasant world, then Max's mother was a shoo-in. Unless she had committed some grave sin he knew nothing about.

"You didn't kill anybody, did you?"

"What? No, of course not."

"You didn't cheat on Dad or commit some blasphemy. In fact, you've spent most of your life trying to make sure I did the right thing, behaved appropriately, stayed honest, that sort of upbringing."

"That's the job of any mother."

"Then you've got nothing to worry about. When your time comes, you'll move on to a beautiful afterlife. I'm sure of it."

That appeared to satisfy Mrs. Porter. She gave him a final nod before sticking her earbuds back in and closing her eyes to somebody's gentle narration. Max waited, but when she did not pop up a question or comment, he sat back with his laptop and resumed watching the world of idiots and baked beans.

Later in the day, Sandra returned and like a tag team, Max jumped from the couch. Instead of a slap of hands, they exchanged a kiss, and before Max's mother could rouse from sleep, he was out the door, in his car, and heading for the office. The case was over, but he still had questions. Particularly about Estelle Lynch.

But not the young lady that squatted in a mobile home and disappeared coincidentally after Robert Sidwell's death. There was a lot to learn about her, about why her photo was in Theo's beloved music room, but those details would not help Max understand why Theo had died. That was the part that kept bothering him. Not only their failure to protect the man, but why he had been targeted in the first place.

Killing Robert Sidwell made plenty of sense. He was a misogynist, a womanizer, or in Drummond's parlance, a cad. Not only could Max see why somebody like Estelle Lynch would murder her boss, he also understood why she might continue to haunt him after his death. But going after his son when Theo had nothing to do with the company? That seemed biblical. In Max's experience, people talked up a good game, but only the rarest circumstances fueled a great enough rage that it would seek retribution through generations.

So, when Max reached the office and sat at his desk, he searched through the life of Estelle Lynch — the one from 1929.

Unlike 2009 Estelle Lynch, this version had plenty of digitized details. It should have been the other way around, and Max struggled to make sense of that. The best he could come up with — the 2009 version strived for anonymity. She understood the internet and worked hard to stay off it. The 1929 version made no attempt to escape her information being archived, and those archives had been put onto the internet long ago. Starting with her birthdate — 1919.

She was only ten years old when she went to work for Loray Mills, only ten when the strike occurred, only ten when the world she knew and understood broke down. That world was comprised of three things — her father, her mother, and work.

Her parents both worked at the mill, too. They lived in the mill town, and thus, Loray Mills was their entire life.

Leonard Lynch, her father, loaded and unloaded trucks in the warehouse. Her mother, Molly Lynch, knew how to use a typewriter, which got her placed with administration. She was a secretary.

"That ain't good."

Max had a strong idea of where this would end up, but to confirm his dark suspicions, he needed primary sources of a more personal nature. A lot could be learned from birth announcements, obituaries, and census data, but understanding the kinds of details he sought required diaries, journals, letters, and other private messages. The problem here was that a ten-year-old girl slaving away her days in a textile mill had little time to write down her deeper thoughts on the experience. Her off-work hours would have been consumed with eating, washing, cleaning their home, looking after her younger siblings, and occasionally playing with a friend. Not to mention that since she was working at the age of ten, she might not have learned how to read or write.

"But her mother knew how to type."

Max started over, this time focusing on Molly Lynch. An hour later, he uncovered an article in one of the raggiest local rags. The sensationalized report revealed enough of the sad tale that he could fill in the rest. The headline — *Striking Child Dies! Police Try To Stop Riot!*

"Crap."

Chapter 24

"THE DEATH WAS RULED A WORKPLACE ACCIDENT," Max told Sandra and Drummond later that night as he paced in the living room. They had waited until after Mrs. Porter had gone to bed, and the built-up energy jittered out of him with each step, with each word. "When challenged by the fact that there couldn't be a workplace accident since there was no work happening, management explained that Estelle Lynch and some of her friends had snuck onto the empty mill floor to mess around. But being kind and generous people, management decided to call it a workplace accident so that the Lynch family received a company payment for their loss."

Drummond hovered in his preferred corner. "That couldn't have gone over well."

"Leonard Lynch, the father — he punched a police officer and served a week in jail for it."

Stretching on the couch, Sandra said, "What about Molly Lynch?"

"She didn't make a statement, but there's this photo." Max brought up the newspaper photo on his phone. It showed a woman cold as concrete on a winter night surrounded by officials and police escorting her out of a Loray Mills' building. She stared dead-eyed into the distance.

"Anything witchy?"

"Not that I could find. The pictures looked benign, and any articles or reports I read didn't include the slightest mention of the occult, strange symbols, or even the merest hint at an unusual feeling. Nothing."

Drummond said, "It's obvious the little girl's death was covered up. There's not a snowballs chance that the company would give a striker a dime for what they claimed happened. Not unless they don't want anybody poking into what really happened."

"I'll keep looking into it. Assuming we want to. Theo's dead. We don't really have a client anymore."

Sitting up, Sandra said, "Could you really let this go? Walk away without knowing why it happened?"

Max chuckled. "No."

"Exactly. And my reason for working on the spell today wasn't an excuse. We need to understand where things went wrong in this case or they'll go wrong again. That includes figuring out what really happened to Theo."

Clearing his throat, Drummond said, "Yeah, on that subject. It might get a bit murkier."

Sandra twisted around to face the ghost. "You found something in the Other?"

"I went through my usual contacts and snitches. Tried to find anything about the Sidwells or Estelle Lynch. Didn't get anything from them. But this one waitress I know, and she's not one I've dated —"

Max raised his hands in innocence. "I didn't say a word."

"You gave a look."

"I didn't —"

"Stop it," Sandra said with the tired impatience of a mother caught between fighting siblings. "Max, stay quiet. Drummond, what did the waitress say?"

The ghost gave a clear look of triumph, but before Max could protest, he lowered to the floor and continued, "She knew a guy who knew a guy. That's the way it works in the Other. Doesn't matter how many dead people are there, you're always only a few steps away from just about anybody. So, I meet up with this reporter, Haywood Drint, who says he knows the whole story. But here's where it gets weird — the Estelle Lynch article he wrote about happened in 1969."

Leaning his elbows on his knees, Max said, "I can't decide if I'm shocked. Part of me is thinking that it figures one-hundred-percent."

"I felt the same way. Mr. Drint had been sent to cover the death of a young lady at the Sidwell Mills. He figured it'd be an easy job and an easy by-line. If it turned out to be a murder, he might even hit the front page. But when he arrived, security wouldn't let him on the premises. They claimed they had to maintain the purity of the scene until the police were done. After the cops left, security refused to let him inside saying that the police would make an official statement, and he could talk with them about anything else."

"Let me guess — the police ruled it a workplace accident."

Drummond snapped his fingers and pointed at Max. "We have a winner. The whole thing smelled bad, and ol' Haywood must've been a heckuva reporter in his day because he smelled a good story in that rot. He started digging around.

"He learned that Estelle worked for Reginald Sidwell. This would be Theo's grandfather, I think. Unless he was an uncle or something. Doesn't matter, though. What matters is that Reginald had a reputation amongst the secretaries, and I'm guessing you can figure that one out."

With a disgusted grunt, Sandra said, "What is it with these Sidwell men?"

Max said, "Unbridled power can bring out the worst in people. Triple that when you've been raised in a pampered household that encourages dominating others."

"That was a rhetorical question, hon."

"The story played out much like you'd expect." Drummond tapped his chin. "Where it got stranger, where it got to the point that Haywood Drint remembered the story, was when he tried to find out anything about Estelle Lynch. He expected to hit obstacles around Sidwell. A wealthy man like that protected himself. But Estelle? She should have been an open book. Only Haywood couldn't find anybody who knew much of anything about her. Job application info was fake. She kept distance from neighbors and co-workers. She barely existed except on paper and the fact that people saw her, that she showed up each day and did her work.

"Best idea Haywood had for what happened — Estelle had

some secret she wanted to keep hidden and Sidwell found out. He tried to blackmail her for sex, and when she refused, they struggled. She ended up dead, and the company covered it up. Probably had a few cops on the payroll to help with that matter."

Sandra pulled out her phone and tapped away. "We've got three women with the same name, each getting involved in the same business, each one playing out forty years apart — 1929, 1969, and 2009."

Max said, "With Theo dead, that probably ends it until 2049. We're off the hook."

"Unless it's happened other decades, too. We may not have found every instance of Estelle Lynch."

"There is that. Hey, Drummond, did you come across any witchcraft with your version of the lady?"

"Not one bit. I kept asking Haywood about that, but he didn't notice anything, and there was nothing about his ghost to suggest spell residue. You'd have to do your research thing to dig up his articles to see what he may have missed in the photos."

Sandra turned her phone towards the men. "Already got it right here."

They crowded together to look through the article. One photo showed Estelle Lynch and Reginald Sidwell standing with several other employees. Reginald lacked the Scrooge appearance of his son but shared the malice in his eyes. Max half-expected Estelle to look exactly like the photo he had from Theo's music room, but this Estelle had light hair, looked taller, and not nearly as bubbly.

Speaking Max's thoughts aloud, Drummond said, "Not the same gal. No hints of magic. Maybe these are just ticked off ghosts."

Sandra said, "I'm not willing to close the door on witchcraft yet. With the witch war going on, plenty of these things could be happening. Plus, we've seen too many bizarre spells to be definitive about saying what exactly is the case here. But the evidence so far points to angry, angry ghosts."

"I'm surprised they haven't gone poltergeist long ago."

"That's the key, right there," Max said, pulling out his phone now. "That's why we can't stop this case. We got hired to save Theo. We screwed that up. But those ghosts are still out there, and based on the near-century of haunting and murder that's in their wake, I'm thinking they won't be satisfied."

"Mrs. Sidwell?"

"It's the next logical target. And here it is." He showed his phone. "Funeral is the day after tomorrow. I think we should be there."

Getting to her feet, Sandra said, "That gives us about a-day-and-a-half to find out whatever we can. She's not going to want to see us, and she won't want to listen to us. So, we'll need to have every argument ready."

"Then let's call it a night and get some rest. We've got a lot of work in the morning."

Chapter 25

UNDER NORMAL CIRCUMSTANCES — normal for the Porters, anyway — Max would have been delighted with an assignment of researching for well over a day. Even knowing the clock ticked away, he would have thrived in the situation. But with the Sidwell case, little about the research brought joy. Each time he opened his laptop, he wondered what the next tragic version of Estelle Lynch might look like, what despicable people in power she had to deal with, and what mysterious end occurred before she vanished.

He had the added problem of dealing with his mother. At Sandra's suggestion, they decided it would be *Bring Your Ailing Mother to Work Day*. Mrs. Porter put up a fight on the grounds that this last-minute decision broke her routine, but when Max and Sandra presented a united front, she agreed — grudgingly.

Since Sandra needed access to the casting circle, Max moved a chair in the corner with the bookcase. He slid over a side table, made sure his mother had a glass of water, and set a blanket over the arm of the chair in case she got cold. Mrs. Porter appeared to like her little reading cranny, popped in her earbuds, and drifted off to another land. As Max settled at his desk, he worried those earbuds helped her disassociate from the world. Then again, if audiobooks and music gave her respite from her pain, he saw it as a good thing.

Drummond poked out of the books and swept across the room. "While you both caught some shuteye, I went back to visit ol' Haywood."

"He give you anything?" Max asked.

"Oh, he did. Doll, can you hear me over there?"

Sandra lifted her head from the floor. "I'm not deaf, and

you're plenty loud."

"I'm excited. See, Haywood couldn't let the story go. Long after Reginald was buried, almost a full year, he arranged for an interview with the man's widow — Katherine Sidwell. Back then, when Haywood was alive, he didn't believe in ghosts or witches or any of it. But floating around the Other is bound to change that view."

"Let me guess," Max said, "Katherine told him about the supposed family curse."

"That's right. He didn't believe it, of course, but she insisted that in the years before Reginald's death, he had chronic pains, weird chills, and night terrors that no doctor could cure. During his final week of life, he had started hearing voices, seeing shadows move, that kind of stuff. Got me thinking. Every time Estelle Lynch shows up, the curse gets worse until a Sidwell dies."

Sandra paused. "But this recent version disappeared after Robert died. There wasn't one around for Theo."

"That we know of."

The same excitement that had Drummond bouncing around infected Max. He opened his laptop with a wide smile. "That's good," he said. "Real good. I'll look through everything we have and whatever else I can find to see if there's more to the pattern. Sandra's working on her spells, but if you don't have a plan for the day —"

"I know. Back to the Other. You got it," Drummond said before disappearing.

Max then spent the rest of the morning combing through the pile of information they had acquired on the case. The work proved difficult. His researching instincts did not co-operate, did not guide him from one intuitive leap to another. The dates and events sat before him, but he couldn't make any good guesses beyond the obvious. And while the overall situation was clear enough — ghosts haunted generations of the Sidwells for wrongs done by the family — that wouldn't be enough to convince Mrs. Sidwell. She already believed in the curse and had suffered the loss of her son from it. The Porters needed more.

Making matters tougher, they had yet to find anything pointing to witchcraft. But for Estelle Lynch to keep returning every forty years as a young woman that would destroy a Sidwell required magic. Powerful magic. The kind of controlled energy that could only be found in witchcraft.

And why Theo? More than most of the troublesome questions in this case, that one gnawed at the back of Max's mind. The previous victims all worked in the mill business, all forced Estelle Lynch into one degradation or another, all abused their power. But Theo? He was a kid when Robert Sidwell did the things that garnered a paranormal vengeance. Was it as basic as making a child pay for the sins of the father?

Max could accept that reasoning from somebody born in the 1700s or earlier, maybe from somebody living through the 19th century. But in the 20th or 21st century, that kind of viciousness seemed antiquated. Not that modern day people couldn't be evil bastards who wanted to see a family suffer. But most folks would prefer to make that suffering more immediate, more public — embarrassing or shameful video going viral and destroying the target's life instead of waiting decades for the next generation to grow up and be ruined in silence.

Two things happened next that not only interrupted Max's flow of research but stopped him entirely. First, his stomach reminded him that he needed to break for lunch. Second, he received an email. When he pulled up his mailbox, he saw that the sender was Jane Porter.

Chapter 26

HAVING MADE A HURRIED EXIT from the office, Max wished he could have been smoother about the whole thing. He regretted leaving Sandra to deal with his mother, but he had to get out of there, and he couldn't talk about why. If he mentioned the email, Sandra would have tried to reason with him, help him work out how to handle Aunt Jane, and what he should write back. Good things, indeed, but not when his mother might overhear. Because if she did, if she caught any of that conversation, the entire world would implode as his mother's fury sucked in all matter and bellowed out fiery guilt. He carried enough of that. Even a simple *How could you do this to your own mother?* had the potential to destroy him. So, he left without a word.

But as he drove along the city streets, considering one restaurant after another for lunch, his body jangled with trepidation. He didn't want to eat anything too rich. For that matter, he didn't want anything too good. With his stomach roiling, anything like that would be wasted. Also, while he needed a space to write a considered response, he didn't want to be sitting amongst the busy lunchtime crowd.

Instead, he opted to grab a sub and head over to Miller Park. It was a large enough park that he could sit in peace at one of the sheltered benches, away from the playground area or the hiking trails. Lunch in the middle of the week would not draw a lot of people, and with the recent storms leaving everything damp and cool, he counted on even less of a turnout.

The food did its job. Filled him up without making him sick. That would make a great review, he snickered. When he finished eating, he threw away his trash and set his laptop on the wooden table.

The email stared at him.

He considered filing it away for later — after the case. But there would always be a case, always an excuse. Waiting for a convenient time amounted to stalling. He could avoid difficult conversations with the best, but he knew that stalling, avoidance, whatever he called it, always led to emptiness.

He set his fingers to type.

"Your wife is worried about you." Drummond chose a dramatic lowering from above until he sat on the opposite side of the table. "Rushing out of the office, no word since."

"Tell her I'm fine. I needed a little space to work something out."

"Tell her yourself. I'm not a phone operator."

Max wanted to point out that nobody born this century would know that reference, but he held back. He didn't want to encourage banter that would stretch this visit out. Lifting his view over the laptop, he saw the ghost glaring back at him.

"Okay, okay." He texted Sandra.

"Thank you. Now you're going to tell me what's the real problem."

"The real problem? Having a partner who knows you as well as your wife, and then having your wife be another partner. I can't escape you people."

Drummond ignored the comment. "I'd normally think you were concerned about the case or the client, but this feels different."

"Leave it alone."

"Can't do that. If whatever this is bleeds over into work, you put your life in danger, the life of a client, and most important, Sandra's life. In fact, she might be the only one I really care about in this scenario."

Max wished he could feel insulted, but he sort of agreed. He put Sandra ahead in importance, too. And that meant telling the ghost the truth. It didn't take long, and showing Drummond the email explained the rest.

After hearing the situation, Drummond looked baffled. "Why are you so stupid sometimes?"

"Ah, wonderful. Another Marshall Drummond pep talk."

"I'm serious. Your generation is too concerned with self-reflection. Sometimes, a man needs to be a man."

"It's great thinking like that which has led to hundreds of wars."

"I'm not talking about that fake, manly crap that sent too many boys to be slaughtered on D-Day, or the kind of chest-thumping that gets weaker guys in trouble. I even applaud the effort of modern guys to do some digging into their souls. But once you've figured out who you are, you don't need to go scrounging around for more like a mangy dog."

"I'm a dog now?"

"A mangy one. But really, with the endless soul-searching that you've done since I've known you — trust me, you've figured out who you are. It's not important to uncover every single facet of your past. How many of our cases do you have to go through before you learn that lesson? Sometimes, the past is buried for a good reason."

Closing his computer, Max said, "Okay. I've heard you. You can go back to the office and report to Sandra."

Drummond shot into the air. "You don't have to be a jerk." He disappeared.

Good, Max thought. He wanted to be alone in the first place. If he sought guidance from a detective dead for over eighty years, he knew where to get that. Clearly, he went to the park for solitude.

Irritated by a damp spot on the bench that had soaked through to his thigh, Max stood and stomped feeling into his feet. Not too far off, he heard giggling and the pitched voices of children. He spotted a mother and her two boys strolling toward the playground.

She stood tall, with a bit of heft, and had dark skin that stood out against a white outfit. One of the boys with her was white and the other looked Korean. If she was their mother, they were most likely adopted. And that made Max think of the Sandwich Boys.

PB and J had lived two full lives already. Before the Porters, the Sandwich Boys had survived a homeless existence. No good options for their future. No guarantee they would live that long. Now, one readied to go to college while the other tried to whittle down the immense opportunities the world presented. What benefit would either young man gain from looking back?

Not only that, but the past had already come back once. Came after PB in the form of his birth-father. That nearly killed PB, and while Max and PB grew closer after that horrible event, they would have been fine without it.

Maybe Drummond was right. Maybe there was a point where self-reflection became self-indulgence.

Yet Max opened his computer again and clicked on the email. Indulgent or not, he still had curiosity. That quality had served him well throughout his life and his career. And what harm could come from reading an email? He didn't have to reply, after all.

The message was short and curt — *I'll meet with you only once. Tell me when.*

He didn't have to reply. But he knew that he would.

Chapter 27

THE PORTERS DID NOT ATTEND THE CHURCH SERVICE. Sandra suggested that if Mrs. Sidwell noticed them in the pews, a bad scene would develop. Possibly one that involved calling the police. Better to wait until after the burial.

So, dressed nicely and standing a respectful distance from the graveside mourners, Max and Sandra waited in the damp. The overcast day dropped the temperature, and the gray weather promised another shower soon. Drummond hovered next to Max.

While they waited, Max scanned the crowd of black clad wealth. Some of those people had to be other textile owners or board members or higher-ups of one flavor or another. He tried to recognize them from the old photos and news articles, but the decades between the photos and this funeral had taken their toll. If he had seen any of them previously, he could not place them now.

He wondered if the ghosts that had caused this trauma came to see the conclusion of their handiwork. Unfortunately, cemeteries tended to be chock full of the dead. Worse than hospitals. Sandra once told Max that a large cemetery could look like a blinding wall of ghost light. And from what he had learned over the years, a lot of the ghosts roaming around their graves had serious problems keeping them from moving on, making the matter worse. Drummond could walk amongst them with no issue, but he felt uncomfortable to be around them for long.

"It's a bit like walking through an old madhouse," he had once said. "You never know what's going to reach out at you, and some of them spout gibberish while others are laughing for no reason."

Not all cemeteries were like that. For a few cases, they had been to some that were rather pleasant. Or, at least, not as dangerous. No matter how Max looked at it, though, cemeteries were not good places for The Porter Agency to visit.

"You doing okay?" he asked Sandra.

She threaded her arm around his and pressed close. "Even without the ghosts, it'd be darn cold out here."

"Yeah, but with them?"

"I'm fine. We're far enough back. Most of them are circling the grave."

Drummond said, "They're wondering what the new guy will look like, trying to size him up."

"Can you see Theo?"

"Not yet. With any luck, he's moved on, but if he didn't, he might be hiding. Trying to, anyway. A lot of folks spend their first weeks in their coffins. Either they don't realize they can come out, or they're too afraid to."

"But can't the others go under the ground and see if he's there?"

Rocking back and forth, touching the tip of his hat to someone Max could not see, Drummond said, "Technically, yeah. Except most ghosts wouldn't dare. Looking into another coffin is rude, invasive, and kind of creepy. Big stigma against it. You won't find many willing to try."

"You've done it."

"For a case, sure. But that's the nature of the gig. We've got to do unpleasant things sometimes to make things right in this world. And if you paid any attention, you'd have noticed I try to avoid doing it at cemeteries where other ghosts could see me. Heck, I try to avoid doing it at all. Maybe you should stop asking for it."

"Sheesh. Sorry. Didn't realize it was such an issue."

"You know it's an issue for me to open locked doors because of the pain, yet you keeping asking for that. Why should this be any different?"

"Careful, there. You're starting to lay guilt like my mother."

In the distance, Mrs. Sidwell approached Theo's coffin. She

wore a black coat over her black dress as well as a small black hat with a veil attached. She had black gloves on, too. And she trembled. Her head bowed and a shudder rolled along her back as she caressed the wooden resting place of her son. At length, she straightened and lifted her head. Leading with her nose upturned in a manner Max had become too familiar with, she faced the small gathering. This far away, Max could not hear what she said, but the murmur of her voice carried to them. She was making a speech — maybe a formal eulogy — and she commanded rapt attention from her listeners.

Pride flowed through that murmur. Pride and sorrow. When she finished, she stepped back, and the crowd broke into two groups. One dispersed toward their cars or into small circles to chat before leaving. The other group formed a line to touch the coffin and offer useless words to the grieving mother. Fifteen long minutes drifted by before the stragglers finally headed away.

"Now?" Max asked.

"It ain't going to get any better," Drummond said.

Sandra started toward the grave, and the other two followed. They hardly had taken a dozen steps when Mrs. Sidwell saw them. Her body stiffened. Her face constricted. But she didn't yell at them or send some younger men to force them away. Rather, she held stone still and waited.

Walking directly to the coffin, Sandra touched the wood. She flinched as if receiving an electric charge. Then, putting on a pitying smile, she turned to Mrs. Sidwell. "We are so sorry for what happened."

"Has he moved on?" The words came out in a monotone.

"We don't know yet."

Mrs. Sidwell's eyes drifted to the coffin and then to the grave awaiting it. "He hasn't. I would have felt relief for him by now." Her chin quivered but before she lost control, she sniffed hard and looked away. With a white handkerchief, she dabbed at her tears under her veil.

In the awkward silence, Max shifted his feet. They couldn't leave without letting Mrs. Sidwell know what little they had learned, but each time he opened his mouth to speak, he stopped. The choice to approach her at the cemetery screamed out as a bad idea. What had they been thinking?

But as Mrs. Sidwell walked away, she said, "Come with me."

Sandra offered a surprised shrug when Max looked to her for an answer, and they fell in step behind the bereaved. She made a straight line to a waiting limousine. The driver — same guy that drove Theo to the clandestine meetings with Max — held the car door open for her. She ducked in and the Porters followed.

Over the course of his life, Max had been inside a few limos, and each one looked different. Some were glorified taxis. Plush and comfortable but no bigger than any other luxury car. One had been a gaudy, neon affair for a bachelor party. That limo smelled stale and dirty and looked ready to fall apart. Max heard that the marriage had fallen apart, too. But the Sidwell limousine, unsurprisingly, was a full-stretch, tasteful display of class and sophistication.

Max and Sandra occupied the back seat with Drummond floating partially through the door. Mrs. Sidwell took a swiveling chair, poured a stiff drink from a crystal decanter, and pressed a button that caused the divider to rise, shutting the driver out of sight. She sipped from her glass and watched the Porters. Observed them. Like they were lab rats. Max squirmed but held his tongue.

Sandra whispered to Max, "This is bad."

Max didn't have to ask. Drummond answered, "All those hazy ghosts are in here."

Looking back at Mrs. Sidwell, feeling the drop in temperature clearer now, Max pictured the gray and white blurs that surrounded her. That's how she knew her son hadn't moved on. She felt the same horrid, icy chill she had always felt while he lived.

"I don't blame you," she said.

The lack of emotion behind her words made them hard to believe. Or perhaps Max wanted to blame himself. He would need some therapy to figure that out. A glance toward Drummond reminded him of what the ghost had said — that too much self-reflection could be as harmful as not enough. He'd have to reflect on that, too.

In a softer tone, Mrs. Sidwell went on, "If I had listened to my instincts, I would have contacted you far sooner. Then, perhaps, we would not be here today."

Sandra said, "We made decisions based on what we saw happening and what we knew at the time. You can't blame yourself."

"I can. I do. And now my son is dead but not gone. He still suffers. I can feel it. I know it in my heart. You said you couldn't tell yet if he had moved on. Does it normally take time? Is there still a chance he will move on if we have patience?"

Max could see Sandra's hand itching to reach out, to console, but he knew that gesture would not be welcomed. He rested his hand atop his wife's and said, "We're sorry, but it doesn't work like that. The initial chance to move on happens when we die."

"That suggests there are other chances."

"We can intervene. After all, we got Robert to move on. And anyone stuck can move on once they've dealt with whatever is keeping them here."

"Except my son is being held back by others. Correct?"

"We don't know for sure," Sandra said. "But probably."

Mrs. Sidwell halted through her next words, leaving enough space to drive an eighteen-wheeler between each utterance. "Then … perhaps … I … still … require … your … services."

"Well, well," Drummond said. "You've got to love it when the client does the job you set out to do."

Max said, "You want us to keep working for you?"

"Partner, keep your mouth shut. You came here hoping to convince her to do exactly what she's about to do. You ever heard about a gift horse?"

With a stronger voice, Mrs. Sidwell said, "My Theo is still here, and that means the same things that tormented him in life are still tormenting him. Isn't that correct?"

Sandra said, "Most likely."

"And The Porter Agency is still the best option for dealing with such instances."

"We think so."

"Then let's see if you can do better than before."

Perhaps sensing Max's urge to question the situation again, Drummond said, "If you say another word, I swear I'll freeze your brain for an hour."

Sandra saved the day. "Thank you for the opportunity. We've felt terrible about this, and we don't like to lose."

"That puts us in a similar frame of mind."

"The team has spent quite a few hours with further investigations that we hope will produce better results."

Mrs. Sidwell frowned. "Can't you repeat what you did for Robert?"

"The problem is that Robert wasn't being attacked by those ghosts. He was amongst them."

"I don't care about the other ghosts. I want my son to move on, to be at peace."

"We do, too. But the spell I used for your husband will only make things worse for Theo."

"Worse? That doesn't make sense."

"Think of it like your son is in an endless ocean. He's drowning. Thrashing around. These ghosts — they're doing everything they can to pull him under. Now, if we cast the spell that I used for Robert, it would be as if a rescue boat came into view, just out of reach, and no matter how much he screamed or splashed, they wouldn't see him. They'd travel away, leaving him behind to think all hope is lost. What happens then?"

With a full gulp of her drink, Mrs. Sidwell said, "He gives up. He allows the ghosts to take him down."

"And we don't want that. Not ever."

"Then what do we do?"

Max said, "We keep searching. We've got to uncover as much as we can until we know why this is happening and why in this way. Once we know that, Sandra can craft the exact spell he'll need. It'll be the life preserver that gets thrown to him. One he can actually reach."

"That's right," Sandra said. "But if you really want us to do that, you'll have to open up about Theo, about Robert, about whatever you know or think you know that might be motivating these ghosts."

Mrs. Sidwell stayed motionless for a long time. Only her shifting eyes suggested a raging debate within. At length, she set her glass down with a clink and reached beneath her seat. Pressing an unseen button, a drawer silently slid out next to her. She paused. Then with a defiant grunt, she lifted out a leatherbound photo album.

Handing it over, she said, "This is everything. Now, go save my boy."

Chapter 28

NOBODY DARED OPEN THE PHOTO ALBUM the entire ride to the office. Even after they placed it on the conference room table, they hesitated. Drummond floated near the ceiling but made no wisecracks to get them moving. Max and Sandra inspected it like it might explode.

The first thing Max noticed was the feel of the book. Though bound in dark leather and marked with the title *Sidwell Memories* across the top, it felt more like a book of witchcraft. Not the worst of witch tomes — not human skin — but it gave off an aura of magic energy. Sandra must have noticed it, too, for she never questioned Max's ginger handling of the album.

It had a lot of pages and many papers stuffed in between, some poking out at odd angles. Perhaps the worst sensations had been psychological. Perhaps the way Mrs. Sidwell had presented the album colored Max's view of it. But if that were true, then why did his ghost partner and his wife react the same?

Drummond was the first to speak up. "I realize none of us want to open that thing, but it's not like she's setting us up."

"Something's wrong about it, though," Sandra said.

"All I'm saying is that I don't think we have to worry about a surprise witch curse with that book. She seemed honest about her fears for her son, and she's right to be afraid."

Max rubbed his hands over the book. "Okay, then. We open it and get started."

Nobody moved further.

"Don't make me do it," Drummond said. "There's no reason I should have to feel the pain of touching any book, let alone that one."

"Right. Sorry."

With a deep breath, Max placed a finger on the top corner and turned the cover open. The pages were browned with age, and the aroma of old binding glue coasted off them. They crinkled and crackled with each turn. From the first photos, Max understood why Mrs. Sidwell had behaved so strangely about the album.

He had expected the hodgepodge of family photographs, articles of achievement, and other celebratory memorabilia, but these fragments of lifetimes were not the usual moments of love and joy. This album chronicled the Sidwell's business dealings and their many unsavory misdeeds. It seemed like a strange record to keep until Max's intuition put it together.

"None of this is on the internet," he said.

"So?" Drummond said.

"That's why I couldn't find anything. Nobody else can, either. If you've got secrets to keep, if you really don't want people knowing things about you or your family or your business, then you make sure it doesn't ever get on the internet. Once it's online, forget it. You'll never get it off there. And even if it's protected behind firewall after firewall on your company server, somebody will be smart enough to hack through it and steal your data."

"You can't steal what isn't there."

"Exactly. Assuming these are the only copies that exist, then nobody can get to this unless they have this album. Breaking into a mansion to steal an album would require a lot more risk than being an anonymous hacker."

The first few pages included photographs of the Sidwell Mills opening. Dated 1930, it showed an oily-haired man and his stout wife. Scrawled at the bottom — *Wendall and Bernice.* Images abounded of various Sidwells throughout the decades, wearing well-tailored suits and expensive dresses, as they strolled across the mill while workers toiled around them. Other pages had letters and memos. One caught Max's eye. It read:

My dearest wife,

You must ignore the gossip of the day. I know you suspect me of greater levels of infidelity than I could ever achieve. No mortal man could have the libido to match your imagination of my failings. And yes, my dear, I do not deny that I have had such failings in the past. My overly-playful behavior with some women has gone too far. But that does not excuse what you have done. Ms. Charlaine Chapel did not deserve a physical assault, and while I have seen to it that the mess you left behind has been disposed of, we cannot continue in this way. Judge Paul has warned me that he has limits. So, please, come home and we shall begin anew. I will shut my wandering eye, and you will cease your jealous abuses.

Yours always,
Preston

Reading over the letter, Drummond said, "Who the heck is Preston?"

Max checked the date. "It's from 1972. That puts Reginald Sidwell in charge. Preston could be a brother or cousin. Certainly another Sidwell bastard who used his power to mistreat female employees. Only this one had a wife unwilling to look away."

"Sounds like she hurt the mistress. Maybe even killed her."

Sandra said, "And he got a judge to help cover it up."

Flipping through page after page, Max said, "There's a lot of work to go through here. This letter alone could account for one of the hazy ghosts haunting this family. Being sexually assaulted by the husband and then murdered by the wife — that's got to put a ghost right on the edge of poltergeist from the start."

Drummond said, "Suddenly, these hazy ghosts are looking a whole lot clearer."

"This is more than I can go through in a week. We'll need to break it up."

"If you lay out a few pages flat on the table, I can look over them, too."

"Marshall Drummond offering to help with research? This is more serious than I thought."

"Keep laughing, funny man, and you'll be stuck doing it by yourself."

Chuckling, Sandra said, "I'll call Brenda to help. What about Osorio?"

"Don't do that, doll. Let the good detective be. He's our man in the police department. Trust me on this — we don't want to overuse that asset. I lost a good friend that way. Best to let Jorge Osorio come to us in most cases."

The album had three metal rings that clawed open and closed. Max pulled them open and stacked pages in four piles. One he handed to Sandra. One he set aside for Brenda. The third he spread out on the table for Drummond, and then grabbed the last pile for himself.

"Good luck," he said as he headed to his desk.

Chapter 29

THE FOLLOWING HOUR consisted of one dastardly discovery after another. The Sidwells had a tremendous amount of blood on their hands — both figurative and literal. If Max had learned of this family a decade or so ago, he would never have believed it possible. Unfortunately, the modern world had shown everybody that the super-rich truly played by a different rule set. Justice did not apply.

Max rocked back in his office chair. "I hate to say this, but maybe we should let the ghosts do their thing. These Sidwells were horrible people."

"You got that right," Brenda said, crouched over the coffee table. "I got a printout of a spreadsheet from 1991 made by Ms. Maggie Sidwell. It reveals every arrest for drinking and drunken crap that the family had buried or washed away throughout the century. It's a long list."

Speaking with a sharp bite, Sandra said, "We are not going to sit back and watch those ghosts devour Theo or his mother."

Max said, "I didn't mean it for real. You know that."

"Listen. Both of you. You're right about the Sidwells. And the more sins we uncover, the greater the anger those ghosts probably have toward that family. In fact, I'm starting to doubt that Robert was haunting his son."

"He wasn't helping the boy."

"I'd be willing to bet that he was being hurt by those ghosts, too. Held back from moving on. Maybe he found some way to blame Theo for that. Doesn't matter anymore. We broke him free. But with what we saw when Theo died coupled with the viciousness of this family, well, some of those ghosts, at the least, must be in the beginning stages of becoming poltergeists. No question."

"Great." Max kicked the edge of his desk as he rolled back. "Do you happen to know how to stop a poltergeist? The few times we've encountered them haven't gone that well."

"We're learning. Once we've finished with this album, Brenda and I will focus on the different approaches to getting rid of that kind of infestation — though, this isn't a haunted house, so we'll have to narrow our search."

Max rocked up to his feet. "I need a breather."

He left the office for a stroll around the block. Avoiding the larger puddles on the cracked sidewalk, he inhaled the gummy air and tried to clear his head. This case pounded in his brain.

On the one hand, he could understand Mrs. Sidwell withholding this album. It was shameful and embarrassing and, in some parts, criminal. She wouldn't want any of that information leaking to the public.

But on the other hand, she had risked her son's life by not sharing the information. Had The Porter Agency been properly informed, they would have utilized a different approach. They could have focused less on freeing Robert Sidwell and more on studying super-pissed off ghosts. Theo might have lived.

Max's phone buzzed in his pocket — an email notification. Propping against the office building wall, he tapped and swiped until he found a reply from Aunt Jane. Like the message before, clear and concise ruled her approach. She gave a two-hour window, an address in Rock Hill, South Carolina, and a phone number. *Text when you arrive. One chance.*

Copying the address over to his maps program, Max saw that Rock Hill was about an hour-and-forty-minute drive. But he had to go through the city of Charlotte to reach the border between North and South Carolina. Specifically, he had to use Route 77 which often got snarled in traffic due to construction that never seemed to end. He might be able to get around some of it, but he didn't know the city streets too well. There was a loop around the city, but his maps app promised the straight route would be the best.

He checked his watch. If he got going soon, he could give himself a decent buffer should anything go wrong. But that meant breaking it to the others. Brenda wouldn't care. Provided she spent time learning from Sandra, she seemed content. Drummond would give him an earful — the ghost wouldn't like having to shoulder more of Max's research work — but he also wouldn't argue. Complain, yes. Argue, no.

The one person Max had to speak with, of course, was Sandra. Less *speak with* and more *apologize*. Well, it had to be done. He hustled back into the office, caught Sandra's attention, and asked to talk in private. So as not to disrupt the others from working, Max and Sandra stepped into the building's main hall.

He gave her the full explanation including the previous email from Aunt Jane and the fact that he had responded. When he finished, she said, "You should go."

"Really?"

"Why would you think otherwise?"

"I thought you'd be angry."

She rested her hands on his shoulders — a sure sign that he had been an idiot. "Look, honey, I knew from the moment your mother first mentioned Aunt Jane that you wouldn't stop until you found her."

"But you sided with my mother. You said I should listen to her and drop this."

She stretched up and kissed his forehead — a sure sign that he had been a big idiot. "I also said that I knew you'd go ahead anyway. I only want you to measure your expectations. Pay attention to how she's behaving in these emails. She's not going to open up much to you."

"Maybe. But I can be pretty persuasive."

Sandra rolled her eyes. "Promise me that when you're done, you'll come back here and get to work. Whatever happens, good or bad, we still have to stop these ghosts, and we need your help."

"Because I'm your superhero."

"If that's what you need to believe."

They grinned at each other and hugged. After two minutes of

kissing, Max grabbed some of the papers to go through later and hit the road. As he left the office, he heard Drummond say, "Where's he going?"

Sandra said, "Worry about getting your pages done."

"Yeah, but what's the point of keeping him around, if he's leaving when we need him most."

Max missed Sandra's reply, but he caught Drummond saying, "Doll, you need to —"

Unfortunately, Max was out of earshot before learning of Drummond's last words as a ghost. He guessed that hours later, when he had finished with Aunt Jane and returned to the office, he would find his detective partner had been whisked far away, perhaps beyond the mortal realm, never to be seen or heard again, by the hand of a charming and beautiful witch. Or Sandra gave him an earful. Either option would keep Drummond from making such a moronic comment again.

The main exit off 77 South into Rock Hill dumped Max on Celanese Road, a highly developed area with a Hooters, an Outback steakhouse, and numerous hotel chains filling out the spaces between the trees and grass. It looked like Rock Hill wanted to hide the commercialized nature of the area. Maybe they did. From what Max knew, much of Rock Hill retained a rural charm that this section lacked.

But he had not come for a taste of South Carolina — real or imagined. He turned left, went beneath the highway overpass, and entered the massive parking lot of Home Depot. He cruised to the far corner and parked in one of the few shaded spaces.

Shutting the car off, Max's leg muscles eased along with his back. The trip had gone smoothly, but a nearly two-hour drive was still two hours longer than he wanted to be on the road. The Sidwell album pages awaited his attention from the backseat, and throughout the journey, he had the urge to pull over and spend a few minutes looking through them. As much as he wanted to meet Aunt Jane, he couldn't deny Drummond's final words.

Well, not the exact final words, the ghost might still be getting chewed out for *Doll, you need to* — but rather the idea behind his previous words — that Max's main skill in the Agency was research, that he was their best researcher, and that was what they needed most right then. Just because Sandra had been understanding in his need to drive out to Rock Hill didn't mean he should be doing it. But Max shook off those thoughts. Right or wrong, he was there now. No point in debating it anymore.

One text and ten minutes later, any consideration of backing out left him. A rough knock on the window announced Aunt Jane's arrival.

Chapter 30

THE WOMAN WHO SAT IN THE PASSENGER SEAT wore a floral dress under a puffy coat. She had dark hair that had been professionally handled to look perfect, and she wore enough makeup to highlight her charming features but not so much as to look gaudy. At her age, somewhere in her seventies, she could have appeared unpleasant — an elderly woman pretending she still could pull off a younger look. Except she did pull it off. Max guessed she had the older men in the area wanting to spend their final years by her side.

"Not what you thought you'd find?" she said — even her voice had a pleasant lilt.

"Sorry, no. Between your short replies and my mother's cryptic talk about you, I figured you'd be a lumberjack of a woman."

She tittered — not a laugh, but a genuine titter. "Don't let me fool you again. I can be a real bitch, if I need to be."

"I consider myself warned."

Her smile dropped, and he glimpsed the fire behind. "I'm not interested in a family reunion, but I also knew that someday you might come find me with questions. So, this is it. Your one chance. Ask anything, and I'll tell you whatever I know."

Max's head whirled off-kilter. "I don't know where to begin."

"You don't get all night."

He paused, focused, and said, "I suppose I should start with the big question. What the heck happened between you and my father? Why did you two stop talking to the point that I didn't even know you existed until recently?"

"You didn't know about me?" She smacked the door with her fist. One hard hit as her teeth pressed inside her lips. "You sure you want to hear this? If you leave now, you can go back to whatever life you've made for yourself and nothing changes. Stay, and I'm going to hit you with a lot of painful truth."

Max held still.

"Okay. You asked for it." Aunt Jane rolled her neck. "Your father had a difficult time in life. Even as a boy. He found it hard to make friends, hard to hold relationships, hard to do anything in a normal way. Nowadays, you'd say he was on the spectrum, but we didn't know about that back then. In fact, I think the only reason he and your mother survived together was that she didn't have a lot of options for men. I know that's rude, but it's the truth. She wasn't ugly, but she was below average. Getting married was the most important thing to her. She had swallowed the wholesome dream — find a man, get married, have children, be happy. But she was pushy and that turned off a lot of guys. Now, do you know about what happened with your father and the truck driving and what went down?"

"You mean his paranormal experiences?"

"That's a good phrase — his paranormal experiences. Well, when those experiences started happening, it drove your mother to the church. For a while, she became quite religious, and she forced your father to join in. I guess she thought Jesus would save her. And this is where the problems with me begin."

"I take it you're not religious."

"Me? I'm an outright atheist. No equivocations in my mind. That religious stuff is crap. There is no god. We're on our own. Now, your father —" Her strength wavered a moment before she pulled herself back. "Your father needed help, and the only thing your mother wanted to do was take him to church and pray. So, I stepped in. He's my brother, after all, and even if I didn't know about the spectrum, I knew how special he was. I understood he didn't process the world the same way the rest of us did.

"But your mother thought I was trying to convert him or poison his faith or I don't know what. I think she needed somebody to blame, and back then, even saying you were an atheist was ostracizing yourself in front of everyone. Still is, but not as bad. I kept my beliefs quiet to most, but not to my brother. You can imagine how things went from there."

Max pictured the worst of his mother's tirades over the years and guessed it was probably worse.

"She decided to cut me out of their lives. I tried writing him, but she must have intercepted the letters. Emails would never get replies, so I assumed she got to those first as well. Basically, every method I could come up with to reach out to my brother, she blocked me. The final straw came shortly after I had moved down here.

"Your father was on the road and somehow found me. Just showed up on my doorstep. We chatted about growing up and the movies we'd sneak into and a lot of memories that meant something to us but were nothing to anybody else. It was wonderful. I remembering thinking that this could work. We could see each other without her knowing, and we'd still be connected. But when he got ready to leave, he said this would be the only time. He wasn't well. He saw weird things. Heard weird things. And it scared him. Your mother had convinced him the religious path would fix things, and he figured that he had to try. Not only for his marriage and his child, but for his own sanity. Talking with an atheist was too dangerous, he thought — or more accurately, your mother had told him — so he wanted to say goodbye." She crossed her arms and looked out the side window. "Broke my heart."

Part of Max wanted to defend his mother. She certainly had the capability to do some of these things, but all of them? And to continue for years? It didn't sound like her. Not the woman he remembered. Maybe the woman she was now — the one getting more religious the closer she came to her end. And perhaps that version of her was similar to the one that leaned on religion to guide her husband away from dark places. Max could comprehend how that person vehemently hated Aunt Jane for being an atheist.

But the woman that raised Max, though she could be plenty stern, had taught him empathy and tolerance. She taught him to be open to other people's beliefs, welcoming of the differences we have, and joyful for the similarities. This was not the same woman. Couldn't be.

Aunt Jane pressed her fingers on either side of her nose before fishing out a tissue from her purse. "I wish you the best. I truly do. But I can't be a part of your life. Your mother blames me for some of the pain your father went through, and frankly, I blame her for the same thing."

"Wait. Don't go, yet."

"I've got nothing more to say."

"If what you say is true, then my father is — is he alive or dead?"

Tears dribbled down her cheeks. She wiped them away without smearing her makeup. "He died a long time ago. Your mother never even told me."

"Believe me, I know she can hold a grudge, but she never would be that cruel."

"No? She never told me about you either. I found out my brother died years later from an old friend. Suicide. I guess he kept seeing those ghosts, and surprise, your mother's religion didn't help him. When I drove to visit his grave, I couldn't stop myself from going to see her, too. I was so angry, I wanted to scream at her until she called the police. But when I got to your home, I saw her walking with you. You were already a young boy."

"But you didn't talk to me. You never reached out to me. Are you that scared of her?"

"I didn't contact you because I feared what she might do to you. Not that she'd hurt you, but that she might isolate you the way she did my brother. So, I left. It's her fault that I don't know you. Just because I can't pretend there's a magic being in the sky that cares deeply how we use our genitals or wants to make sure women are subservient or … I'm sorry. When I get angry about religion, I tend to spout off without thinking."

"It's okay. And thank you."

"You're thanking me for ruining your memories?"

"You didn't ruin anything. Besides, knowing the truth is more important."

She put out her hand. "It's been a pleasure meeting you."

With one firm shake, she exited the car. He watched her walk several rows over and get into a heavy-duty pickup truck. Once she had driven out of the parking lot, he pressed his hands into the steering wheel.

He shouted. Screamed. Punched at the roof. And cried.

Uttering a slew of swears, he started his car and got onto the highway back home. At least he had a solid ninety minutes or so before he had to face his mother.

Chapter 31

NINETY MINUTES WASN'T ENOUGH. He didn't relax at all. Not that he sought some soothing forgiveness to wash over him, but he wanted to reach a less aggravated state. When he spoke with his mother, he wanted to hear the truth. If he burst into the house red-faced and shouting, no good would come from it. But sitting in the driveway, he didn't think he could do much better than slamming doors and yelling at her about how she had betrayed him.

He needed time to process everything before he dared speak to her. Needed to reach a point of self-control. And maybe he should never talk with her about it at all. She wouldn't be alive much longer. What good could possibly come from blowing up the one blood connection he still had?

That itched at him, too — gaining and losing Aunt Jane. She struck him as a formidable woman. He wanted to know her, know the life she had lived. From the little details — what jobs had she done throughout the years? — to the larger ones — did she have children? can he meet them? — he wanted to know about what he had missed.

But that would never happen.

He glanced at his house and tried to understand. His mother had acted out of fear. Her husband appeared to be losing his mind — talking about voices and ghosts. She turned toward religion, and when his mother committed to something, she went all the way. Aunt Jane never stood a chance.

Yet where had that religious fervor gone while raising him? Not that he wanted it. He suspected that a few heartfelt conversations with Aunt Jane and he'd be an atheist, too. But for his mother to drop away from religion for so many years …

unless she blamed religion for not saving her husband.

He clasped the key to turn off the idling car. Perhaps she blamed herself, too. Her failure. Like he blamed himself about Theo. For that matter, Mrs. Sidwell blamed him, too — even as she pointed her finger at her own cold heart.

Max groaned. This would not be a fun talk. Maybe he should speak with Sandra first. Maybe discussing it with her, venting about it until he felt spent, maybe that would be enough.

But that would have to wait. Dealing with his mother would have to wait, too. Thinking of Mrs. Sidwell reminded him that he had a case to focus on, and he had promised to get back to work once he finished with Aunt Jane. He set the car in reverse and backed out.

But the idea of walking into the office and facing those enquiring looks from Sandra and Drummond and probably Brenda, too — no, he wasn't ready for that. Instead, he drove out to Wake Forest University and the Z Smith Reynolds Library. His favorite.

Except when he found a parking space, he sat still. The researcher in him wanted to rush across the campus, breathe in the books, settle into the meditative quiet, and lose himself in the work. Pretend for a while that nothing had changed. The son in him wanted to explode into another bout of raging screams, storm into the library, and blast through the work he had promised to do. Act like it didn't matter as much as his mother's horrible secrets.

Neither was good. Neither was true. And both would sully the sanctity of a building he revered.

Picking up the stack of album pages, he adjusted his seat back a bit. "It's another work in the car day."

After texting Sandra that he was okay — upset, but okay — and that he had found a quiet place to work for a bit, he settled into the rhythms of research. He read about Peter Sidwell, a cousin who ran the sales department under Robert for ten years. Peter's father turned out to be Preston Sidwell — author of the letter to his wife concerning a judge covering up her actions. Peter learned from his father. He made sure to reward his top salesmen with special trips to foreign countries where high-class, underage orgies were easily arranged. Many of these salesmen were married, so Peter would plan the entire thing to coincide with a work retreat or some other fictitious event. Of course, billing for this could not be done on the books, but it still had to be done. Nobody wanted to pay out of their own pocket. So, Mrs. Sidwell had gathered flight information, bank records, and even a few naughty photos to put the pieces together. While disgusted by the facts, Max was impressed with Mrs. Sidwell. She could have been a great criminal forensic accountant.

Hoping to find a less nauseating subject to focus on — though, he doubted that was possible — he flipped through several pages. Until he noticed a name leap out — Molly Lynch. Mother of Estelle.

The name blinked like a neon sign — huge letters and a flaming arrow pointing at it. Pasted on the album, there were a few news articles and a series of letters from Molly to her mother. Reading over these, the truth rose through the ashes of the past. Max knew the feeling well. His skin bumped and his chest tightened. His heart raced. He read through it again to make sure he had it right. But he had not been mistaken.

When the Loray Mills strike began, Molly continued to show up for her job. Because Leonard worked on the labor side and Molly worked in the admin offices, the Lynches tried to thread a thin needle. The father joined the strikers while the mother continued to draw a paycheck. They got away with it for a short time because neither one meant much to management. They were cogs. Nothing more.

But they had a child.

Max imagined little Estelle was left on her own for the first time in years, maybe the first time ever. Some days, she joined her friends running around, making up games, and exploring. On occasion, her father brought her along to the strike, but that would have been a special thing — times when other children were there to celebrate a particular advance in the cause or to hear a speaker of note. Otherwise, Max thought Leonard would keep his daughter away from the dangers inherent in a mass of disgruntled striking workers. On rare occasions, Molly would take her daughter to the Loray Mills' offices. Max could not imagine what would have spawned such an occasion — perhaps no other option had been available — but it clearly happened at least once. The little girl died because of it.

Based on two letters from Molly to her mother as well as reading between the lines of the news articles, Max pieced together that the day Estelle went to work with Molly, Molly had expected her boss to be out. He was one of several vice presidents, and he behaved as if the secretarial pool was his personal playland. That day, he had been called in despite scheduling a trip out of town. The man was not in a good mood.

He called Molly into his office and wasted no time. She wrote her mother that the boss had been unusually aggressive, rubbing against her leg, squeezing her breasts, and attempting to kiss her at every turn. She had been able to ignore his behavior, but he never acted so angry before. In the past, she always escaped him with a playful smile along with a firm *no,* and he laughed it away. There were other secretaries willing to satisfy him further. But this day, he wanted to win at something, he wanted her, and he refused to play games. Molly wrote:

> *I've never been so scared. I was sure he would do something terrible to me, and how would I ever explain that to Leonard. My husband's a good man and doesn't deserve that. The whole thing made me sick. I nearly threw up, and only the thought of how violent things might become if I ruined the carpet kept my lunch down. Do you remember when I was little and I had to eat boxes of salt crackers when my stomach was upset? I was struggling against his big hands, and that's what I thought of. I couldn't stop thinking about salt crackers. But that's when the worst of it happened. That's when Estelle came in.*

Molly skipped over the rest, writing that her mother surely had read the papers and knew little Estelle was no more. Max had read enough to figure out how it went down. Anything he thought unclear, notes had been provided that stated the truth.

These notes came from Summer Sidwell, the daughter of Wendall Sidwell, the vice president at Loray Mills and Molly Lynch's boss. How Summer discovered what her father had done wasn't provided, but Max imagined a lot of hushed conversations floated around the Sidwell home during that time. It would not have been difficult for her to overhear on purpose.

Wendall did not deny trying to take advantage of Molly Lynch. "One of the perks of the job," he said to his wife one night, according to Summer. He added, "You get my wealth and my name from my hard work. This is the least that I should expect."

But as he fought with Molly, he saw a strange look overcome the secretary. She no longer looked fearful at him, no longer squirmed to get away. Instead, her horrified eyes turned toward his office door. With his pants around his ankles and his underwear askew, he twisted back to find a little girl in the doorway.

Neither Molly nor Summer detailed how it transpired from there, but from what Max could piece together, Wendall moved to hit the child. Little Estelle dodged around the office, enraging Wendall. Poor Molly must have been trying to calm her boss and get hold of her daughter. It would have been chaos. At some point, Wendall caught Estelle. He either shook her, threw her away hard, or hit her. Whatever the case, little Estelle tumbled down the stairs to the front door.

Molly wrote to her mother that such a gruesome account would not bring back her little angel. It would only feed the vultures of the press. She wrote her last letter not to give her own account but to urge her mother to travel to Gastonia. She needed her mother's presence, her mother's grounding, and most of all, her mother's love.

Max folded the letter back and turned the page. He wished he could be shocked by what he had read, but he expected it all along. A single page, a memo from a Loray Mills internal investigator, described in broad, non-confrontational language that the death of Estelle Lynch had actually occurred in the offices of Wendall Sidwell. However, the investigation showed no wrongdoing by Mr. Sidwell, and further suggested that the child's mother may have been at fault. She should have known better than to bring her child to work. As a result, the author of the memo listed several people who should receive payments to ensure this story did not become widely known. Beyond offering payments to the Lynches, there were two judges, a detective, and several secretaries. The worst of it, though — the memo suggested promoting Wendall Sidwell, perhaps giving him a branch mill to call his own. After all, if any suspicions or outright accusations fell upon Sidwell, Loray Mills could then claim they obviously knew nothing about it; otherwise, they would never have promoted him. He would have been fired.

"Not only did that bastard get away with it, but he got a promotion." Max pushed the pages aside.

He wanted to throw up. He wanted to punch something. How could people be expected to keep living in a world that went against them so often? And this happened nearly a hundred years ago, yet nothing had changed. Those with money and power could get away with literal murder, and though plenty of others knew what had happened, it didn't matter. Even if one of the secretaries found the courage to stand up, the bribery list included two judges who would have no trouble quashing any real case. Sidwell Mills was founded in the blood of Estelle Lynch, and nobody had stopped it.

Max called Sandra. "If I don't have the reason behind this figured out, you might as well fire me."

"Does this mean you're ready to get back to work?"

"I've been working, but yes, I'm ready to get back to the office. I've got a lot to tell you."

Chapter 32

RELATING THE COMPLETE STORY OF ESTELLE LYNCH and her family didn't take as long as Max thought it would. Sandra and Brenda sat quietly and took notes. Drummond never interrupted. That last fact gave it away — Sandra must have prepped the others to say nothing so Max would get through it fast. He wanted to be angry, but he felt rather amused. Perhaps his body was tired of the anger it had burned through already for one day.

"That's good stuff," Drummond said when Max had finished. "I think you've nailed down the start of the Sidwell's problems."

"It's this album that's done the work for us. It's a roadmap of the family's crimes."

"It goes deeper than that, and you found it. Take the compliment."

"Um, thank you."

Sandra said, "Since we agree Estelle's death is what started this, that creates a new problem. How is it that the ghost of a ten-year-old who may not even understand why she died in the first place, how is it that she keeps coming back every forty years? And how can she act like a mature woman when she goes to lure the Sidwell men to their demise?"

"What's to figure out?" Drummond said. "You don't think we keep learning in the Other?"

"Do you?"

He moved around the office as if his coat itched the center of his back. "It's not that we can't learn anything new. I suppose some do take the time. The thing is that it's hard to justify. Not for me, of course. I work with you and so I've had to learn about computers and such. But if you died in 1804, learning how to type isn't going to change your afterlife prospects. Dead is dead. For most, there's no job applications. They're doing nothing but existing until they work through whatever's holding them back from moving on."

Noticing Brenda's discomfort, Max gave her a quick rundown of the conversation. At this, she brightened. "I think I can answer this."

She hurried across to the bookshelf, located one volume, and brought it back to the coffee table. It was a worn book of spells and lore. In the tradition of many such tomes, it had been titled *Spells and Lore*. Witches could be so creative in how they hurt their enemies, but when it came to book titles, they usually failed.

"The last few days, we've been working with the spells in this book. But I figured out there was a lore side, too." She winked. "The title gave me a clue. Do all y'all know much about possession?"

Max said, "We've had a few brief touches with it."

"That makes sense — the brief part. I got interested in it because of what happened to me." Before working for The Porter Agency, Brenda had been a client. "I saw how hard it is for a ghost to inhabit a living person. It doesn't happen nearly as much as the movies make it seem. The ghost has to expel a tremendous amount of energy, and that's assuming the target has opened themselves up to it."

"Like using a Ouija board?"

Sandra pulled the book closer to read. "That's right. There are also some religious practices that do it on purpose, too." To Brenda: "Are you saying that little Estelle Lynch has been possessing people?"

"It would take her a long time to build the kind of energy and learn the kind of power she would need. Say maybe forty years."

"And then when she was done, she'd have to start over if she wanted to do it again. Another forty years."

Max drum-rolled his hands on the table. "That's perfect. Not only does it make sense with the timeline, but that would explain how the other versions of Estelle Lynch showed up with no real background and disappeared without a trace. She never really existed."

"I'm not convinced," Drummond said. "How are we to believe that a ten-year-old girl is going to figure this out? How does she learn to possess somebody?"

When Max repeated Drummond's questions, Brenda said, "I had the same thought. You could argue that she's been dead a long time, so she could have learned a lot of strange stuff. But let's say she meets a dead witch. That witch could have taught her a lot. The problem that I see is what happens after. She ends up in the body of a young woman who works for Sidwell. Okay. Now what? What does a ten-year-old know about getting an apartment, driving a car, using a credit card? How could she possibly have functioned?"

Sandra said, "It's worse than that. Even if we give her the greatest benefit of the doubt possible and say she learned how to possess and how to live as an adult, she still had play into Sidwell's sexual desires. It's hard to believe a ten-year-old from 1929 knew enough about sex to pull that off. And I don't care if she bumped into Casanova himself in the Other, nobody can teach that aspect of life from books alone. You've got to actually do it for yourself."

Heading back to his desk, Max said, "Then I guess it's not possession. But I feel like we're on the right track."

Brenda said, "Hold on. I wasn't finished. This is possession, but it's not Estelle Lynch doing the deed. We need a woman who has the knowledge to handle society, the adult knowledge to handle the sexual nature of the case, and the strength to motivate getting involved. Only one person makes any sense for that."

Sandra shut the book with a thump. "The mother."

"Molly Lynch," Max said. "Of course. She's furious about what happened to her daughter, about what happened to herself, and most of all, about the fact that the Sidwells never got punished for any of it."

"That's why she's doing the punishing," Brenda said.

As the pieces clicked into place, Max's intuition leapt forward. "Robert truly didn't want to hurt his son. I mean, he wasn't *haunting* his son. He stayed around to fight against Molly and the others."

"But he hated his son."

"Yeah. But his son was the only heir. Sidwell didn't want to see his line end with Theo."

Drummond said, "That's why he attacked you. He wanted to stop us from forcing him to move on. Leave his boy unprotected."

Building on the group's enthusiasm, Sandra said, "After Robert was gone, Molly and the others lost control. They dipped into poltergeist territory and slaughtered Theo. But that wasn't enough to satiate their hatred. So, now they want to destroy whatever's left of him and the Sidwells."

Back on his feet, Max said, "This sounds right to me, except that leaves us with the big question — what can we do about it?"

"First, we double-check our hypothesis against the information we have. If we're still convinced that we're right, then we put together a spell that'll blow it apart."

Chapter 33

AS MIDNIGHT APPROACHED, Max stretched across the backseat of their car while Sandra drove them to the Sidwell mansion. Brenda sat in the passenger seat, and Drummond hovered above them all. Max knew his partner wanted more space, but after the emotional wringer he had gone through that day, plus the long hours of driving to South Carolina and back, Max needed the rest. The risks they would soon be taking required the clearest mind he could offer.

But rest fought with his anticipation. Not helping matters — the recent rains had failed to cool temperatures enough, leaving the world muggy and swarming with mosquitoes. Even with the car's air conditioner running full blast, Max felt sticky. Trying to ignore his discomfort, he frowned at Sandra.

She had come up with a solid plan based on the information available and her ever-growing knowledge of witchcraft. "It's a simple spell in structure but complicated to cast. Not because of the steps — it's rather basic to lay out on the floor — but it requires a great level of concentration. Buddhist monks would be perfect at casting it."

"I'll never doubt you," Drummond said, "but can you handle it?"

"Not really. Not on my own. But with Brenda's energy and our combined concentration, I think we have a good shot at pulling this off."

They had entered worse situations with less. Making it harder, Max would have to give Sandra his focus yet also manage the interactions with the ghosts. If he was going to serve this spell with his best, he needed to sleep. At least, a little.

Unfortunately, he couldn't close he eyes without seeing Aunt

Jane's pleasant appearance, without hearing her unpleasant accusations, without feeling the rising burn towards his mother. He didn't want to hurt her, and he knew if he confronted her with what Aunt Jane had said, his mother would be forced to deal with the past. She could deny things, maybe even prove that Aunt Jane had fabricated it. Yet if she did so, then while it would absolve his mother, Aunt Jane would become the betrayer. That woman would have gone out of her way to meet with Max and poison him against his only living parent. Which would bring him back to wondering why and what did Aunt Jane actually do to cause the initial falling out with the family. By returning to where he had started thinking about this, his pain and anger grew. He couldn't see a path with a good outcome.

Sitting up and allowing Drummond to ease into the seat next to him, Max tried to push everything about his mother out of his head. He would have to deal with it eventually, but none of those concerns would help him now. They had ghosts to face. Poltergeists. And while he didn't expect magic beams burning out of an old television set, he wouldn't discount the possibility. For the sake of all, he needed to be both clear-headed and focused. By the time they pulled up to the enormous house, Max thought he could manage one.

Because Sandra had called ahead, their heartwarming friend, Timothy the butler, awaited their arrival. He stood at attention by the front door, and though he said nothing, Max could feel the impatience as if it were a finger tapping on his shoulder. As he and the others walked to the house, the butler took one perturbed step back. Without a word, Timothy ushered them inside and led the way through the maze of hallways.

Sandra had told Mrs. Sidwell they needed to cast their spell at a location central to the sources of anger. Mrs. Sidwell suggested the ballroom or the music room, but those were sources of her anger, not the ghosts. When she finally understood the requirements, she knew the exact place to go — Robert's office.

In most homes, this room would have been used as a master bedroom. In a mansion of this size, the office looked adequate. Surprisingly, the room did not appear like a typical workspace for a tyrant. The desk had been chosen for functionality, not to be an imposing centerpiece. Nor were there intimidating towers of books with odd bits of taxidermy strategically placed to look down upon visitors. Rather the room had been decorated to feel inviting, friendly, perhaps even warm.

Max thought that the butler had taken them to the wrong place, but the way Sandra looked around, he knew she saw the hazy ghosts. This was the right room. And knowing that, Max realized the true word that described this office — *disarming.* It put nervous secretaries at ease, helped lower their guard, convinced them that Robert wasn't so mean, that maybe his previous inuendoes had been misinterpreted. The room set these women up for Robert's capricious appetites.

An L-shaped couch had been built into the wall of one corner. Max tried not to think about the horrors that occurred over there. In fact, he decided it best to stand far away from that section of the office.

With no preamble, Sandra produced a boxcutter from a bag that Brenda had carried in and started ripping up the lush carpeting. Mrs. Sidwell took one step forward, ready to object, but Max touched her on the shoulder and shook his head. Stepping back with grim acceptance, she hugged herself as if suddenly cold.

Max looked to Drummond. The ghost nodded. Well, at least their targets had joined them.

Once a large, jagged section of carpeting had been torn out, Sandra and Brenda chose two colors of chalk — white and green. Max waited until they had drawn the outline of the casting circle. As they filled in the detailed symbols, he positioned eight black candles, evenly spaced, around the edge.

Ten minutes later, Sandra clapped chalk off her hands and brought the Sidwell album out of the bag. She handed it to Max. "You sure you're okay doing this?"

"Somebody's got to. Besides, I've got you protecting me."

She didn't look so confident. "These are poltergeists. Not the ghosts you're used to dealing with."

"Goes with the job."

"I know, but —"

"You said that you and Brenda have to keep casting the spell throughout the process. That means I do the rest. Unless you want to trust Mrs. Sidwell, and I doubt you want to do that."

"Maybe if we —"

"Hon, stop trying to stop me."

"It's just that —"

He wrapped her in a tight hug. "I know. I love you, too."

"Okay, you two," Drummond said, "that's enough. You got nothing to worry about. I'll be here the whole time. Any one of these hazy, blurry, angry ghosts gets out of line, they'll be getting a taste of my fists."

As Sandra joined Brenda at the southern end of the circle, Max moved toward the north. He tried to walk with assured steps. Unfortunately, the butler watched from next to the door, and Max could feel the man's mocking disbelief. Glancing at Mrs. Sidwell didn't help, either. She continued to shiver a mix of ghostly touches and lack of confidence. Only reason she had given up the album or continued working with The Porter Agency — she had no other choice.

"It's going to be fine," Max said to her.

Nobody believed him.

Chapter 34

BRENDA LIT THE CANDLES, whispering a short phrase before each one. Sandra made sure to meet Max's eyes, then Drummond's, before she knelt at the circle. That familiar tingle struck Max's skin — the sensation of energy in the air being redirected by the will of his wife.

"We are about to face a dangerous group of ghosts." She spoke with authority and conviction. "These are not ghosts to be reasoned with." Mostly, she spoke to help everybody focus on the same goal. "These no longer carry the memories of the human beings they once were." Sandra wouldn't want the client interrupting once the spell got underway. "They must recapture that essence of themselves. That is our task. Remind them of what they were so that they can face the traumas that put them into their current state. Only then will they be able to move on. Only then will we be able to help them."

Brenda brought over a palm-sized, stone bowl. Trying not to show his fear, Max's heart quickened. Sandra had not mentioned the use of blood magic — probably because she knew he would have objected. He glanced at Drummond. The ghost acted calm. All the time Max had spent driving to South Carolina, Drummond had spent with Sandra and Brenda. He knew this was coming, and like the others, he had avoided saying a word.

Max couldn't let this happen. Surely, a better spell existed. One that didn't require going down such a dark road. He started to step forward, but Drummond swooped in front of him. The ghost turned his head side-to-side and put a finger to his lips.

Grinding his teeth, Max looked over at his wife. She had not produced a knife, yet. There was still time to stop this. Still time to —

In one swift motion, Sandra's hand went wide. A sizzle sound. A spark. Whatever Brenda had prepared in that bowl spouted flames.

Not blood magic at all. Some kind of herbal-fire-thing.

Drummond winked and floated back towards the ceiling, leaving Max to stand there feeling foolish. He should have trusted his wife. It was meeting Aunt Jane that had him second-guessing those he knew and loved. If he allowed the revelations Aunt Jane had presented about the family to worm into his heart, he would start doubting everybody that mattered. That would isolate him. Lead him to self-destruction.

"Focus," Sandra said. "Everybody must focus. Look into the circle. Try to see our troubled ghosts."

Pushing away these intrusive thoughts, Max poured his attention towards the casting circle. Brenda knelt next to Sandra, and the two chanted in unison. A gentle sound. A soothing sound. Not quite musical but pleasant to the ear. Max thought the spell might act like a lure. His fingers clenched the Sidwell family album as he readied to fulfill his task.

A few seconds went by with no change. But then the ghosts appeared. Though Max had been told the spell would make them visible, though he had seen them before with the office spell, he still startled back a step as they swam in and out of view — not completely defined but not hazy blurs, either. They looked like people drifting by in a thin, morning mist.

Sandra never looked up from the circle, but her voice cut into Max's head as if she stood next to him. "It's time."

Holding the album against his chest, Max checked Sandra for the final signal. Drummond came aside, adjusted his hat, and said, "Anything goes wrong, you feel the slightest thing is off, don't be the hero. I can jump in at any moment."

Max nodded. He appreciated that Drummond had his back. He didn't appreciate that Drummond felt the need to remind him. To Max, it suggested that this was far more dangerous than he wanted to consider.

Keeping her head down, Sandra raised one hand, snapped her fingers twice, and pointed to the circle. "Enter and be heard."

Through the many years of spells and curses, magic and witches, Max had stepped into his fair share of casting circles. Some voluntarily. Some not. But each one shared a common sensation of warmth and prickling energy. Yet each spell had its uniqueness, too. This one — this one shoved his heart up into his throat like he had missed several stairs and dropped unexpectedly.

He stumbled toward the center. His breath held. His mouth dried. The room took on a bluish hue as if he watched the sharks swim by at a city aquarium.

But these sharks had faces. Their bodies still lacked form — more like shredded cloth streaming in an unseen wind — but he recognized Molly Lynch immediately as if she had walked right out of a picture. Estelle Lynch, too. The little girl floated a couple feet from Drummond, staring at the detective, perhaps confused at seeing a ghost that was not part of the group.

"It'll be okay, kid," Drummond said.

Estelle hissed and shot off, smacking into a corner lamp. The bulb flashed and shattered. Mrs. Sidwell and Timothy jumped.

"Tell them," Sandra said. "Remind them. Bring them back."

Max adjusted his legs into a wider, firmer stance as he slung the album open. He turned to a random page, saw the photograph of a woman with auburn hair and an innocent smile, and he searched the ghosts to locate her. Didn't take long. She hovered above Robert's desk, glowering at it.

"Ms. Broker." Max spoke like a professor taking roll. "Ms. Lily Broker."

The ghost lifted its morose gaze toward him.

Max then said the simple phrase Sandra had drilled into him for about ten minutes before they left the Agency office. "Listen to me. Hear me and remember." He scanned a letter from Lily to her closest friend, Ann. "In 1972, you got hired at Sidwell Mills as a secretary. You were thrilled. It was your first job that made you feel worth something. Your first adult job. Less than a week in, Rich Sidwell — a cousin visiting the mill for the day — offered to take you out on a date. You thought the stars had aligned for you. Told Ann that if you played it right, you could be set for life. Rich was handsome, well-connected, and the way he looked at you gave you butterflies." Pasted on the album page next to the letter, Max read over an obituary and a police report. "Your body was found dumped in the woods north of Winston. According to police, Rich said he had a pleasant time with you, dinner and a movie, dropped you off around eleven. He had receipts. Nobody ever investigated his story further." Max looked straight at Lily Broker's ghost. "But you remember what happened. We know, too. Rich hurt you, didn't he? Rich murdered you."

Lily's mouth dropped, creating a grotesque black hole. She grabbed the desk, lifted the edge, and slammed it down. Again and again.

With a cry, Mrs. Sidwell backed away. After two stuttering steps, she must have realized that nowhere in the room would be safe. At Sandra's silent behest, Brenda walked to Mrs. Sidwell, acted calm, and returned the frightened lady to her position.

"It'll be okay," Brenda said. "This is rough stuff for the ghosts to hear. It's upsetting."

To Max, Sandra said, "Another."

Picking another random page, Max said, "Listen to me. Hear me and remember. Mrs. Juliet Romano. 1950. Widowed with three boys. You worked on the floor for many years. Hard work. You never complained. Never caused trouble. When your youngest got sick, you asked for a day off to tend him. The floor manager understood and approved the request, but Mr. Wendall Sidwell happened to walk by at that moment. He fired you. When you begged for mercy, he struck you across the cheek. This started a spiral of misfortunes. Lack of income, no access to doctors, to food, to anything. The boy died. You lost hope and took your own life."

Mrs. Romano had drifted into the circle, the slash across her throat like a wide grin beneath her mouth. As she absorbed the story, her face shook. She shrieked and bulleted around the room, knocking paintings askew and throwing anything at hand — papers, a book, a letter opener. With greater speed she circled and circled, building gusts of icy wind.

"Stay focused," Sandra called out. Once more to Max: "Another."

"Listen to me. Hear me and remember," he said. "Mr. Guy Bauer. 1925. You worked the floor at Loray Mills alongside Wendall Sidwell. You thought he was your friend." The ghost of a handsome man in overalls from a century ago flew into the circle. "You worked hard for the company and had enough education that you figured you had a good chance for a promotion. But it never came. Wendall became the floor manager. It didn't take long before he saw that you were fired, and it took a shorter time before you learned that he had orchestrated the whole thing. Turned the company against you and took credit for your good work. He fired you so you wouldn't be able to get the truth out. All the Sidwells' success and wealth stem from betraying you."

Mr. Bauer roared. He swept across the floor, overturned a chair, and threw a trashcan at the door. Timothy shoved Mrs. Sidwell over and ducked as the metal can left a dent in the wood.

"More," Sandra said.

Max looked over the next tales of horror. So many of them played out the same. With disgust, he said, "Listen to me. Hear me and remember. Ms. Sharon Reston, 1985. Ms. Melody Chambers, 1937. Ms. Jennifer Smith, 2004."

Three ghosts bobbing mid-air suddenly snapped awake. As Max spoke, they drifted closer to the circle. Each one becoming more visible, more solid in features. Throughout it all, Mrs. Romano continued to grab and throw pieces of the office.

"You were the secretaries unfortunate enough to work directly for a Sidwell boss. These men treated you like toys for their pleasure. They never saw you as human. Just something to satisfy their urges. Ms. Chambers, you were called to a late-night meeting to take shorthand, but instead found Mr. Sidwell naked and drunk. He was too strong to resist, and nobody came to help you. Ms. Reston, as Sidwell Mills modernized, you were one of the few people who had embraced computers early. You had the knowledge they needed. So, when Mr. Sidwell suggested you meet in his office to show him what this new technology could offer, you were thrilled. Finally, somebody appreciated what you had learned — especially in a field that had been a boy's club from the start. But Mr. Sidwell had no intention of discussing computers with you. And Ms. Smith, you thought the modern 21st century world had changed from those olden days of disrespect and skirt-chasing bosses, but you ended up in this room, sprawled against that desk, learning of the depraved depths many in power possess."

All three bashed in and out of the walls. Each time a loud bang reverberated throughout the room. Mrs. Sidwell flinched with each the sound.

Before Sandra could command for another, Max said, "Listen to me. Hear me and remember." He turned the next page and landed upon the one he knew would come eventually but had hoped to postpone. "Molly Lynch."

All activity ceased.

The instant silence pressed upon Max as he lifted his head to see what had happened. Every ghost gazed at the single form approaching the circle. Molly moved with a sultry, hypnotic sway like a cobra lost in a snake charmer's song. But Max could not be sure if the spell charmed her or if she attempted to charm him.

"You were wronged, hurt, abused. Worst of all, your dear Estelle —"

Before Max could finish the name, Molly's screech sent sparks flying from the electrical outlets. She raised her hands, clawing her fingers like talons, and shot forward. Drummond soared into the circle, but she tossed him aside with no effort. He spun out of the way, and Max saw the shock on his partner's face. It surely matched his own.

Outside the circle, a hurricane arose. The ghosts swam in every direction, smashing furniture, breaking through walls, throwing anything loose. Brenda covered Sandra while Timothy fought the winds to reach Mrs. Sidwell. Drummond strained towards the circle, but he might as well have tried to cross the track during the Indy 500.

"Listen to me. Hear me and remember," Max repeated,

hoping the words would get through. "We want to help you. We know you're in pain. We know you're angry. But your rage is keeping your daughter stuck in this ghost form. Don't you want her to move on? To be free?"

Molly's face would not hold one image. At times, she appeared as she must have in her prime — a powerful woman even with the hardships life had piled upon her. But as Max watched her, his body numb and alarmed, he saw her as a decaying corpse, long dead, long forgotten by most.

"You've had your vengeance. The Sidwells have paid. Save yourself. Save your daughter. You remember her." Max reached for the photo in the album. "Estelle Maria —"

The ghost screeched again, a rusty wail of anger and lament. She lunged forward, yanked the album away, and sent it spiraling out of the circle. It smacked into the butler, breaking his nose, and sending a splash of blood into the howling ghost winds.

Molly rushed her face right up in front of Max. Her third face — a terrifying visage of bloodless hatred. Her lidless eyes allowed no escape from her gaze. Her lipless mouth turned a skeletal grin into the teeth of madness. And Max swore he smelled the grave — earth and decay. He could hear the worms crawling over her.

Hands of ice burned against his skin as she took him by the shoulders and crashed his head against the ceiling. Twice she slammed him upward before letting his dazed body collapse to the floor. Sandra bolted to her feet. The casting fell away, and along with it, sight of the ghosts. But they continued to damage the room, continued to spin up a storm. Appearing like a traditional haunting, the room danced in destruction.

Cradling Max's head, Sandra showed no concern for the poltergeist rage surrounding her. Then again, Max's brain wobbled in his skull, so perhaps he misinterpreted the signals from his eyes. He did hear Drummond, though.

"Lady, you got a lot of nerve hurting my friend."

Max smiled. His partner wouldn't be caught by surprise a second time.

Chapter 35

MRS. SIDWELL CALLED IT THE SEWING ROOM, but Max didn't think anything had been sewn in the space for generations. The sewing machine parked in one corner looked untouched, and the spool on top had faded from black to gray. A long table for cutting fabric dominated the center of the room — not a thread or fiber upon it — and a longer couch ran the length of one wall. Compared to the rest of the house, the room was small, downright cozy.

Sandra tried to ease Max onto the couch, but she lost her balance as he flopped down. She toppled over his knees. "Sorry," she said. His head swam too much to respond.

Standing in the doorway, Brenda watched over everyone like a nurse ready to pounce on any sudden need. Drummond arrived last, readjusting his hat and tie. He acted a bit winded, but the satisfied roll of his shoulders suggested he had subdued the attacking ghosts — at least, for the moment.

On the other end of the couch, Mrs. Sidwell tended to Timothy's broken nose. Blood dried over his chin and down the front of his suit. "Keep your head back," she demanded.

"Yes, ma'am." Timothy tilted his head as she struggled to open a first aid kit. Her hand would not stop shaking.

Sandra's hands shook, too. She kept pressing her head against Max's neck, kept squeezing his shoulders and kissing his cheek, before checking him over for injury again. When she repeated *I'm sorry* for the third time, Max reared back to get her into focus — his sight hadn't quite returned to normal.

"Am I missing something? I'm not dead, am I?"

"No." She half-laughed, half-cried. "You're fine. Nothing bad happened."

"I wouldn't call getting intimate with the ceiling fixtures a good time."

"I should have salted the circle. I thought I understood what we we're doing, that we needed the ghosts to enter so they could interact with you. I thought my spell would be protection enough, and we had Drummond there, too. You should never have been hurt."

As she checked him over again, he looked to his ghost partner. Drummond gave a slow nod. More than acknowledgment, though, Max saw the same worry that Sandra displayed. "How close to dying was I?"

"Any closer," Drummond said, "and I would've started picking out a nice casket."

Max's stomach shriveled as his heart punched his chest four times. Facing possible death never got easier. He licked his dry lips and forced out a few shuddering breaths. That usually worked to calm the anxiety racing up his chest and out to his fingers.

During Molly's attack, Max felt her strength and her fury, but even as she pummeled him senseless, he never thought he would die. He trusted his team. And they had saved him, so that warranted the trust. Yet the way they spoke now …

He thought of his mother. The work the Porters did was dangerous. Deadly. What would happen to his mother if he died before her? PB and J would have to take responsibility for her. If they got home in time to find out. Otherwise, the state might get involved — and that would not have a healthy, happy outcome. The Sandwich Boys would be forced into a red-tape nightmare trying to save her from the System, and in the end — well, Max didn't want to think about it any further. It didn't matter because he didn't die.

"I don't know what went wrong," Sandra said.

Max said, "I swear I'm fine."

"I meant about the rest of the spell. Those poltergeists should have been reformed not reinvigorated. That's why I wanted them to enter the circle with you. They should have come in and heard you and found their old ghost selves. Then we would have had a room full of ghosts that could move on — either on their own or we could have cast a spell to assist them. But these things got so much angrier."

Brenda said, "Maybe if we do an entwining spell like we did for Mr. Robert?"

"Even with the research we've done, you know it might take us weeks to figure it out. I'm not sure Mrs. Sidwell can wait that long."

Drummond said. "Even if she's willing, the ghosts here will have burned the place to cinders by then."

"You can't leave me like this." Mrs. Sidwell stood, dropping the bloody towel she had used to help Timothy in his lap. "I hired you."

Sandra threaded her fingers with Max before she turned away. He gave her hand a squeeze. They both needed to feel each other, to know they were still alive, still okay. He appreciated it more when she spoke in a kind but firm voice to Mrs. Sidwell.

"We've said this already, so please believe me — you have nothing to worry about. We do not abandon clients. We won't stop working on this until the problem is cleared."

"I should think not. This is your fault, after all."

"Now hold on," Max said, scooting forward and immediately regretting it when the world dipped into a spin.

As he settled back, Sandra said, "We have done everything in our power to help you. But you have continually withheld information."

"This again," Mrs. Sidwell said. "You cannot shift the blame when it is obvious that you aren't up to the task."

"We have an incredibly good success rate. And you hired us because we are the best around."

"Maybe I should have looked further out."

Sandra's hand tensed around Max's. Taking great care with each word, she said, "Unless you want to take even greater risk by entering a witch deal, nobody is going to do more for you than us."

"Was getting my son killed part of your great service, too?"

Brenda stepped forward, her body language that of a mother

scolding her unruly kids. "You better not be going any further down this road. You're acting like all super-rich folk act. The moment anybody says anything you don't like, you attack. Never once willing to consider you might be wrong. Never admit to anything. Well, we're not having it."

As if she had heard the vilest insult, Mrs. Sidwell's face dropped in shock. "I am speaking with your boss. You need to learn —"

"You better not be thinking about saying *your place.* We can walk straight out of here right now and leave you to die with these ghosts. Wouldn't bother me one bit. I'm sick of people with more money than anybody could possibly need acting like the rest of us don't work hard enough. You didn't earn a dime. You married into it. And your husband was born into it. Look at you now. You're scratching your arms and wriggling in your shoes because you know what I'm saying is true, but you refuse to admit it. That's the rule — never admit to anything but praise. Deflect the rest."

"I do not deflect. I work hard, and I listen to the people around me, and if I make a mistake —"

"You mean *when* you make a mistake."

"I mean *if,* and if that happens, then I own my mistakes. Isn't that right, Timothy?"

Pinching the bridge of his nose, Timothy lowered his head. "Ma'am, with respect, my name is Dylan."

Mrs. Sidwell looked down at her butler, her face contorting as her brain tried to process. It reminded Max how many people reacted when first encountering the supernatural. This woman had come upon too many world-shaking changes in such a short period, he couldn't expect her to accept another.

Yet to his surprise, her shoulders fell and her chin rose. Not in defiance, but rather with humility. "Of course. I appear to have quite a few mistakes to own up to." To Dylan: "Why would you never correct me?"

"I did, ma'am." Dylan's broken nose made him sound stuffed and ill. "Several times. However, you ignored me each time, or yelled that you couldn't be bothered then. Please don't be angry.

I meant no disrespect. It just seemed simpler to let you call me whatever you pleased."

"But your name?"

"Unfortunately, I work in near-dead profession. Finding placement as a personal attendant is difficult to achieve. I did not wish to lose this valuable post over something so minor."

She snickered. "You don't really look like a Timothy." She frowned. "Can't say you look like a Dylan, either. But if that is your name, then that is what I will call you."

"Thank you, ma'am."

"And …" Mrs. Sidwell swallowed, opened her mouth, licked her lips, and continued to strain. At length, she said, "And I'm sorry. You have my sincere apology."

The lights flickered. Drummond said, "Will you look at that?"

At first, Max thought he referenced the miracle of Mrs. Sidwell both admitting she had been wrong and apologizing for it, but then he saw his wife's eagerness. Sandra got to her feet and stared above Mrs. Sidwell.

"What's wrong?" Mrs. Sidwell's nerves ignited.

Sandra said, "I saw it, too."

"Saw what? The lights?"

"The ghosts. When you gave your honest apology to Dylan, a flutter of energy rippled through the ghosts around you."

"And what does that mean?"

Drummond said, "Don't get too excited. They still look plenty angry."

Trying to sit forward again, and discovering he could manage that much without losing consciousness, Max said, "It means they're listening. It means there's hope yet." To Sandra: "Right?"

Whirling toward Brenda with beaming excitement, Sandra said, "We have a chance."

"Anything you want," Brenda said.

Returning to her sharp voice, Mrs. Sidwell said, "I want to know what is going on. Now."

"She's trying to save your life. Isn't that obvious?"

Before Sandra could plaster a smile and grit her teeth, Max said, "I think I know. Those ghosts liked hearing you admit what you did to Dylan. If you want to end this, you're going to have to admit it all. Everything you and your family have done to these poor souls."

"Forgive my ignorance in asking," Mrs. Sidwell said with no hint of regret in her tone, "but haven't we already tried that? Dylan got a broken nose, and I'm not sure your head is yet functioning quite right."

"I'm feeling much better, thank you. And *we* didn't face the Sidwell crimes. I did. Tried to, anyway."

"He's right," Sandra said. "The only way you're going to be rid of these ghosts, the only way they won't destroy this house and drag you to your death in the process, is for you to go through that album yourself. So, Mrs. Sidwell, it's up to you. This is the solution. Will you do it?"

The war between the fiction Mrs. Sidwell had built around her life like a battlement and the storming armies of the truth raged on her face. Max had seen her go through this too often in the short time he had known her. But she looked stronger now. More determined.

Clutching her hands to her chest, she gazed upward. "Theo, if you can hear me, I'm sorry. I'm so sorry for everything I've ever done knowingly, unknowingly — I'm sorry, I'm sorry. Please forgive me. I love you."

"That's a good start." Sandra helped Max to his feet. She looked to Mrs. Sidwell. "I'm afraid it's going to take a bit more than that, though. And it won't work here. What happened in the office showed me that."

"Then where?"

Sandra looked over at Brenda. "I need you to drive back to the office and get *Spells for the Haunted and Wicked.* It should be on my desk. Meet up with us as fast as possible. This'll best be done at one of the witching hours, and there aren't that many left tonight."

Brenda said, "Okay, but I've got the same question — where?"

The answer struck Max, and he groaned. "You've got to be kidding."

Chapter 36

SIDWELL MILLS. Located southeast of Winston-Salem. Defunct textile mill since 2015. The surrounding unofficial town — never incorporated — was dying by 2012. In 2020, Covid killed off half the remaining residents and forced the final ones to flee. Driving through the empty streets lit only by the moon gave the place an eerie, hollowness like the eyeholes of a skull.

Up ahead, Dylan navigated the Sidwell limousine through the old streets. In the scope of the wide beams, each image of boarded up windows, of vines crawling along the walls, of weeds breaking through the sidewalks left Max with impressions of the apocalypse. If a horde of leather-clad, motorcycle-riding maniacs busted through a door crying out for gasoline, he wouldn't have been shocked.

At the front gate of the mill, Dylan parked and walked over to unlock the chains before swinging open access. While waiting, painted in the red of the limo's brake lights, Max had to ask, "What happens if this doesn't work?"

From the backseat, Drummond said, "Thanks for the positive attitude."

Sandra rubbed Max's knee. However, her words were less soothing. "If Sidwell can't do exactly what we tell her, I don't see how she lives through this."

"And the ghosts?" Max said.

"We'll have to figure something out. We can't let a bunch of poltergeists loose to create havoc in the world."

"Both of you are going kill me a second time with your happy thoughts. Look, if Mrs. Sidwell screws up and dies, those ghosts are going to calm down. For a little while, anyway. Most of them will probably hang around here or the mansion for a century or two, or until some moron comes along and disturbs them. What I'm saying is that we'll have plenty of time to do what we do and send them on their way. And if we find that too hard, we can always call in a priest for an exorcism."

"Wait," Max said. "Are exorcisms real?"

"I saw a couple when I was alive. Looked pretty real, but I don't know for sure. Doll, you probably know."

"I haven't looked into that aspect of ghosts much. From what I've read, exorcisms can work if the possessed victim is a believer. Or the poltergeist, in this case. You'd have to find out what religion the ghost followed and perform their rituals. I suppose an exorcism is the same as witchcraft — casting spells by focusing energy."

"Here's an idea, you two — let's focus on not getting our client killed. Then we don't have to worry about exorcisms. Also, clients tend not to pay when they're dead."

Dylan hurried back into the limo and drove onto the mill property. Max followed. They curved upward, passing an enormous and empty parking lot until they reached a central area. Several blocky buildings loomed around the edges. Marked roads led off with signage for truck drivers to docks for either unloading raw materials or loading finished products. Four stained rectangles along the side of one building suggested where dumpsters once stood. Next to another building, a row of refrigerators and bookcases lined the brick wall. Whereas the town looked dead and decaying, the mill looked abandoned and waiting — ready for a new tenant to bring it back to life.

Once again, Dylan parked the limo and exited while it idled. He motioned toward the Porters to stay put as he strode toward a building with a stately façade — the main offices, according to the sign posted to the right of its door. He fumbled out a ring overloaded with keys and entered the building.

Sandra's phone dinged a text. "Brenda's got the book and wants to know if there's anything else we need."

"Since we have no idea what we're doing," Max said, "I think the book will be enough."

As Sandra texted back, she said, "I've got to agree with

Drummond — you're being awfully negative. We've handled things like this before."

"Not a gaggle of poltergeists."

"No, but we've dealt with the unknown before. We try, we make mistakes, we learn. How is this any different?"

"Theo's dead, for one. We've never lost a client before."

Drummond said, "He's not the client, and that wasn't our fault. Besides, we've had clients die before, just not in this way. And before you start nitpicking, let me remind you that I've been around a lot longer than you both. If you haven't figured it out yet, death is part of the gig."

"I know that. I do."

Sandra said, "Then what's wrong?"

He shrugged. He wanted to say that seeing Molly Lynch rush toward him, her face shifting with menace, and feeling her dead cold as she battered him had given him a few doubts, but he held back. That didn't feel like the truth. She had shaken his confidence for the moment, but as the others had pointed out, they had been through these kinds of things before. This was something else.

"What if," he said, thinking the words out as he spoke. "What if Mrs. Sidwell is holding back more information? Theo died because of that. We could have been killed, too. And then she has a change of heart and gives us this album, but it still isn't enough. Couldn't there be more secrets?"

"Partner, with a family like the Sidwells, there are always more secrets."

"Then why are we doing this? If we can't trust the people we're trying to help, what's the point?"

Sandra said, "Hon, you've had a few big days lately. Meeting your Aunt Jane —"

"This isn't about that." He paused. "Maybe it is. I don't know. But I'm saying we shouldn't trust Sidwell. Whatever she does, assume there's more going on. I think if we do that, we'll be better off. Safer."

"Can't argue with that," Drummond said. "But then, that's pretty much how I approach everybody in the world."

A loud clunk came from within the building. Two floodlights mounted on the roof burst into life. Overly-bright light washed the area as if providing for a midnight road crew.

When Dylan returned, he opened the limo door for Mrs. Sidwell to exit. Max shut off the car. "Guess it's showtime."

Chapter 37

THE NIGHT AIR CONTINUED TO COOL as a breeze picked up. A thick blanket of clouds rolled in. Soon they would block the moonlight.

"Everybody here?" Max asked.

Drummond said, "And more. Molly and the crew from the mansion are buzzing around Sidwell, but I can see lots of pale glows poking out the windows, the doorways, floating above. A lot of bad things have happened here."

Mrs. Sidwell surveyed the mill as if she could see those ghosts. She turned to Sandra. "Shouldn't you draw a circle in the dirt or something?"

"Not this time," Sandra said. "We've tried enough casting circles. The ghosts after your family are beyond that now. It's going to be up to you."

"Me? I already told Theo I was sorry."

"And I already told you that wasn't enough. You're out of chances. If you don't do this tonight, now, these ghosts will kill you."

"Maybe that's better."

"Not for Theo. He'll go on being tortured by them, and you won't be around to stop it. Might go on for eternity. Is that what you want?"

Mrs. Sidwell looked away. She aged with every shake of her head. Max walked up to her and gestured forward.

"It's not so scary," he said.

"I'm not afraid." She sounded terrified.

"I was. I am. My wife is one of the best witches out there, yet every single time I have to enter a casting circle or commune with ghosts or deal with magic at all, I find it frightening. I think it should be. Most of us are not meant to handle these things."

"The ghosts do not worry me."

"No? They worry the heck out of me."

"None of this is about them. It's about my family. It is about paying for the lives we have enjoyed and for the freedoms we have been granted."

Max glanced back at Sandra and Drummond. They stood by, watching, offering nothing but a nervous gesture that he continue. But he didn't know what else to say. He wanted to point out how self-centered she acted. However, he couldn't blame her for thinking the sensible thing was avoiding a confrontation with supernatural entities that wanted to kill her.

He settled on the hard truth. "You can't back out. It's not only your life and Theo's afterlife that concern us. If you don't follow through here, there's a good chance those ghosts will spread out beyond your family. Now, I realize the Sidwell name is not synonymous with giving a crap about others, but you're here to change that."

She didn't yell with indignation, didn't storm off to her limo and leave, didn't challenge anything he said. That was an improvement.

Max went on, "All families have things in their past they wish could be different. Your family has more than others, but we're basically the same. We've got to forgive ourselves. Most of what has been done was not done by us. My family — the things I want to be altered from the past happened when I was little. Some of it before I was born. Besides, the past is over. It can't be changed. The future, however — that's a different matter. We can change that. We must. It's the only way we can grow."

Mrs. Sidwell continued her silence. At length, she walked forward. Her feet crunched the pebbles and dirt as she moved into the middle of the lot. Rubbing her arms, she gazed over at Dylan and the limo.

Damn. Max had hoped she received his message, hoped it was more than meaningless rambles, but by the longing way she leaned toward the limo, he knew escape tempted her. She could dash for it. Dylan would help her race away.

Instead, she kicked at the ground, marking a spot. Taking a firm, even stand, she raised her voice and spoke into the wind. "I am Penelope Sidwell. My husband was Robert Sidwell, and my son was Theo. I am here to address the wrongs done to you."

Max returned to Sandra and Drummond. "What are the ghosts doing?"

Sandra scanned the area. "The ones around those warehouses look confused. I doubt they've been addressed by the living in a long, long time. Maybe not ever."

"Yeah," Drummond said, "but our poltergeist friends are paying attention."

"Maybe you should move a little closer to her. Just in case."

Lowering his hat at an angle, he clicked his tongue. "Anything for you."

As he drifted toward Mrs. Sidwell, a ghostly swagger to his movements, Max thought of the endless ways this could go wrong. "Push on through," he said. "Right?"

Sandra chuckled softly. "Always."

Mrs. Sidwell continued, "I'm not sure what you want to hear. I know a lot of you have suffered because of my husband. He's not here. But I guess you know that." Despite her assertive manner a moment ago, her words now slipped out unassured. "I … I'm sorry for what my husband did. If I could have stopped him, you must believe me that I would have done so."

"I'm not buying a word of this," Drummond said. "They ain't either."

The windows on the main office building cracked. All of them. All at once.

Mrs. Sidwell crouched, anticipating falling glass, but the ghosts didn't take it that far. Yet. She looked back, her face paling.

"It's going to be okay," Sandra said. "You have to speak honestly. From the heart."

Max whispered, "I'm not sure she's spoken an honest word her entire life."

Clearing her throat, she clutched her hands at her waist like a teacher imploring a specific point. "You need to listen and be patient. I am not good at this. I haven't had to —"

Her shoulder flung back, and she screamed. Drummond shot forward and put up his fists. "No more of that. The lady is trying to make things right. Give her a chance."

Keeping her voice down, Sandra said, "Several of the ghosts are acting wary of Drummond."

"He fought them before," Max said. "They've got to remember what that felt like. What about Molly?"

"She's hovering near Dylan. Not a threat to him, I don't think. Looks more like she's observing Sidwell."

"Observing? Like a general watching a battle?"

"Maybe. But she better not think she has that much control over her troops. Poltergeists are not known for appreciating strict order."

Impressing Max with her gumption, Mrs. Sidwell straightened her hair and said, "I am truly sorry for what has happened here. I wish I could change the past for you all, but the damage has already been done. You need to move on now. Get over it and go to a better place."

Sandra winced. "That was not a good thing to say."

As Drummond swung his fists, he dodged to one side. There were too many ghosts, though. As Sandra narrated the scene, Max pictured the three men with mangled faces slamming through Mrs. Sidwell. She couldn't scream this time — her lungs had no air — as she tumbled to the ground. Dylan rushed over to help her up.

Molly raised a hand. The ghosts pulled back. But Sandra said the trouble hadn't gone away. They obeyed Molly, but it wouldn't last. They looked like chained dogs — eager and angry, ready to maul when let loose.

"Come on," Drummond said to the crowd of ghosts. "I've fought worse than you."

As Dylan escorted Mrs. Sidwell back towards the Porters, Max leaned closer to his wife and said, "This isn't going to work. She can't do it."

Mrs. Sidwell wrenched her arm away from Dylan. Her frustrated glower wrinkled her forehead while shrinking her mouth into a tighter and tighter dot. With her hands splayed at her sides as if she didn't know what to do with her fingers, she shook her head at the Porters. "Why aren't you helping me? I hired you to fix this, and every plan you have makes things worse. I ought to sue you into oblivion."

Sandra's hand went to her hip as she stomped closer to Mrs. Sidwell. "You do not talk to us like that. It's that arrogance that got you in this mess in the first place. You and every other Sidwell."

Drummond continued his standoff with the ghosts, but from his swiveling attention and darting eyes, Max didn't think it would last long. While some of the ghosts must have worried about confronting Drummond, most probably held back to see what happened.

"This is ridiculous," Mrs. Sidwell said. "I tried being polite to these creatures and they attacked me."

Sandra whipped out a warning hand. "We didn't tell you to be polite. And those *creatures* — they are the remnants of the human beings your family destroyed. They don't want you to be polite. They want you to be sincere."

"I told them I was sorry, and I am. I regret everything that Robert did, everything all those Sidwells did over the years. It was wrong. It was cruel. And it should never have happened. You heard me out there. I said as much, and they still hurt me."

"You're still playing at this."

"I assure you I am not. My son is …" Her entire body stiffened before she could croak out, "He's dead. And they are the reason for it."

"Cut the crap, lady." Max thundered over. "One moment you're weeping and weak, contrite and fearful. The next moment you act like a prima donna. All that money you have has ruined your humanity."

"Says the man who cannot wait to get some of my money."

"As payment for work. And here's a big difference — for us, that money means food. It means a roof over our head and clothes to wear. For you, it means more money. It's a number so large it says you don't have to think about anything serious. To you, it's power to do what you want, to whoever you want. It's a lack of consequences. And I don't care. I really don't. Some people are rich and some aren't. Some earn their money, some are born into it, and some — like you — marry into it. I'm sure screwing Robert made you feel you earned every dime."

"You don't know anything of my life before Robert. And you do not need to know."

"I know you've lived your privileged life for so long, you can't see anybody as a person anymore. Maybe you once lived a normal life, but now … it's disgusting. We've been trying to help you."

"I don't have to listen to this."

"That's been your problem your whole life."

Max didn't wait for a response. He went to his car, throwing his arms in the air as he continued to argue with her in his head. Jerking the car door open, he ducked in, grabbed the Sidwell album, and hastened back to the others.

"This is your last chance," he said as he brushed by Mrs. Sidwell. Without look back, he said, "Get moving."

"I do not answer to rudeness, and I will not bother with you anymore."

"Then you're going to die." Max continued to walk away.

Chapter 38

KEEPING HIS FOCUS AHEAD, Max strode toward the central point of the lot. A few seconds later, Mrs. Sidwell joined him. Drummond no longer fought any ghosts, and he didn't appear to be threatening them, either. Good. It looked as if Max had gotten their attention.

"Listen up," he said like an officer addressing his troops. "People like Mrs. Sidwell here have a hard time accepting reality when it doesn't fit with what they want it to be. She truly cannot comprehend the harm she has caused. But I'm going to give it one last try. Please, don't hurt her. She's got enough hurt coming."

He glanced at Drummond. The ghost assessed the threats before he gave a single nod. Max swallowed. If this didn't work … but he buried that thought away. Catching Sandra in his peripheral vision, he refocused. Push on through. That's what needed to happen here. Push on through until Mrs. Sidwell accepted the truth.

Opening the album, he leafed through the pages until he found one that they hadn't dealt with yet. "Conner Stokes, died 1938. He tried to reignite the passions for a strike. The newspaper article here says he died from a heart defect, but there's a medical report here, too. No defect. No health problems at all. The Sidwells hired a fixer." He leaned towards Mrs. Sidwell. "That's a polite way to say they contracted a murderer."

Mrs. Sidwell pointed at him, opened her mouth to utter a defiant defense, but then her gaze shifted to the emptiness around them. The emptiness filled with angry ghosts. Closing her eyes and speaking with the strained patience of a frustrated teacher, she said, "Mr. Stokes, if you can hear me, I don't know what more I can do but repeat that I am sorry. But that was in 1938. My own parents hadn't been born yet."

A metal whine from down one of the roads was followed by the crash of heavy containers falling. The lighting dimmed.

Drummond said, "Doesn't sound like Mr. Stokes accepted her heartfelt apology."

"That's not good enough," Max said to Mrs. Sidwell. "If you keep denying what I'm telling you, this has only one possible ending."

"They can't hold me accountable for what happened so long ago."

"They can, and they do," Max said.

"But how was I to stop any of that when I didn't even exist?" She had lost her vigor once more. This time, Max noticed a new desperation in her eyes. Perhaps she finally understood this was the last straw.

"Oh, come on. They're not stupid. They don't blame you for what other Sidwells did long ago. But you continue to benefit from those things. You benefit from the horrors these people went through. Look here — 1974, Joy Chiswell. She worked on the main floor and noticed several problems with old machinery that not only endangered your employees, but made them less efficient. When she brought it to the attention of management, she thought they would be happy. Update the machinery and the company could be more productive and avoid potential claims for injury. Instead, you fired her."

She whimpered. "I didn't. I was a child."

The main office door flew open with a bang. The wood splintered and the top portion broke off its hinge. It continued to slam open and closed as if something attempted to rip it free.

"Not only that," Max went on, "but the Sidwells spread the word about Ms. Chiswell — said she was difficult to work with. Made it hard for her to get a decent paying job. She ended up homeless and traveled north in search of work. Died on the streets in the blizzard of '78."

"I can't be punished for that. I can't be asked to sacrifice for that."

"You built your wealth on the hell of others."

With less conviction, she said, "We all have. But ... but it is true that I came from a family with money. Not Sidwell money, but we were comfortable. Still, even the poorest in this country can trace what little they have to the broken backs of others. None of us are innocent."

"Maybe not. But you have gone beyond what is acceptable. Look at the advantages you've had. How is this not enough for you? You've ruined these, and you still want more. You've got the best clothes, the best car, the best food, the best servants. You've had so much money, you could've stopped at any time and been more than comfortable to your last day. That's got to be enough."

With the last gasp of anger, Mrs. Sidwell said, "Who are you to decide how much is enough?"

Max did not need Sandra or Drummond to tell him what happened next. He felt the cold touch of several ghosts whisk by him. Mrs. Sidwell dropped to her knees, ducking to avoid the icy fingers she felt along her back. But the ghosts didn't stop to harm her. They rushed by, turning their anger toward her limousine.

Dents formed in its sides. The safety glass shattered at once, sending sparkling pebbles across the lot like fireworks burst upon the ground. The tires popped and hissed, and smoke billowed from the hood. Dylan jumped at each piece of damage, but he stayed by Sandra's side.

Squatting down, Max grabbed Mrs. Sidwell by the wrists. "Why are you being so stubbornly stupid? Haven't you lost enough? Why is it so hard for you to admit that you're greedy? You want to know how I can decide when it's enough — the answer is easy. It's not a number. Nobody faults you for being wealthy. But when your wealth comes at the detriment of others, that's when it's too much."

She tried to look away, but he shook her wrists.

"You could've lived a simpler life off that money. A happy life. You could've been generous with the rest. Helped others."

"I had no say. It was Robert's money."

"You weren't a helpless secretary. You were his wife. You had to have some influence. But even if that wasn't in your nature, even if you wanted the best of everything, you could have made a little less profit so that your hard-working employees were safe and cared for."

"It wasn't me. I didn't. I never knew what he was doing."

"Sure you did."

"No, I swear. Not until it was too late."

From behind, Drummond said, "Hold on, partner."

Without looking back, Max said, "What do you got?"

"One of the old ghosts, the non-poltergeist type, says there are letters in the album."

"Yeah, we know. A bunch of letters."

"Not those. Different letters. She said it again — they're *in* the album."

Though still fueled by adrenaline, Max stood with slow control. He paused to look down upon a woman whose world crumbled around her. It would not take much now to break her, send her mind spiraling into an emptiness of denial. That would make things worse. These ghosts fed on anger and hatred toward the Sidwells, yet they clung to some sense of vengeance. If Mrs. Sidwell would understand this, she would see that the Porters had tried to satiate that vengeance without it turning violent.

He picked up the album and looked over the cover. Brushing his fingertips over the surface, he didn't notice anything. He opened the book and checked the inside flap. Nothing. He flipped to the back and there it was. A clear bump to the paper lining the inside of the back cover. Three tries, but he finally slipped his fingernail under the lining and pulled it back enough to get a good grip.

With a more dramatic flourish than he had intended, Max ripped the rest out of the album. It made a long tearing sound as it released from the sticky glue, and Mrs. Sidwell quaked the entire time. Max dropped the album to the ground as he held yellowed pages overhead like a television lawyer presenting his case-winning evidence.

"You had to know we would find these letters. You gave us

the album." Max looked at the first page with its Sidwell letterhead. "You couldn't have forgotten these were in here. So why? You too afraid to admit in your own voice what you know to be true? Do I have to be the one to read your words?"

If this had been a trial, opposing counsel would have objected to his badgering the witness. But the judge and jury were wisps of the dead, and they had already decided guilt decades ago. If anything, this was a sentencing.

"Those aren't my words," Mrs. Sidwell growled into the ground.

Max waited as long as he dared, but Mrs. Sidwell did not move. If she read the letter out loud or admitted to what he thought it contained, their chances of success would be high. But having him read it — that would be no better than when he presented the album back at the mansion. For this to work with Max reading the letter, she would have to be the one to listen. Not the ghosts. She would have to hear the truth.

Drummond watched the main road leading up to the lot. "You should know that those ghosts hiding around the town and around other buildings are coming out for this. If it comes to it, I'll do what I can to protect you, but if this goes south, forget about our client. Grab Sandra and run."

Max took the paper in both hands, hoping his grip would keep it from shaking too hard to read, and angled it against the floodlights. He took a big breath. And he read.

Chapter 39

To the new Mrs. Sidwell,

It is with a warm heart and honest goodwill that I welcome you to our family. Being a Sidwell means gaining the best of everything. I know you will enjoy it, as I have, and I wish you many happy years and a long, fruitful life with plenty of grandchildren for me.

No fairytale is without its villains, though, and no family is without its secrets. This album you now hold is filled with ours. It began when Mildred Bernice Browning married Wendall Sidwell. For her own safety, and possibly her sanity, she started keeping records of his misdeeds. When her son married, she wrote the first letter and handed the album to the next generation. Sometimes, depending on the nature of the husband, this album has served as a shield against the husband's worst impulses. Sometimes, this album is a threat that you expect to keep the promise of the life you will become accustomed to. When you have children of your own, this album will protect them and their futures.

Within these pages, there are many hard things to read. And you will add more. You will face disrespect, infidelity, and shame. But I do not weep for you. You made a devil's bargain, as all of us Sidwell women have, and this album is one of the burdens we must share.

Max peeked over the edge of the letter. Mrs. Sidwell had not moved. She no longer shook, no longer wept. Her mind had been stripped, and each sentence he read out whipped against her back with precision. But the time for mercy had long passed. He read on:

> *I know this sounds cruel and heartless, but you will understand once you have absorbed these pages. Do not fool yourself into thinking my dear son, Robert, is any different from the Sidwell men before him. Do not think you have fooled me with declarations of love. I know my son. He is an ugly man. Ugly and selfish. I know you, too. Deeper than you can imagine. You have enough beauty to find a man far better natured than Robert. However, you may not have the beauty to meet one so wealthy as him.*
>
> *I do not write this to insult you, but rather to be honest. I know this is true of you because I was the same. I married Reginald because I knew the security his wealth would bring me. I lived a hard life. A poor life. And if you think I have whored myself out for a pocket full of gold, then so have you.*

Max paused. Mrs. Sidwell had turned to stone. Fearing the shock may have caused a stroke or heart attack, he waited to see her body rise and fall with a simple breath. He waited for her to speak. This entire nightmare could end if she would simply speak the truth.

But she said nothing. Wishing otherwise, he returned to the letter:

> *In this album, you are to keep track of everything wrong Robert does. He will steal for no reason but the thrill of getting away with it. He will take many women, and some will willingly go with him for the hope of dethroning you. He will cut every corner with his company at the expense of others. The Sidwell men have raised each generation to*

believe they not only earned the money which they inherited but that they are entitled to walk over those who stand in their way. Be prepared. You may have to do the same to keep your position.

After you have read this letter, you should do what we Sidwell women have done before. Burn it. Keep the album going and forget the things you learned. Once you place a horror into its pages, allow it to be erased from your mind, from your life. If you don't, you'll never be able to sleep again.

Finally, we will not speak of this. Not ever. If you ask me, I will deny it. There are crimes in this album that could destroy the family reputation and others that will destroy the family outright. You are their guardian. If you wonder why I am giving you this responsibility and why I do not fear handing over this leverage, you should know that I've watched you carefully since you first arrived in Robert's life. I've hired private investigators to vet you. And now that I know you, I know you will not destroy the Sidwell family with this album. Doing so would mean destroying yourself, and you are far too selfish to do such a thing. As I have been. As we Sidwell women have been.

I look forward to being your mother-in-law, and I pray that we will not only enjoy many happy years together, but that you will have the least opportunities to fill these pages.

With much love,
the old Mrs. Sidwell

Max lowered his hands to his sides, the letter making small cracks and snaps as the wind gently blew. A burnt oil stench wafted from the wrecked limousine. He barely noticed. His focus had turned to Mrs. Sidwell. Without looking, he knew the others — living and dead — watched this crumpled woman, too.

Hunched over herself, she made it difficult to get a read on her mental state. But like an actress savoring the beats before her big moment, Mrs. Sidwell rolled her back and shoulders until she sat on her knees like a demure young lady.

Max's heart sank. Everything they had endured, and still they had failed to break through her defenses. As she stared up at him, he could feel the growing insolence within her. Soon, she would spout something offensive, and there would be no holding back the ghosts. He turned slightly towards Sandra — ready to run.

But Mrs. Sidwell's eyes widened. And welled. She didn't shake or shudder, but tears streamed down her cheeks. Until she gasped, Max missed that she had stopped breathing. But when that gasp came, a howling cry followed.

She clutched the sides of her head and ripped out two fistfuls of her hair. A louder scream erupted from deep within her chest. Another gasp. Another howl.

With chunks of hair poking between her fingers, she beat her thighs and chest — hard enough that bruises would form. One hand opened — the wind taking her hair away — and she slapped her face, leaving a red welt behind. The loudest cry yet followed.

"You!" The single word rang out with accusation and rage. She thrust to her feet, her bloodshot eyes glowering at Max. "You!"

Before he said anything or acted against her, Drummond said, "Not you, partner."

Max saw it now, too. Her wrath went through him, beyond him. She placed a firm foot ahead. Then another. Her mind so consumed with its fury, it had little room to remind her legs how to function.

Turning around, Max saw the subject of her hatred — the Sidwell office building.

"All of you!" Each word echoed as it slammed from wall to wall. "Take, take, take." Throwing her entire body into the action, she shouted a long, high wail at the offices.

When her lungs could no longer support the sound, she collapsed. Now she shook. Now she shuddered. Now her gasps filled with sorrow, her cries with regret. And as she rolled onto her back, she opened her arms, palms facing the sky, and she said the most important words of her life. "Forgive me."

Max shot a look at Sandra, then Drummond. Both nodded — the ghosts were listening.

Through shamed tears, Mrs. Sidwell said, "I did nothing. I should have, but I did nothing. I don't know what I could have done against a man like Robert, against a family like the Sidwells. I never tried. He would bring home a secretary to babysit Theo, and I saw the fear in her eyes. He would dazzle me with a new diamond and say that the company had a great quarter, and I knew the blood drenching that gift. I knew, and I did nothing."

Gesturing to the ghosts, Drummond turned to Max. "Almost there. Don't let her off the hook."

"It's not enough," Max said, hoping the humble phrase didn't break her. "Keep going."

She lifted her head, looked at him as if he spoke a foreign language, then dropped back. "What more can I say? I lived in luxury while others suffered, and I didn't care. I'd give to a charity and pretended that was enough. I served on boards and thought I did something good with the money that came from the evil of my husband. It was no more than a fabrication. And I knew it. I could find any excuse, and I believed my excuses. I'm like any other person. I'm willing to ignore the pain around me because I suffer my own pain, and maybe that seems like too much to handle. But it isn't. It was easier to think that, though, because I felt absolved from doing anything, risking anything. Yet no matter what I say, the truth is always the same — I never stopped Robert. I never did anything. And you lot listening to me, you bore the pain. I am sorry. I don't deserve your forgiveness, but I ask for it anyway. Forgive me. And, please, forgive my Theo."

Drummond said, "That's it, partner. I think she's done."

Chapter 40

LITTLE POCKETS OF WARMTH formed around the area. The ghosts were leaving. They were moving on. To the sound of Mrs. Sidwell crying, they disappeared. Even though Max could not see them, even if he hadn't felt the shift in the air or the sudden rise in temperature, he could see the results on Sandra's face. She watched the angry, hurt souls lift into the light of the afterlife, and she smiled.

All the violent activity — the banging doors, bashing cars, cracking glass — all the noise ceased. The electric sensation of so many beings filling the mill slowly dissipated, and Max felt as if a heavy blanket had been lifted away with a gentle touch. The seconds ticked by to the sound of Mrs. Sidwell's muted cries.

"Almost there," Drummond said, as he came alongside Max. "The mill ghosts are going, moving on, and our poltergeist friends have calmed down, but they don't look ready to leave."

Max watched Mrs. Sidwell, searching for any indication that she could put herself through more. But she had spent her strength to get this far. Her reality had disintegrated. If the ghosts demanded more of her, she had nothing left to give. Except her life, and Max refused to let that happen.

"You've done a good thing," he said, lowering to her side and helping her sit up.

"Theo? Did it work for him? Has he moved on?"

Max glanced at Drummond, and the ghost shook his head. "The ghosts are moving on. A little at a time. I think," Max said, "your son will be the last to go. The others won't let him leave until they've been satisfied."

Sniffing, she said, "But what more could they want from me?"

Putting out his hand, he said, "Come. Let's join the others

and we'll figure it out."

"I'm not going to leave. I won't give up. I'll go through every page, if I must. I'll address each person, one by one. I'll give them what they need to —" But she coughed and pressed a hand against her chest.

"Nobody's giving up. But your part is done for now."

"Promise me."

"I promise. We're not leaving here."

"Then I'll have patience."

With an arm around her shoulder, Max escorted the broken woman toward Sandra and Dylan. Drummond flew ahead to meet them. Once they reached the others, Dylan quickly took over care of Mrs. Sidwell.

"How's it looking back there?" Max asked.

Sandra said, "Getting better."

Drummond said, "Don't get too excited, though. We're still going to have to deal with the hardest one."

The name came to Max, at once. Who else could it be? "Molly Lynch."

"She's standing where Mrs. Sidwell fell to the ground, and Theo's right next to her. The threat is pretty clear to me." Drummond tilted his head toward Sandra. "I got nothing, and I don't expect Max has anything, either. You got a plan for this or are we out of ideas?"

Headlights splashed across as a car rumbled toward them. Sandra raised an eyebrow. "I think my last idea is arriving right now."

When the car reached them and parked, Brenda exited. She carried the book Sandra had requested. "Hey, boss," she said, walking over. She glanced at the destroyed limo. "Everything going okay?"

"One final bit of business," Sandra said, taking the book.

Chapter 41

WATCHING HIS WIFE SEARCHING through *Spells for the Haunted and Wicked,* Max shared the anticipation and confusion of the others around them. He wanted to ask her a dozen questions, or even just one, but refrained. Better to let her handle this at her own pace. Dylan and Mrs. Sidwell would not be so forgiving, though, so he walked over to them. "She'll explain in a moment."

"We'd rather you explain right now," Dylan said.

But Mrs. Sidwell pressed her hand on Dylan's forearm. "No, no. None of that anymore. I no longer have the right to demand things. We will wait until she is ready."

When she found the right page, Sandra handed the book to Brenda who rushed back to the cars to get supplies. Sandra then approached Mrs. Sidwell. "I'm going to cast a spell, a very old spell, and I think I'll be able to convince Molly Lynch to act like the other ghosts, to move on."

"What spell?" Max asked, noticing that Brenda returned with a candle, a container of salt, a clay plate, and several long feathers. "You'll need chalk, won't you?"

"Not that kind of spell." Sandra placed her hands around Mrs. Sidwell's hands. "The spells I used before were witchcraft. But there is older magic. Ancient magic. Magic before witchcraft."

As Brenda approached, Max plucked the book from her filled hands. The slipcover for *Spells for the Haunted and Wicked* came off, but the title printed into the hardcover did not match. He couldn't read the language, but it was a single word. "What are you doing, hon? What is this?"

Sandra whispered something to Mrs. Sidwell before walking over to Max. "I'm trying to do my job."

Drummond peered at the book. "This looks like something

the old Brotherhood would use."

"We've tried everything else. My spells couldn't do the trick. Either they weren't strong enough or witchcraft itself isn't enough or I'm not. What we did tonight, however, that worked — that was the old magic."

Max waved his hand at where the ghosts had been. "That wasn't old magic. That was talking to the ghosts. That was admitting her guilt and culpability."

"It may not have seemed like magic, but both of you should trust me — plenty of magic was being used. It kept her alive. Reading from that album, the energy of her breakdown. That's how the old religions worked, the old magic — it was emotional, cathartic, and it thrived on those high states. Most important, it's been the only thing that's gotten through to these ghosts."

"I'm hearing you," Drummond said, "but I don't like it. Isn't that old stuff unstable? That was part of the problem the Brotherhood had."

"That's why this is a last resort."

Max turned a few pages in the book. He couldn't read the writing, but it unnerved him. Diagrams of spells had been placed next to aged drawings of skulls, burning souls, and bloody corpses — he didn't like this at all.

Before he said as much, she clapped her hand over his mouth. "You have risked your life several times on this case already. It's upsetting and worrying, and I sat back and let you do it. I did that because it's what we do. We take these risks when there are no other options. That's where we are now. If you see another option, I'll listen. No? Drummond? You have anything?"

"Um, no, ma'am."

"Okay, then. I'm going to give our client the best we have."

Sandra seized the paraphernalia from Brenda, leaving behind the salt, and strode out into the open lot. Nobody dared to stop her. Max took a step to follow, but Drummond put out a hand.

"You can't do anything to help," the ghost said.

Brenda called out, "Don't you want the salt?"

Lowering to her knees, Sandra said, "That's for you."

Dylan made a production of coughing and clearing his throat.

"Perhaps you could be so kind as to loan us the use of your car. I can take Mrs. Sidwell home."

"I am not leaving," Mrs. Sidwell said. "But if you wish to go, then you should go. I promise you won't be penalized for it."

Max watched a moment of indecision cross the butler's face, but then Dylan said, "No, ma'am. If you insist on remaining, then so will I."

Neither displayed further emotion, but Max swore he could feel them both warming toward each other. Not in a romantic way, but rather the beginnings of a found family.

While Sandra set her candle in place and mouthed the words of her spell, Brenda opened the bag of salt and drew a line encircling the group. Drummond made sure to keep his distance until she finished.

"This will protect us?" Mrs. Sidwell asked.

Max said, "With regular ghosts, it usually does. But Molly is not a regular ghost."

"Should we be worried?"

"Did you hold anything back? Are there more secrets about her and the Sidwells?"

"No. I promise you, if there is more, I know nothing about it."

"Then there's no reason for her to come after you anymore."

Brenda walked to Max's other side. "Don't worry about that. If the spell works, we'll be able to see Molly. We'll know if she starts getting angry."

Though only Max could hear, Drummond said, "I'll defend them, too. It'll be a lot easier only having to fight one ghost instead of a horde."

"One?" Max said. "What about the other poltergeists?"

"They're moving on. She's the only one left. Well, Theo's still here. And the daughter, Estelle, but I don't expect to be fighting a kid."

Sandra struck a match, and the bright flame took on greater volume in the late night. She lit the candle. Circling the air above the flicker, she called out a series of strange words. With one hand, she picked up the feathers and set each one on fire. Thick, red smoke plumed off each feather — far more smoke than such a small object should make. She set the burning feathers on the clay plate, and the smoke thickened.

As the crimson smoke spread, a figure became visible within. The form shifted in and out as the smoke billowed around, but after a few words from Sandra, it settled. The smokey shape held in place enough to be clear.

Molly Lynch.

Chapter 42

THE SMOKE CONTINUED TO POUR out of the burning feathers like a hard wind flapping a flag, and each puff strengthened the visibility of Molly. Though young, she carried a proud fire within. Max could see her wishing to walk the picket line with her husband, hating that she had to continue working for the company that harmed so many, but willing to do so to feed her family.

Sandra must have seen the same thing because she opened with, "You love your family. It's always been the most important thing to you. I understand. I love mine every bit as much."

When Molly spoke, the rusty smoke puffed around her words. Her voice came through the sizzling of flames making it difficult to understand, but not impossible. "Leave us alone, witch."

Despite her statement, Max could see that Molly's rage had subsided. She spoke in a commanding tone, but the threat to Sandra appeared far less dangerous. Drummond noticed, too. He glanced back at Max with a satisfied nod.

"You've done what you came for," Sandra said. "It's time to move on to the next stage of your afterlife."

"No."

"Look around the mill. Your army of ghosts knows it's over. They've moved on. They've accepted Mrs. Sidwell's words."

"No." This second time, Molly's single-word response carried greater depths of pain. Max heard more than anger, more than hatred. He heard sorrow.

Whispering to Drummond, he said, "Tell her that Molly's regretting something."

"I'm sure she regrets a lot of somethings. I'm not disturbing

Sandra's spell to tell her the obvious."

Indeed, Sandra confirmed Drummond's assessment when she said, "You've spent nearly a century haunting this mill and this family. You won. You've had your vengeance. Don't second guess your victory. Don't let any other thoughts keep you stuck here."

"I'm not done. Not until the Sidwells end."

The smoke shot high overhead, glowing like fire, and Sandra fell back. Max stepped to the edge of the salt line, his heart jumping against his chest. But Sandra returned to her knees. She rushed through the spell again, including the hand motions over the candle, and the smoke eased down to its previous state.

"You've killed Robert Sidwell. You've killed Theo Sidwell. The line is severed. Taking the mother's life will not change that."

Molly glared across the lot at Mrs. Sidwell. "She doesn't matter anymore."

"Then what is it?"

Max's mind flashed through the case. He thought about the Loray Mills strike and the Lynch family's involvement during that time. Could Molly's husband have been caught up in something with the Sidwells? No. Wendall Sidwell probably had no idea who Leonard was — or any of his employees, for that matter. Sandra pointed out that the vengeance against Wendall had been served. What else could Molly want? Maybe when she wrote her mother …

The letter!

"Drummond, tell Sandra there's a letter from Molly to her mother in the album. Molly glosses over the details by saying she wants her mother to come visit."

Before Max had finished speaking, Drummond dashed over the gravel and pavement. He leaned close to Sandra and whispered in her ear. As Drummond returned, Sandra gathered the album from the ground nearby and opened the letter.

When she finished reading, her jaw dropped. "It's not that you don't want to move on. You can't."

Molly jumped upward like a superhero flying away — except

the smoke snaked around her. Even as it revealed her, it chained her down.

"Let me go," she said.

"You didn't tell your mother everything, did you?"

Straining against the smoke, Molly's face twisted. "Don't do this to me."

"What happened that night?"

"You have no right."

"After so many decades, don't you want to be rid of this burden? Let us help you."

"She doesn't need to know."

Sandra looked to her side. "Estelle? Why hide anything from her now? She's seen you possess people, destroy them so that you can murder Sidwells."

Dropping any pretense of fighting the smoke, Molly's shoulders slouched forward. "She's my baby. My child."

"She's also over a century old. Just because she didn't get to live and mature into a woman, doesn't make her a fool. Tell us what happened the night your daughter was killed."

"I … I …" She bowed her head. A body-wrenching sob erupted from her core. She arched back, and the blood smoke pulsed around her. "You want to know? Do you all want to know?"

Max suddenly thought he didn't really need that answer, but Molly thrust her hands out to her sides. The red smoke shot outward, cutting through the air with erratic, jagged lines of lightning. She then pointed her hands at Sandra. Veins of smoke stretched between them.

Sandra's head wracked back. The floodlights atop the building burst in showers of sparks. But as those lights went dark, the fiery smoke created an eerie iridescent glow. The burning feathers brightened, and the candleflame shot upward. It stretched seven feet high, a thin pillar of fire, and Max could feel its intense heat. With a hefty bang, the candle exploded. Bits of wax shrapnel burst off. But as the flame lowered, still the feathers burned, still the smoke poured forth, still they held Sandra in their grasp.

"No," Max whispered.

"I've got this," Drummond said.

Yet when both moved forward, the jagged lines reached outward towards them. Max turned his head, intending to warn the others to stay behind the salt. He watched as these branching blood-red smoke veins slipped across the salt and around Dylan's head. Then Mrs. Sidwell. Then Brenda. And as the thought hit that the smoke was not Molly's ghost but merely made her visible and thus, the smoke had no issue crossing a salt line, it wrapped around Max's head, too.

Chapter 43

SEVERAL TIMES OVER THE YEARS, ghosts had giving Max visions of their past. It often proved painful, and each time, Max wondered if his brain might finally break under the pressure. The human mind had not evolved to process such things. This time felt worse. Where the usual experience reminded him of watching a movie — only one he could feel, too — this one placed him in the subject's head. What Molly saw, heard, smelled, touched, and tasted — so did Max. She created a full-bodied moment in time to be more than witnessed. He became the main character in her memory.

As Max's eyes cleared, he had his back pressed into the corner. His felt the pain on the chair rail had chipped away. Little splinters stung his back where his blouse had torn. His skirt dug into his thighs like teeth. Wendall Sidwell menaced the office with his lanky arms, his oily hair, and his lecherous grin. With his tie askew and his shirt pulled, he looked as out of sorts as he was out of sense. By his hand, Max saw a silver picture frame — a black-and-white wedding photo of Wendall and Bernice Sidwell. Neither newlywed looked happy. Bernice glared beyond Wendall as if she could see through the photograph, see him lunge forward, struggling to pin Max/Molly against the wall while he pawed under that biting skirt. Max pushed his hands into Wendall's shoulders, into the man's face, but despite Wendall's slim build, he had greater strength.

A thought struck — and Max understood these were not his thoughts but Molly's — that maybe he shouldn't fight back. Let it happen. Get it over with. He had heard the stories at lunch.

The man never went further than groping — and only with one hand. Max wouldn't be the first secretary to suffer this fate. Listening to Wendall's heavy panted grunts as he played with himself. It turned Max's stomach. He swallowed the burning bile racing up his throat. But not to fight back? How could he live with himself?

Fate, however, had other plans. Before he could make that choice — and he knew he could never live with the shame of not fighting — he heard a gentle voice that chilled his skin.

"Mommy?"

Wendall paused. Pants around his ankle. Underwear half-down. The reek of whiskey hot from his lips. As Max/Molly scurried out of the corner, away from the sweating man, he noticed Estelle stood in the doorway, her face scrunched as she tried to make sense of what she witnessed.

Clamping down his tears, shutting off the terror that wanted to scream up his throat, Max/Molly rushed over to Estelle. "Hi, sweetie. Did you get bored? It's late. We should get home."

He ushered her back to the outer-office, the sound of his heart pounding hard enough to shake the building into the ground. He grabbed his purse and reached the top of the stairs before Wendall spoke — a hoarse cry of *Wait!* Pathetic. One of Loray Mills prized vice presidents looked more like an awkward schoolboy as he had pulled his pants up and swooped his hair back.

"Mrs. Lynch," Wendall said, finding a more authoritative tone. "I think we can agree that this meeting did not go well. We may have moved you into the offices too fast. You don't seem able to handle the workload."

Max/Molly narrowed his eyes. Tears stung even as his jaw locked. Barely opening his mouth, tasting blood from the inside cheek, he said, "I'm sure there are other vice presidents who might prefer a more traditional secretary."

"I don't know if that's the best for the company."

The cocky way Wendall spoke — Max/Molly wanted to choke the man until his eyes bugged out of his head. Feel the pulse weaken beneath his fingers as he watched the bastard's life leave. Instead, he plastered on a smile. "Then I'll go back to working on the floor with my husband."

"Unfortunately, the workers, including your husband, have chosen to strike against us. I'm sorry, Mrs. Lynch, but I don't see any option but to let you go."

Pressing his lips tight, Max/Molly tried not to think about how few jobs were out there. He stood motionless, staring in disbelief at Wendall. Once he thought he had control over his voice, once he saw few good options in front of him, he said, "This strike is getting a lot of attention from the press. Plenty of reporters out there. If you fire me, I'm sure they'll find my story interesting. Sensational, even."

Max/Molly had hoped the threat would shut him up, but Wendall laughed. "Nobody will believe you."

"Maybe not. But your reputation won't stay spotless. Your wife might not like this kind of attention, either."

Taking a handkerchief from his inside breast pocket, Wendall patted his upper-lip. It scratched like sandpaper — the man needed to shave. "Oh, I think my reputation will be fine. Might even improve with some of my business partners. You, however, will have to explain to your husband why he shouldn't think you're a whore. Seducing your boss with those curves and that sway in your walk. Why, I'm sure a smart man like your husband would draw the same conclusion as any red-blooded American."

"My husband loves me, and that means he trusts me."

"You better hope so. Now, little Estelle's heard quite a lot, too. You'll be explaining things to her tonight. Things she's too young to hear. What kind of mother are you? Bringing a child to this environment. During a strike, no less. Disgusting."

"You son of a bitch."

"Vulgar mouth, vulgar behavior. You go to the press, and the world will learn what a terrible parent you are. The government might even show up and take away your child. A sweet one like Estelle should be protected."

As Wendall turned away and strolled to his office, Estelle said, "Mommy, you're hurting me."

Max glanced down. He had squeezed the child's hand. But

when Estelle wriggled that hand free, when Max no longer had that hand to channel his rage, his mind went blindingly blank. Flashes of the brown walls, the metal desks, the black phones. Sounds of Estelle calling for him. The hard floor click-click-clicking with each step in his heels. Heels that made his feet swell at the end of a long day. Heels that angered him every morning he put them on.

He kicked those heels off, picked one up, and darted after Mr. Wendall Sidwell, vice president of bastards and scumbags. Uttering a banshee scream, Max slammed the point of his heel into Sidwell's shoulder blade. Max and Molly gave a satisfied cheer in Max's mind as they felt the slight resistance and then sudden give of Sidwell's skin when it burst open. Blood spritzed around the narrow point.

Whirling back, Wendall tried to reach the shoe. As he thrashed his body about, he banged his desk. The wedding photo fell to the floor; the glass shattering like thin ice. Though he failed to get the shoe, his wild movements dislodged it.

Breathing heavy, peering through his oily hair that had fallen over his eyes, he bared his teeth. "How dare you?"

Max/Molly formed a fist and attempted a haymaker. But like many men of his era, Wendall had boxed in his teen years. He shifted his head back out of the way, then returned with a sharp jab to the chin. Lights sparked in Max's eyes. His legs wobbled as he stumbled back.

Wendall lurched forward and threw another short hit — this time to the gut. As Max/Molly doubled-over, the muscles locking, he couldn't breathe. Wendall's hand cupped Max's neck. He pushed Max back, back, back. Max's legs rushed to stay upright as they blitzed through the outer-office. With a furious roar, Wendall threw Max/Molly away.

He hit the floor and rolled over, bumping against something hard at the door. Hard? The screech of a little girl hit Max's ears. He raised his head in time to see Estelle spilling back into the empty support of the stairwell.

Molly screamed as she scrambled for her daughter. The sheer terror thrust Max out of Molly — nobody could hold on to that bronco of emotion — and deposited him up at the ceiling. Like a ghost watching from above, he saw her snatching the emptiness in front of Estelle's panicked hands. The little girl went over. Each thump on the staircase resounded through the floor and walls like military drum hits. Cries and thumps and cries and thumps and a snap. Such a tiny noise for such a monumental end.

The sickening silence that followed was worse.

Molly's mouth had locked open in soundless anguish. Her eyes could not open wider as tears rivered down her face.

Standing over her, Wendall gazed down at the dead child. From the ceiling, Max could not tell if Wendall cared or not, but he heard the powerful man break the quiet with a minor, "Huh."

Chapter 44

THE BURNING SMOKE reduced to the deep red of embers as it receded from each person's head. It snaked back to Molly, returning to its original purpose of making her visible. Max watched Sandra's heaving sobs as she reached out a hand toward the ghost, oblivious to the destroyed candle and the bits of wax that peppered her clothes. Molly reached back, crying as well, but with the control of someone who had shed too many tears over the same, unhealing wounds. The smoke thinned as the feathers neared their conclusion.

Leaving the others behind and stunned, Max walked to his wife. He got onto his knees and held her. Gazing up at Molly, he said, "Thank you for giving us the truth."

Sandra wiped her face and shook off the last shiver. "I'm so sorry for what you went through. No woman should ever have to face that."

She paused. Max nudged her. She knew what needed to be said, and they both knew that he could not be the one to say it. Molly would never hear anything from a man. A greedy, self-centered man destroyed her life. And when she returned forty years later, the same thing happened. And forty years after that. Each time one of these Sidwell men had a chance to abuse their power, they took it. She made them pay, but it never ended her pain. It never fixed the past.

"You've done enough," Sandra said. "The Sidwells are done. There are no more men to try for these crimes. It's over. They're over."

The smoke had become more black than red. Sandra rose on her knees. "A horrible thing happened to you. A thing that should never be allowed. But you have let it define your existence for too long. You've let it hurt you again and again, and in doing so, you've let Wendall hurt you again and again."

Molly said, "What am I without this pain? If I go on, I can haunt the Sidwell land, keep it poisoned forever, never let their unpunished crimes be forgotten."

"People already have forgotten. Most have never heard of Loray Mills, let alone Molly Lynch or Wendall Sidwell. A hundred years — it wipes away everything." Sandra stood. "I know your pain is still real, but if you go on, you'll be hurting someone else, too."

Molly's gaze lowered as a smoky hand appeared out of the darkness. "Oh, my little sweetie." Crouching to her daughter's level, Molly stroked Estelle's hair. "I'm sorry. Mommy's been angry, but I hope you never thought I was angry with you."

The thinning smoke surrounded Estelle long enough for Max to see the girl shrug.

"Oh, sweetie, no." Molly clutched the girl to her chest. "I love you. I could never be that mad at you. No matter what."

Wriggling free of the hug, Estelle looked around the empty mill. "Everyone's gone."

"They've moved on. Do you remember what that means?"

She swung her hands back and forth. Reciting her words as if rushing through the alphabet, she said, "It means that we're not alive anymore, but not to be sad because all things die, and once they've died, they can move on to whatever comes after."

"That's right. Very good."

"But I want to see my friends."

She kissed her daughter's forehead. "You will, sweetie. I promise." She shared a looked with Sandra before turning a dark eye upon Mrs. Sidwell. Forcing a smile to return, she then shifted back to Estelle. "Do you see this nice man?"

"Uh-huh. He was in a wheelchair."

"When he was alive, that's right. The two of you are going to move on now. You'll get to join your friends and probably meet some new ones."

Estelle pouted. "What about you?"

"I still have to finish here, but I'll be as quick as I can. Like the blink of an eye. And once that's done, I'm going to move on, too. So, don't worry. I'll find you, and we can be happy again."

"No more angry days?"

"None. See this lady and her husband?" She pointed to Sandra. "They're helping me so that I won't be angry anymore."

"Thank you, lady."

Sandra laughed and cried simultaneously. "You're welcome."

"It's settled, then," Molly said.

She stood, kept hold of her daughter's hand, and allowed the last of the red smoke to disappear.

Chapter 45

TWO WEEKS LATER, Max sat behind his desk at The Porter Agency and worked at learning the history behind an old consignment shop downtown. The owners swore the place was haunted, but so far, Max found nothing to suggest they were right. Drummond said from the start that these new clients acted too looney. They were an eccentric couple, but that didn't mean they were wrong.

"No," Drummond said, "but it does mean they're prone to embellishment. I looked, and they've got rats in the basement. I'll bet you that's causing the midnight noises they're hearing. I'd even wager if you talked to their doctors, you'd find they're hypochondriacs, too."

From her desk, Sandra said, "Come here. Look at this."

"You find something?" Max said.

"What? No, not for the case. There's an article about Penelope Sidwell. She's funding a new organization that fights child labor in other countries."

Drummond clicked his tongue. "Nothing like being tormented by poltergeists to get a person acting noble."

"What's wrong? Run out of waitresses to date?"

"My dating life is none of your business."

Max laughed. "Then why do you insist on telling us about it? I can probably name the last five you've gone out with."

The office door opened, and Dylan entered with Mrs. Sidwell following. Sandra rushed over to great them. "We were just talking about you. We saw the article."

"Oh, that." Mrs. Sidwell waved away the praise as she took a seat on the couch. "I wish they'd stick to promoting the organization and not focus on me."

Drummond straightened his tie and set his hat at an angle. Every time Mrs. Sidwell visited — which she did every few days — Drummond behaved the same. Apparently, the old detective had started a friendship with Molly Lynch. He promised there was nothing romantic at hand.

"We both lived during the same time," he had said. "It's nice to have somebody I can talk with who really understands me, understands what the world once was like."

He put his arm out, and though Max could not see Molly, he had no trouble picturing her taking that arm so the two could stroll off to the Other for an afternoon. The surprising part came from Mrs. Sidwell.

"Did she leave?"

Sandra said, "For a bit. She'll be back. How did you know?"

"I suppose I've gotten so accustomed to her being near me that I can feel when she's gone. There's a chill in the air that disappears. Does that make sense?"

"Absolutely."

"Do you think she'll ever leave me alone for good? Or even move on?"

"You know she will. Once you've made full amends."

Mrs. Sidwell opened her purse and dug around. "I am working hard at that. Funding projects gets some press, and I've started a few scholarship programs, too. But the big work is something that Dylan is going to help me with. Isn't that right?"

Stepping forward, Dylan said, "Yes, ma'am. I promised you that I would help."

"He's being modest. Dylan is going to lead the project for me, and keep it on track."

Max asked, "What's the project?"

"I want to find our former employees. Not only the ones that Robert and the other Sidwell men hurt, but every single person who ever worked for us. If they're no longer living, then I want to track down their descendants. I'm going to set up a trust that will produce a sizable amount of money each year. That money will get distributed to them all. I realize cash is a poor apology, but if I can drain away the Sidwell riches by giving it to those who created it — well, I can't think of anything better to satisfy Molly Lynch. She wants the Sidwells to end, and this will do it."

"It's a wonderful idea," Sandra said.

"Ah, here." Mrs. Sidwell produced an envelope from her purse and handed it to Sandra. "I think that should be the last payment I need to make for your services."

"You've already paid us."

"Consider it a bonus."

Sandra opened the envelope, peeked in, and blushed. "This is too generous. We can't accept this."

Faster than a comic book superhero, Max sped across the room and snatched the envelope away. "Of course, we can." He glanced at the check — enough to cover the next six months. "That is quite a lot."

Mrs. Sidwell said, "You do good work. There are people who need you, and I do not want to find out that those people aren't getting help because you can't afford the rent. Once I have done everything I need to do for Molly, once she's moved on, if there is anything left, I'll send it to you. The Porter Agency is too important to let something as silly as money get in the way."

With that, she said some pleasant parting words and promised to stay in touch. Dylan escorted her out of the offices. Max waited until he was sure they couldn't hear anything, and then he bellyflopped onto the couch with an ecstatic whoop.

"Do you realize," he said, "that this money takes the pressure off us? At least, for a little while."

Sandra sat at his side and stroked his back. "I'm glad it will relieve some stress for you."

He looked over at her and frowned. "What's that tone mean?"

"Nothing."

"It's something. What is it?"

"I suppose it's occurred to me that if you're feeling so much better, you'll be in the right frame of mind to deal with our other situation."

"What other situation?"

"Your mother, of course."

Max pushed up to a seat. "I walked right into that one, didn't I?"

"You certainly did." She handed him the car keys. "Get going."

"Now?"

After a short negotiation, Sandra agreed to drive to the house with him. She had a few things to do at home, anyway. But she made it clear to Max that he needed to work things out with his mother on his own — and that those things included the details of how they would survive together under the same roof.

"I'm not living like this anymore," she said. "Too much tension — for all of us."

Max had parked in the driveway and turned the car off, but neither had made an effort to go into the house. A light drizzle spattered against the windshield. He watched the gentle drops slide down the glass, finding other drops, forming streams that met others until they became a fast-moving river racing to the wipers at the bottom. "I don't want to cause her so much stress that she has an MS attack. Too many unwelcome stimuli and she could end up speeding down what little road she has left. Smash at the bottom."

"Oh, please. Your mother is an ox. You just don't want to tell her the truth — about anything."

He peeked up at the house. "She's never going to go for this."

"That's fine. You know what to do."

He considered offering Sandra an early dinner at one of her favorite spots — just the two of them — but the moment he opened his mouth, she cast a look that not only said she had read his mind and rejected the thought, but guaranteed that any further cowardice would be met with swift action. He raised his hands. "I give up. I'm going."

When he entered the side door to the kitchen, he decided to detour to the bedroom and grab the Parker House pamphlet. Then to his mother's room. He found her staring out the window at the backyard. He pulled up a chair. Sitting knee-to-knee, he held her hands. "How was your day?"

She shrugged.

"We had a great day. We got paid a bonus for our last case. You know, the one that you didn't like because it kept messing up our schedule."

She said, "Glad something good came of it."

"It did. And that money gives us — gives you — an opportunity to make some choices."

"About what?"

"Your life. I know you want to be here with us, to be close to us —"

"I want to be close to you. Sandra's okay, I suppose."

Poking his finger in the air at her, he said, "That's part of what we need to talk about. We're happy to have you living here, but it's not going to work if you keep up this attitude."

"I don't have an attitude."

He placed the pamphlet on her lap. "You want to live with us, there are going to be some rules. Rules about respect and behavior. Frankly, these are things you taught me as a kid. But if you don't like what we have to say, I understand. That's fine. We have the funds to set you up at a lovely independent living apartment."

She pushed the pamphlet onto the floor. "I knew it. I shouldn't be surprised. Sandra never wanted me in this house, and she's got you riled up and twisted around. You really intend to push your own mother out of your house? Cart me off to some nursing home?"

"It's not a nursing home. You get to live in your own place again. Remember how badly you didn't want to leave your old apartment? This will be like that, but you'll be in a community of people your own age. And if you need it, they have a full medical staff that can help you."

"It's lipstick on a pig."

He threw his arms up but spoke calmly. "It's up to you. Either agree to some ground rules for living in this house, or we can help you move to an independent place. With your MS getting worse, those are the only options."

"Why not get me a nurse with that money you got today?"

"That would be part of our agreement. If you stay with us, we'd have to hire a nurse for the times Sandra or I can't be here. You'd have to agree to your behavior not only for us but for the nurse, too. And you'll have to agree to get out of the house, to make friends, to keep living."

From the angry squint, Max expected his mother to burst into a verbal tirade. She glanced at the pamphlet on the floor before finally looking him in the eye. "I won't go to a place like that. So, I guess I have no choice. I'll try to be nicer to Sandra."

"*Try?*"

"I'll be nicer. I don't mean to be rude. Really. But on the bad MS days, it takes such effort for the simplest things that I don't have energy for smiles and kindness. But I'll try."

He kissed her hands. "Thank you."

"I want you to agree to something, too."

Bracing himself, he said, "What is it?"

"I want you to stop looking for Aunt Jane. I know you're still at it. A mother can tell. Please, you have to trust me. That woman is a poison to this family, and no good will ever come from you hearing whatever she would want to say. It'll only make your life more difficult."

Max chilled. But it only lasted a second. He gave her a nod. "I'll stop. I promise."

Later that night, as he curled in bed with Sandra, he told her in detail about the conversation. When he finished, she propped up on an elbow to look straight at him.

"So, what exactly did you tell her?"

"I told her I'd stop looking for Aunt Jane. And I have stopped."

"Because you found her."

He sat up, scratching the back of his head. "There was a moment, just a flash really, where I considered telling her everything. I could have said that I met with Aunt Jane and that I heard her version of events. And then what? Mom and I have a big fight? I confront her, and force her to rewrite her past."

"Rewrite it with the truth."

"My mother is not Mrs. Sidwell. The truth is not a century of criminal behavior in the family. My mother isn't being haunted by poltergeists that want to destroy her. If she has any ghosts to deal with, they are the kind in her head. Isn't that torture enough?"

"But —"

"How much time does she have left? That's what really went through my mind when she asked for my promise. With Mrs. Sidwell, she fought for her son's life, and then for his afterlife. But with my mother, nobody is being threatened by her secrets. Aunt Jane doesn't want contact with us, and I've satisfied my curiosity."

"Have you?"

"Mostly, I guess. Enough to keep me quiet until my mother's days are done. I might dig around for the full truth after that. Because you're right. The truth matters, maybe it matters most, and I need to really understand it all. But for my mother — nothing good will come from that fight. It won't change anything for her, and the stress of it might hurt her more. Worst case, she might leave for Parker House and never speak with me again. There are lines that people cannot cross and come back from. This might be one of them. I'm not willing to risk finding out with her."

Sandra pecked him on the cheek and eased him back down. She snuggled under his arm and kissed his chest. "I suppose I get it. But it's still a lie."

"Yeah," Max said with an uncomfortable sigh. "But it's a lie of love."

He hoped that was true.

Afterword

Thank you, once again, for joining me on another Max Porter journey. Your constant support in reading these books, and spreading the word so others discovery this witchy world, is what keeps me writing the series. I hope you enjoyed this latest. But let me get right into why you really want to read this afterword:

It should come as no surprise to readers of this series that the Loray Mills strike of 1929 is true. All the details, including the murder of the police chief and the questionable judicial process afterward are true. There are only a few books covering the entire run of the strike, and those that exist are more scholarly than most people seek out, but they do exist if you are interested. When the strike became a matter of national (and later, international) attention, several people received their fifteen minutes of fame. While none of those names lasted in our national awareness, for a short time, the public knew of those struggling in Gastonia and the fight against the big companies that wanted to crush them. The tale of Molly and Estelle Lynch, however, is fictitious.

Likewise, the Harriet-Henderson strike of 1959 is also true, as is reference to the numerous strikes that occurred throughout the state.

The Sidwell family is a fiction, though.

Because textiles and tobacco continue to rule this state, I had considered delving into the Hanes family (yes, as in Hanes underwear), but they are more privacy driven than the Reynolds family (which are also quite a private family). And, really, we don't need their dirty laundry to make our entertainment. Where they choose to be public, as with Reynolda House, I will use what I can, or as in the murder of Z. Smith Reynolds, when private events become public record. Otherwise, I try to respect their privacy.

On the lighter side, Baggerz Saloon is a real biker bar that plays live music. According to the internet (and from driving by the location), the bar may have closed. However, I was there just last year, and they have been around for quite a while, so if you're doing a Max Porter tour through the area, you may want to check out the place to see if it's still around.

Finally, and obvious to regular readers, Speedy's is a real, and excellent, Lexington barbecue joint that I highly recommend. Of all the research I must do for these books, I promise that I will always give you my earnest dedication to trying out these wonderful venues. It's a burden my tastebuds must carry.

Acknowledgements

I am going to depart from the usual list of names here. After nineteen books, those of you who have helped out know who you are. You have my eternal thanks. I do have to mention my wife and son, though, without whom none of the books in this series would have ever succeeded. Also, I have to live with my wife, so I better make sure to thank her.

This time, however, I want to focus on the most important of you, my readers. I always make a point of thanking you in each book, but I want you to know how much I truly appreciate your support. After the last book, *Southern Kin*, I waited nervously to see what people thought. It had been eighteen books, and did you really care anymore, and maybe I had run out of new ways to tell The Porter Agency's stories.

It became clear, quite fast, that you still love Max. In a time of worldwide, economic instability, you continue to purchase these books, allowing me to continue creating them. I can't express enough the joy I receive when reading your emails or catching a positive review or hearing from you on social media.

Often, when I'm at a convention or a conference, I am asked if I'm going to write more Max Porter. I have always answered that as long as you keep buying them, I'll keep writing them. I figure you'll let me know how you feel and if you want me to stop. Based on the last book (and hopefully, this one), your answer is that you want more and more and more.

I aim to deliver.

So, thank you. Always.

About the Author

Stuart Jaffe is the madman behind the *Nathan K thrillers, The Max Porter Paranormal Mysteries,* the *Ridnight Mysteries,* the *Parallel Society* novels, *The Malja Chronicles, The Bluesman, Founders, Real Magic,* and much more. He trained in martial arts for over a decade until a knee injury ended that practice. Now, he plays lead guitar in a local blues band, *The Bootleggers,* and enjoys life on a small farm in rural North Carolina.

www.ingramcontent.com/pod-product-compliance
Lightning Source LLC
Chambersburg PA
CBHW030519310726
48979CB00010B/1727/J

* 9 7 8 1 9 6 3 5 1 7 2 0 0 *